The VIRTUES of CHRISTMAS

A HOLIDAY NOVELLA DUET

GRACE BURROWES

New York Times Bestselling Author

Published as a two-novella compilation, by Grace Burrowes Publishing, 21 Summit Avenue, Hagerstown, MD 21740.

Cover design by Author's Lifesaver, Inc.

Cover photos by Period Images.

ISBN: 1941419380
ISBN-13: 978-1941419380

Respect for Christmas

GRACE BURROWES

Dedicated to those who spend the holidays with family members who will never get it. When it comes to family, the season of miracles is 365 days long, or sometimes 366.

CHAPTER ONE

My Dearest Brenner,

You will forgive a friend of long-standing for not using your newly acquired honorific. Old habits die hard, though I suppose even an Irish barony is due an occasional nod. In ten or twenty years, perhaps, I will acquire the knack of addressing you as my lord. Perhaps not. In any case, I hope this letter finds you well and anticipating the holidays—or the holiday punch—with much joy.

The time has come for you to repay that small favor I did you several years ago—the favor that resulted in you eluding capture, torture, and death at the hands of our then-enemies. My request is laughably simple to accomplish for a man of your skills, which is fortunate, for the matter has become urgent. My solicitors tell me I'm in want of a wealthy wife. One must approach the matrimonial lists confident that no stain will mar one's bachelor escutcheon in the eyes of prospective in-laws.

Did I ever tell you that I deserve sole credit for raising the celebrated Henrietta Whitlow from the status of bumbling housemaid to consort of dukes and nabobs? The tale impresses even me, who more or less wrote it...

Henrietta Whitlow—a bumpkin's name, of a certainty—joined my domestic staff shortly after I came down from university. A more shy, unworldly, backward creature you never met. She took pride in blacking the andirons and in polishing the candlesticks. She took pride in shining the windows until every parlor reeked of vinegar. She took a painful degree of pride in every domestic chore imaginable, but no pride whatsoever in herself. I changed all of that, though it was a thankless and tedious chore...

"I tell you, John Coachman, there is no room at this inn!" The innkeeper banged a palm on the counter, as if knocking down goods at auction.

The coachman, a substantial specimen of middle years, leaned forward so he was nose to nose with the innkeeper.

"Your stable is nearly empty," he said, a Scots burr in every syllable. "Your common room boasts exactly one gentleman awaiting a meal, and you *will* find accommodations for my lady."

Lord Michael Brenner, Baron Angelford, the gentleman in question, sat before the common's bow window, which was close enough to the foyer that he heard every word of the argument between the coachman and the innkeeper. Beyond the window, an enormous traveling coach with spanking yellow wheels and four matched chestnuts stood in the yard. The horses' breath blew white in the frigid air, and one of the wheelers stomped a hoof against frozen ground.

No crest on the coach door, but considerable fine luggage lashed to the roof. Why would an innkeeper with rooms aplenty turn away a wealthy customer?

"I'm expecting other parties," the innkeeper said. "Decent folk who expect decent accommodations."

A woman emerged from the coach. She was attired in a brown velvet cloak with a cream wool scarf about her neck and ears. She was tall and, based on her nimble descent, young. The second woman, a shorter, rounder specimen in a gray cloak, emerged more slowly and teetered to the ground on the arm of a footman.

What self-respecting innkeeper refused accommodations to two women, at least one of whom was quite well-to-do? Michael waited for a drunken lordling or two to stagger from the coach, or one of London's more notorious gamblers—he knew them all—but the footman closed the coach door.

The taller woman removed her scarf and wrapped it about her companion. Michael caught a glimpse of flaming red hair before the awning over the inn's front door obscured the women from view.

Ah, well then. The puzzle began to make sense.

"If you're expecting other parties," the coachman said, "they won't be underfoot until sundown. My lady needs a room for only a few hours, while I find a blacksmith to reset a shoe on my off-side leader."

"My guests might arrive at any moment," the innkeeper shot back. "The sky promises snow, and I don't give reserved rooms away."

The front door opened, an eddy of cold air reaching even into the common room.

"He's being difficult, ma'am," the coachman said to the red-haired woman. "I'll make the cheating blighter see reason."

"Mr. Murphy's difficult demeanor is one of the reliable institutions on this delightful route," the lady said. "Rather like the potholes and not quite as inconvenient as the highwaymen. Fortunately, Mrs. Murphy's excellent housekeeping is equally trustworthy. How much, Mr. Murphy?"

The woman's tone was cultured and amused, but also just a shade too low, a touch too knowing. Had the common been full of men, every one of them would have eavesdropped on the conversation because her voice was that alluring.

"No amount of coin will produce an extra room," Murphy retorted. "Your kind think everything can be bought, but I run a proper establishment."

"*My kind* is simply a cold, tired traveler far from home and willing to pay for warmth and privacy. A room, please."

Coin slid across the counter. Murphy watched the lady's gloved hand and then studied the gold glinting up from the worn wood.

"I told you after your last visit, Henrietta Whitlow, you are not welcome here. Now be off with you."

"And you call yourself an innkeeper," the coachman sneered. "A woman willing to pay you good coin for a short respite from the elements, and you send her back out into the cold when anybody—"

"Excuse me," Michael said, rising from his table and joining the group at the front desk. "I couldn't help but overhear. Miss Whitlow is welcome to use my rooms."

"But, sir!" Murphy expostulated. "You don't know to whom you're offering such a kindness. I have good, substantial reasons for not allowing just anybody to bide under this roof."

Michael well knew to whom the innkeeper was being so rude.

He passed Miss Whitlow's coins to the coachman. "The holidays are upon us, Mr. Murphy, which means the weather is nasty, and travel is both dangerous and trying. The lady and her companion are welcome to use the parlor connected to my bedchamber. The hospitality extended is not yours, but mine, and as my guests, you will please show them every courtesy. Miss Whitlow."

He bowed to the redhead, who executed a graceful curtsey in response. Her companion had come inside and watched the goings-on in unsmiling silence.

"My thanks," Miss Whitlow said. "Though to whom am I expressing my gratitude?"

"Michael Brenner, at your service. Mr. Murphy, the ladies will take a meal and a round of toddies in your private parlor once they've refreshed themselves above stairs. John Coachman and madam's staff will similarly need sustenance and hospitality. Do I make myself clear?"

Murphy scowled at Miss Whitlow, who regarded him with the level stare of a cat deciding whether the menu would feature mouse, songbird, or fricassee of innkeeper.

The scandal sheets and tattlers didn't do Henrietta Whitlow justice. Her features were just one degree off from cameo perfection—her nose a shade too aquiline, her mouth too full, her eyebrows a bit too dramatic, her height an inch too grand—and the result was unforgettable beauty. Michael had seen her from a distance at the theater many times, but up close, her impact was… more than physical.

Duels had been fought over Henrietta Whitlow, fortunes wagered, and her amatory skills had become the stuff of legend.

"Mr. Brenner, might I invite you to join us?" Miss Whitlow asked. "You are our host, after all, and good company always makes time pass more pleasantly."

The invitation was bold but, at a coaching inn, not outlandishly improper.

"I was awaiting my own midday meal," Michael said. "I'll be happy to join you."

Michael's day had been laid out according to a careful plan, but plans changed, and opportunities sometimes came along unlooked for. A man didn't have a chance to share a meal with London's most sought-after courtesan every day, and Michael had been growing damned hungry waiting for Murphy to produce a bowl of soup and some bread.

* * *

Nothing about Lord Angelford's demeanor suggested he expected Henrietta to repay his kindness with intimate favors, though she knew better than to trust him. British gentlemen were randy creatures, particularly wealthy, titled British gentlemen.

Though his lordship had chosen not to mention that title. Henrietta and Angelford hadn't been introduced, but Michael Brenner would soon learn that newly minted barons had almost as little privacy as courtesans.

His lordship was tall and handsome, though not precisely dark. His hair was auburn, and his voice bore a hint of Ireland overlaid with plenty of English public school. He was exquisitely attired in tall boots, breeches, brown riding jacket, and fine linen, and his waistcoat was gold with subtle green embroidery vining throughout.

Newly titled, but a lord to the teeth already. Such men took good care of their toys, from snuffboxes, to hunters, to dueling pistols, to mistresses.

Henrietta was heartily sick of being a well-cared-for toy.

Lord Angelford ushered her into a cozy parlor with a blazing fire and a dining table set for four. Lucille trundled along as well—she was fiercer than any mastiff when it came to Henrietta's safety—and passed Henrietta her scarf.

"If madam will excuse me," Lucille said, "I'll step upstairs for a moment while we're waiting for a meal."

"Take your time," Henrietta replied, then fell silent as Lucille bustled off. A courtesan excelled at conversation, Henrietta was exhausted, however, and fatigue predisposed her to babbling. A self-possessed quiet was always a far better course than babbling.

"May I take your cloak?" his lordship asked.

"Of course." She passed him her scarf, then undid the frogs of her cloak and peeled it from her shoulders. In London, Henrietta would have made sure to gild the moment with a brush of fingers or a lingering gaze, because a courtesan never knew who her next protector might be.

London, thank the Almighty and John Coachman's skill, was many snowy miles to the south. Henrietta hoped never to see its smoky, crowded, noisy like again.

Nothing in Angelford's gaze lingered—another small mercy. After he hung Henrietta's cloak and scarf on the hooks on the back of the door, he held a chair for her.

"Have you far to go?" he asked, taking the opposite seat. He'd put Henrietta closest to the fire, and the heat was heavenly.

"Another day or so, weather permitting. What of yourself?"

The distance Henrietta wished to travel, from the pinnacle of the demimonde clear back to respectability, was far indeed. Some had managed, such as Charles Fox Pitt's widow, but she'd taken years and years to accomplish that feat and had called upon a store of charm Henrietta could only envy.

"I am traveling to my estate in Oxfordshire," his lordship said, "and tending to some business along the way. Will you celebrate the holidays with family?"

Henrietta's brothers and their wives hadn't cut her off, but Papa was another matter. "My plans are as yet unconfirmed. Have we met before, Mr. Brenner?"

She wanted the dangling sword of her former occupation either cut loose from over her head, or plunged into her already bleak mood.

Damn the holidays anyway.

"We have not been introduced, though I'm sure we have mutual acquaintances. The Duke of Anselm and I have invested in the same ventures on occasion."

Henrietta's last protector, and the best of a curious lot. His Grace was married now, and happily so.

The varlet.

"Then you are aware of my reputation, *your lordship*. If you'd prefer my maid and I dine without you, I'll understand." Henrietta wished he'd go strutting on his handsome way. Men either wanted something from her, or reproached her for what other men paid handsomely to take from her. The hypocrisy was as stunning as it was lucrative.

"Miss Whitlow, I make it a habit not to judge people on the strength of reputation. Too often, public opinion is based on hearsay, anecdote, and convenience, and when one meets the object of gossip in person, the reality is either disappointing or dismaying. The beef stew here is above reproach, though I've sustained myself mainly on bread, cheese, and ham."

A serving maid brought in a tray of toddies, and the scent alone nearly made Henrietta weep. She was cold, exhausted, angry, and should not be taking spirits, but these toddies would be scrumptious.

"I asked you to join me for the meal," she said, "so Murphy would not serve me boiled shoe leather with a side of week-old cabbage. You mustn't think me hospitable."

His lordship set a steaming toddy before her. "I think you tired, chilled, and in need of a meal. As it happens, so am I. Happy Christmas, Miss Whitlow."

He touched his glass to hers and waited for Henrietta to take a sip of hot, sweet, spicy heaven. The spirits were good quality—not fit for a duke, but fit for a retired courtesan. When his lordship launched into a discourse about the potential for increased legal trade in Scottish whisky—of all the undrinkable offenses to pleasurable dining—Henrietta wondered if the baron might be that rarest of specimens, the true British gentleman.

* * *

Michael was already engaged in thievery, a skill he'd hoped never to rely on again. He was stealing the trust of a woman who would doubtless prefer he take her last groat or the clothes off her back. He didn't need her money, and he didn't want her trust.

The yearning to remove the clothes from her back filled him with a combination of self-loathing, amusement, and wistfulness.

"Happy Christmas, your lordship," Miss Whitlow said, taking a sip of her toddy. "Why did you introduce yourself without the title?"

He hadn't noticed that blunder—for it was a blunder. "Habit," Michael said, which was the damned sorry truth. "My last employer was of such consequence he could command favors from the sovereign. A barony was the marquess's way of thanking me for years of loyal service, or so he claimed."

Miss Whitlow held her drink in both hands, and even that—the way she cradled a goblet of hot spirits with pale, unadorned fingers—had a sensual quality.

"You refer to the Marquess of Heathgate," Miss Whitlow said. "A refreshingly direct man, in my experience, and he hasn't a vain bone in his body. My path hasn't crossed his for years."

Arrogant, Lord Heathgate certainly was, but the lady was right—the marquess was not vain. "What you call direct, others have deemed shockingly ungenteel. I suspect hanging a title about my neck was Heathgate's way of getting even for my decision to leave his employ. A joke, by his lights."

She traced her finger about the rim of her glass, and Michael would have sworn the gesture was not intended to be seductive.

"The marquess's jest has not left you laughing, my lord."

If he asked her to call him Michael, she'd probably leave the table, if not the inn. "When I turned in my notice, the marquess wasn't laughing either." Though Heathgate had probably known Michael was contemplating a departure before Michael had admitted it to himself. They'd been a good fit as lord and lackey, a rarity for them both, particularly prior to the marquess's marriage.

Miss Whitlow took another leisurely sip of her drink. "Is this where you lament the terrible burden placed upon you by wealth, consequence, and the sovereign's recognition?"

Mother Mary, she was bold, but then, a courtesan had to be. "I was born bog Irish, Miss Whitlow. You could hang a dukedom on me, and the stink of peat would still precede me everywhere. I respect coin of the realm as only one who's done without it can, but I don't give a counterfeit farthing for titles, styles, or posturing."

The maid intruded again, this time bearing bowls of steaming soup, a small loaf of bread, and a tub of butter.

She'd bobbed half a curtsey and headed for the door when Michael thought to ask, "Would you like a pot of tea, Miss Whitlow? Or chocolate, perhaps?"

"Tea would be lovely. Gunpowder, if it's available."

He would have taken her for a hot chocolate sort of a woman, but he liked that she'd surprised him. So few people did.

"If titles, styles, and posturing don't earn your respect, what does?" she asked.

Michael knew what she was about, turning the conversation always to him, his opinions, his preferences, and yet, he liked even the fiction of interest from her.

Which was not good at all.

"I admire honesty, courage, learning, and determination." *Says the man bent on deceiving a woman who's done nothing to deserve the slight.* "What about you?"

She tore off a chunk of bread, there being no serrated knife on the table. "Honesty is too often counted a virtue, even when it causes an unkind result, and education is largely a privilege of wealthy men. I value compassion, tolerance, and humor. Determination has a place, provided it's tempered by wisdom. Would you please pass the butter?"

A lady would have waited until somebody produced the proper sort of bread knife and recalled to pass her the butter rather than make do and speak up. Such ladies likely endured much needless hunger and unbuttered bread.

"I'll trade you," Michael said, passing over the butter and appropriating the rest of the loaf. "Where do you suppose your companion has got off to?"

Miss Whitlow dabbed a generous portion of butter onto her bread, considered the result, then added more.

"Lucille is exhausted from packing up my household, getting the new tenant settled, and organizing my remove to Oxfordshire. I suspect the poor dear is fast asleep on the sofa in your parlor. I can fetch her down here, if you would rather we have a third at the table."

She turned the same gaze on him she'd treated the innkeeper to: feline, amused, and subtly challenging. No wonder princes and dukes had vied for her favors.

"I'm sure, Miss Whitlow, that my virtue, or what's left of it, is safe in your hands. Unless you're concerned that my behavior will transgress the bounds of your tolerance, we can allow Lucille her rest."

She popped a bite of bread into her mouth. "Your virtue, and the virtue of the male of the species generally, is safe from my predation. I've retired from that game, not that I ever had to stalk the poor, defenseless male. Behave how you please, provided you don't expect me to allow the soup to get cold."

Henrietta Whitlow had retired? Michael belonged to several clubs, though not the loftiest or the most expensive. He owned gaming enterprises among other businesses, rubbed shoulders with journalists and Bow Street runners, and remained current on all the gossip as a matter of business necessity.

Also, old habit, and he'd heard nothing of her retirement. "Am I the first to learn of this decision?" He'd known she was journeying to Oxford for the holidays, as she had every year for the past five, but not that she'd removed from the capital entirely.

She gestured dismissively with the buttered bread. "My comings and goings are hardly news. The soup is good, compared to some I've had. Mr. Murphy apparently respects your custom."

"Or my coin," Michael replied, taking a spoonful of steamy beef broth. "May I ask what precipitated your decision to quit London?"

He ought not to have inquired. The question was personal as hell, and a criminal's professional detachment was integral to achieving Michael's objective.

"I'm not simply quitting London, my lord, I'm quitting my profession. My reasons are personal, though boredom figured prominently among them."

She took a dainty spoonful of soup, when Michael wanted to salute her with his drink. She'd been bored by the amatory attentions of aristocrats and nabobs? Bored by the loveliest jewelry the Ludgate goldsmiths had on offer? Even the king had expressed an interest in furthering his acquaintance with Henrietta Whitlow, without apparent result.

On behalf of the male gender, Michael acknowledged a set-down all the more devastating for being offered with casual humor.

"Maybe you aren't bored so much as angry," he suggested.

Miss Whitlow drained her toddy. "My upbringing was such that my temper is seldom in evidence. I do find it tedious when a man who barely knows me presumes to tell me what sentiment holds sway over my heart. Boredom and I are intimately acquainted, my lord. I try to keep my distance from anger."

She wrinkled her nose at the dregs in her cup.

Michael suspected Henrietta Whitlow's temper could cinder London, if she ever cut loose, and every red-blooded male over the age of fourteen would line up to admire the spectacle at peril to his own continued existence.

Men were idiots, as Michael's four sisters constantly reminded him. "Shall I order more toddies?"

"The tea should be along shortly, and my appreciation for a hot, sweet cup of pure gunpowder rivals my love of books."

Another surprise. "Books?"

"You know," she said, dipping her buttered bread into her soup. "Pages, printing, knowledge, and whacking good stories. Growing up, my brothers were given free run of my father's library. I was limited to sermons, lest my feeble female brain become overheated with Mr. Crusoe's adventures. I'll have the rest of the bread, if you don't care for it."

An Irishman treasured fresh bread and butter almost as much as he favored a good ale. Michael passed her the remains of the loaf.

"What's your favorite book?"

As they consumed their meal, Miss Whitlow gave up a small clue to her soul: She knew her literature, as did Michael. He'd come late to his letters and had studied learned tomes as a way to compensate for a lack of education. Henrietta Whitlow had a passion for books that had probably stood her in good stead among Oxford graduates and comforted her on those occasions when the Oxford graduates had proven poor company.

The maid arrived to clear the plates, a half-grown boy on her heels bearing a tray.

"Mrs. Murphy sends along the plum tarts with her compliments," the maid said, setting a bowl down before Miss Whitlow, then a small blue crock of cream.

"How very gracious of her," Miss Whitlow said as the maid served Michael his portion. "The soup was excellent, and the bread perfect. Please thank everybody from the scullery maid who churned the butter to Mrs. Murphy. The kitchen here is truly a marvel."

From across the table, Michael watched as Miss Whitlow offered the maid a smile so purely warm-hearted, the half-grown boy nearly dropped the tray and the serving maid's curtsey would have flattered a queen. That smile made all right with the world and gave gleeful assurances of happy endings just waiting to come true.

Harmon DeWitt, Viscount Beltram, still spoke fondly of that smile, even as he plotted against the woman who bestowed it.

"My thanks as well," Michael said. "Would you be so good as to ensure that Miss Whitlow's maid has some sustenance? She's enjoying a respite in the parlor adjoined to my bedchamber."

"Certainly, sir. Come along, Gordie."

The lad tried for a bow, but kept his gaze on Miss Whitlow the entire time. She winked at the boy as he backed from the room.

"You'll spoil him for all other ladies," Michael said.

The smile faded into a brittle light in Miss Whitlow's eyes. "Good. We should all exercise the greatest discernment when choosing with whom to share our time and our trust. If I've preserved him from a few scheming chambermaids —for chambermaids are not to be trusted where juvenile males are concerned— then he's better off."

Nothing in her tone suggested even mild annoyance, and yet, Michael sensed reproof again—no creature on earth was less of a threat to anybody than a harried chambermaid—or… something sadder.

Bitterness, perhaps. Well-earned, entirely appropriate bitterness.

Happy Christmas, indeed.

CHAPTER TWO

...Seducing a housemaid ought to be the work of an evening, one doesn't have to be a peer to grasp that fundamental truth. Henrietta had a deceptively strong will, however, and her morals did not yield easily to seduction. After much importuning and not a few stolen liberties, some of which might have borne a slight resemblance to threats to her livelihood, insight befell me.

What the poor thing wanted more than a good tumble was simple attention. She wanted my company, not my cock, for she'd been raised in the household of some selfish old Puritan and a pair of equally gormless brothers. For all her awkward height, her unfortunate red hair, and her Cyprian's form, she thought herself invisible.

And thus, to many she was. But being a man of discernment, I saw her potential...

Baron Angelford did not conform to Henrietta's expectations, though it took her half the soup and most of the bread to recognize the source of her annoyance. He was supposed to steal a glance at her breasts, then smile at her, as if his leering were not only a compliment, but a clever, original compliment.

He should have stolen a sip from her drink then treated her to a smug grin, as if in the history of the male gender, no other fellow had ever been so subtle in his overtures, or so worthy of her notice.

He might have at least accidentally brushed his boot against hers under the table.

Instead, he'd confided that he memorized Shakespearean insults in an effort to impress the English boys with whom he'd gone to school.

"Did that work?" Henrietta asked around a mouthful of plum tart.

"Not exactly. A two-hundred-year-old insult usually falls flat, but I gained a reputation for knowing the Bard, and thus earned extra coin tutoring those upperclassmen unequal to the subtleties of *Hamlet* and *Othello*."

"I would have given much to read those plays as a girl," Henrietta said. "I bought myself a complete, bound edition when I'd been in London for less than a year. My first Christmas token to myself."

She still had that gift and had spent many a night at the theater longing to be home with the Scottish play, rather than smiling at some randy earl.

"What would you like for Christmas this year?" his lordship asked.

What Henrietta wanted was impossible. A succession of titled, wealthy men and her own choices had seen to that.

"Books are always a good choice," she said, "though they come dear. Good tea, and I'm perilously fond of warm stockings." The toddy on top of the fatigue had pried that bit of honesty from her.

Or perhaps she could blame his lordship's ability to truly listen to a conversational partner.

"We can agree on the stockings," he said. "I have four sisters, and I value their knitting skills almost as much as their abilities in the kitchen. I'm fond of a good Irish whiskey, particularly in a cup of strong coffee with a healthy portion of cream."

"Sounds like a waste of good cream." Henrietta liked knowing his lordship had somebody to fuss over him and keep him in good stockings. Truly, she'd consumed her spirits too quickly. "You're letting that plum tart go to waste, my lord."

"I'm not fond of plums, while you appear to relish them." He passed his bowl across the table, and for Henrietta, the moment became fraught with bewilderment. Men stole a bite of her sweets, they did not offer their own, whole and untouched.

"Take it," his lordship said. "I cannot abide food going to waste or a smoking chimney."

Henrietta took a bite of his tart. "What else can't you abide?"

In the course of the meal, he'd become less the titled gentleman and more the hungry fellow enjoying good fare. How had he gone from bog Irish to baron? The journey had doubtless required calculation and daring, much like becoming a wealthy courtesan.

Henrietta had decided by the end of her first year in London that the appellation "successful courtesan" was a contradiction—what female could consider lost virtue a hallmark of success?—but "wealthy courtesan" ought to be a redundant term.

"I'm not fond of winter travel," his lordship said. "For business reasons, I undertook many journeys on the Continent when wiser men would have remained at home, far from war or wintertime coach trips."

Those journeys had doubtless been lucrative, but they'd clearly taken a toll as well.

"All of that is behind you," Henrietta said. "You're titled, wealthy, have all your teeth, and know some excellent insults. The holidays find you in possession of many blessings."

Teasing men was the natural result of having grown up with an older brother and a younger one. *Tease and be teased, lest Papa's sternness suck all the joy from the marrow of life's bones.* Henrietta wasn't teasing her companion, though. She was offering him the same philosophical comfort she offered herself.

It's in the past. No use crying over spilled virtue. You'll never know want or have to step and fetch for another man. Never.

"You look wistful," the baron said. "My mother used to detest the holidays. I can't say all the folderol is much to my taste either."

"Is that why you're repairing to your family seat rather than remaining in Town?"

His smile was crooked, charming, and entirely unexpected. "It's not my family seat, is it? It's simply the real estate I purchased in hopes my great-grandchildren might think of it as home."

Lord Angelford was a bachelor. Henrietta kept track, because she had never, ever shared her favors with engaged or married men.

"To have great-grandchildren, you'll first have to acquire a few children, my lord. Perhaps next Season you'll start on the prerequisites for that venture."

Bride-hunting, in other words. Year after year, Henrietta had watched the marriage machinations from the outer periphery of polite society, half-affronted on behalf of the young ladies, half-envious of the respectability that was the price of admission for the race to the altar.

"If I seek a bride," his lordship said, "the social Season won't have much to do with it. In addition to four sisters, I have two brothers, and one has obliged me with three nephews. They are naughty, rambunctious, entirely dear boys, and any one of them would make a fine baron."

"I have nephews." Another unplanned admission. "They both have my red hair, and the youngest…" Henrietta had a niece as well, though she'd never met the child.

At some point, his lordship had shed his jacket—the room was toasty—and he'd turned back his cuffs. Each departure from strict propriety made him more attractive, which ought not to have been the case. Henrietta had learned to appreciate—and mentally appraise—masculine tailoring down to the penny.

What lay beneath the tailoring was usually a matter of indifference to her.

"Those small boys are why you quit London," the baron said. "You love them madly."

"A courtesan doesn't love, my lord. She adores, treasures, or is fond of." Eventually. At first she loved, and then she learned to be more careful.

"You love those children. My youngest nephew is a terror. The child scares the daylights out of me, and I can only guess at the prayers my sister-in-law has said to keep his guardian angels ever vigilant."

"You're a Papist?"

"Church of England, though my mother has likely harangued the Deity to correct that mistake since the moment she gained her place next to St. Patrick."

His tone said he'd been fond of his mother, and worse yet, he missed her. Henrietta had been missing her own mother for more than twenty years.

"I used to dress in widow's weeds and slip into the back of St. George's on rainy Sundays." Only Lucille knew this, though Henrietta was certain her secret was safe with his lordship. "I missed services, though my father would say my attendance was blaspheming."

His lordship patted Henrietta's hand. "Papas are the worst. My mother often reassured me of that, and I pass the sentiment along to my nephews."

His touch was warm and surprising for its pure friendliness. The contact must have taken him aback as well, because when the maid bustled through the door, his fingers yet lingered on Henrietta's knuckles.

"Madam's coachman is come back," the maid said. "He be cursing something powerful in the common, and I do believe it's starting to snow again. The smithy's gone off to Oxford to spend the holidays with his sweetheart's family. Murphy could have told John Coachman as much. Don't know why he didn't."

She piled dishes on a tray as she spoke, and Henrietta's sentimental reminiscences collided, as sentiment so often did, with hard reality.

"I'll have to bribe Murphy into renting me a room," Henrietta said, taking a last sip of tepid gunpowder. "You will excuse me, my—"

She'd started to rise, but the baron stayed her with a raised hand. "My room is available to you, should you wish to tarry here for the duration, though you might be weeks waiting for the smithy to return."

One of the greatest pleasures of falling from grace was learning to curse. Henrietta instead fell back on the words of one of her few old friends.

"Blasts and fogs upon this weather. I cannot take your rooms from you, my lord. I'll probably end up buying a horse before I can journey onward, and it will be the most expensive nag this village ever sent limping onto the king's highway."

"You quote *King Lear*," the baron replied. "And you need not tarry here at all. I'm traveling on in the direction of Oxford, and you're welcome to share my coach. I can see about hiring you a spare horse when we reach the next coaching inn."

He offered assistance, with no apparent thought of anything in return.

Years of disappointment made Henrietta cautious. "I will pay for any horses myself, my lord."

"Will you at least accept my company as far as the next coaching inn?"

She shouldn't. She really truly should not, but he'd surrendered his plum tart and understood the desperation with which she loved her nephews.

"As far as the next coaching inn," Henrietta said. "No farther."

* * *

"Mordecai MacFergus, as I live and breathe. What are you doing so far south of a proper Scotsman's home?"

Despite the cold, the stingy innkeeper, and the dodgy off-leader, MacFergus's heart lifted at the sound of his native Strathclyde accents.

"If it isn't wee Liam Logan," he said, extending a hand and striding up the aisle of the stable. "How long has it been? Two years since I laid eyes on your ugly face?"

Logan shook hands and offered his flask. "At least, and we were on the Great North Road, God rot its ruts to hell. Tell me how your family goes on."

In the relative warmth and privacy of the stable, they caught up, as two coachmen will, passing the time happily with news of home and news of others who plied their trade. Like most coachmen, Logan was a healthy specimen, his cheeks reddened by the elements, his face weathered, and his grip crushing.

"So who's the fancy gent?" MacFergus asked as the horses munched hay and winter breezes stirred bits of straw in the barn's dirt aisle. The smell of the stable would ever be his favorite—horses, leather, fodder, and even the occasional whiff of manure.

Nothing fertilized a garden like good old horse shit.

Logan made a fancy bow. "You see before you the coachman to Michael, Baron Angelford, and he's anything but fancy. I'm working for an Irishman, MacFergus, one with a proper estate not forty miles on and a proper title, though he's an Irishman among the English."

The English and the Scots had an uneasy tolerance for each other, while the Irish, who'd attempted a rebellion as recently as 1798, didn't fare as well on English soil. They had their peers and grand estates, but in the hierarchy of peerages, the Irish duke ranked below his English and Scottish counterparts and was seldom allowed to forget it.

"Lonely business, being Irish among the English," MacFergus said. "My lady is no stranger to loneliness. I've been driving for Miss Whitlow since she acquired her first coach and team, nearly eight years ago, and you never met a better employer."

Logan tipped his flask up and shook the last drops into his mouth, then tucked the empty flask into his pocket.

"That's always the way of it, isn't it? Them as the Quality disdain can be the most decent, while the earls and dukes will leave good horses standing in the cold for hours outside the Christmas ball."

A gelding two stalls down lifted its tail and broke wind in staccato bursts.

"Caspar agrees with you," MacFergus said. "Your baron was right considerate of my lady, despite Murphy's pernickety airs."

A barn tabby leaped down from the rafters, strutted along a beam, then hopped to a manger and to the floor. Logan picked up the animal and gave it a scratching about the ears.

"So it's like that, is it?" he said. "My Mary got by as best she could before we married. Many a village girl does when she comes to London. Many a Town girl does too, and some of the goings-on at the house parties, Morty MacFergus, would shame the devil."

Miss Henrietta did not attend house parties, and her household conducted itself properly, but for the comings and goings of the gentleman with whom she'd contracted a liaison. Those comings and goings were undertaken discreetly, which Lucille claimed was a written condition signed by both parties.

"My lady was a good girl, from what I hear," MacFergus said, "and then she went into service. Been some time since a gent treated her proper."

"A pity that, but the baron's no stranger to them with poor manners. His own family can't be bothered to join him at the holidays. He'll be all alone in the great hall come Christmas morning, and that's just not right. I've had more than a few wee drams with my lord over a hand of cards, though you mustn't tell any I said that."

Coachmen were privy to an employer's secrets. They knew who called upon whom and who was never at home even when they were clearly within the dwelling. They knew who was invited to which entertainments, who skipped Sunday services, and which gentlemen paid very-late-night calls upon the wives of friends.

A baron sharing a flask and a frequent hand of cards with his coachman, though... Not the done thing.

"My lady travels to see her family at the holidays," MacFergus said, "and they barely welcome her. She stays at an inn rather than with any of them and calls on her brothers as if she were some distant cousin. Her own father won't stay in the same room with her, though my lady never complains of him."

Lucille, usually as taciturn as a nun, ranted about Squire Whitlow's treatment of his daughter. As the holidays came closer, Lucille became more grim, for nothing would dissuade Miss Henrietta from her annual pilgrimage to Oxfordshire.

"Damned rotten English," Logan said. "My oldest—you recall my Angus?—has three girls. He'd never treat one of his own so shabbily, much less at Yuletide, or my Mary would serve him a proper thrashing and I'd cut the birch rod for her."

Quiet descended, underscored by the sound of horses at their hay and the cat purring in Logan's arms.

"Logan, we're a pair of decent, God-fearing men, aren't we?"

Logan set the cat down and dusted his hands. "You're about to get me in trouble, Morty MacFergus, like that time you suggested we put that frog in Mrs. MacMurtry's water glass."

"You're the one who came up with that idea." Always full of mischief, was

Liam Logan. "Your baron is lonely, my Miss Henrietta is lonely, and they're rubbing on well enough as we speak. All I'm suggesting is that we take a wee hand in making their holidays a little brighter."

"No coachman has wee hands."

"And nobody should be alone at Christmas."

"Can't argue with that."

"We're agreed, then," MacFergus said, slinging an arm around his friend's shoulders. "I have a few ideas."

"You have a full flask as well, or my name's not Liam Patrick MacPherson Logan."

"Aye, that I do." MacFergus passed the flask over. "Mind you attend me, because we'll have to be subtle."

Caspar broke wind again as the two coachmen disappeared into the warmth and privacy of the harness room.

* * *

Most of Michael's travel on the Continent had been aimed at gathering intelligence while appearing to transact business. An Irishman, assumed to be at odds with the British crown, had a margin of safety his English counterparts did not, and Michael had exploited that margin to the last limit.

Missions went awry all the time, and this encounter with Henrietta Whitlow had just gone very awry indeed. The dratted woman had scrambled his wits, with her smile, her ferocious love for her nephews, and her wary regard for all assistance.

"Shall we transfer your trunks to my vehicle?" Michael asked.

Wrong question. Miss Whitlow tossed a wrinkled linen serviette onto the empty table. "I see no need to impose on you to that degree."

"I have sisters and know that a lady likes her personal effects about her. Even if the next coaching inn is more obliging, you might spend a few days there, depending on the availability of a blacksmith."

Michael could have reset a damned shoe, provided a forge was available. He'd been hoping his quarry would either spend the night at Murphy's establishment, where she'd broken her journey before, or bide long enough to allow a thorough search of her effects.

A loose horseshoe was a metaphor for the course of most missions—good luck mixed with bad, depending on perspective and agenda.

"I'll fetch a small valise of necessities," Miss Whitlow said. "Give me fifteen minutes to rouse Lucille and assemble our immediate needs."

Before Michael could hold her chair, she rose and swept from the room. In her absence, the little chamber became cramped instead of cozy, the peat fire smoky rather than fragrant. In future, Michael would have more respect for Mrs. Murphy's toddies, and for Henrietta Whitlow's legendary charm.

He paid the shot, summoned his coach, and gave instructions to his grooms to prepare for departure. By the time those arrangements had been made, Miss Whitlow and her maid stood at the bottom of the inn's stairs, the maid looking no less dour for having stolen a nap.

"I don't like it," Miss Whitlow's coachman was saying. "The weather is turning up dirty, yon baron has no one to vouch for him, and this blighted excuse for a sheep crossing likely hasn't a spare coach horse at any price."

"Then I'll buy one at the next coaching inn and send it back to you, MacFergus," Miss Whitlow said. "His lordship has offered to tend to the purchase if the next inn is as disobliging as Mr. Murphy tried to be."

Michael strode into the foyer, Miss Whitlow's cloak over his arm. "I understand your caution," he said to the coachman, "but as it happens, Miss Whitlow and I are both journeying to Oxfordshire, and if need be, I can deliver her to her family's very doorstep. Your concern is misplaced."

He draped the velvet cloak over Miss Whitlow's shoulders when she obligingly turned her back. The urge to smooth his hands over feminine contours was eclipsed only by the knowledge that too many other men had assumed that privilege without Miss Whitlow's permission.

"My concern is not misplaced," the coachman retorted. "See that my lady's trust and her effects aren't either."

"MacFergus, the baron has no need to steal my fripperies," Miss Whitlow said, patting her coachman's arm. "Enjoy a respite from the elements, and don't worry about me. Lucille is the equal of any highwayman, and his lordship has been all that is gentlemanly."

Lucille smirked at the coachman, who stomped off toward the door.

"I'll be having a look at the baron's conveyance," he said. "And making sure his coachman knows in what direction Oxford lies."

"Don't worry," Michael said to the ladies as the door closed on a gust of frigid air. "My coachman is Scottish as well. He tells me two Scotsmen on English soil are under a blood oath not to kill each other by any means except excessive drink. The Irish try to observe the same courtesy with each other, with limited success."

"It's the same with those of my profession in London," Miss Whitlow said. "My former profession. We never disparage each other, never judge one another in public. Why bother, when polite society delights endlessly in treating us ill?"

Lucille cleared her throat and stared at a point beyond Miss Whitlow's left shoulder.

"Shall we be on our way?" Michael offered his arm, and Miss Whitlow took it.

Murphy was not on hand to see his guests off, which in any other hostelry would have been rank neglect. As Michael held the door for the ladies, the serving maid rushed forth from the common with a closed basket.

"From the missus. She says safe journey."

Lucille took the basket as the girl scampered back to the kitchen.

Michael handed the women into his coach, which boasted heated bricks and velvet upholstery, then climbed in and confronted a dilemma. Lucille had taken the backward-facing seat, while Miss Whitlow sat on the forward-facing bench.

A gentleman did not presume, but neither did he willingly sit next to a maid glaring daggers at him. Michael was on the point of taking the place beside Lucille anyway, when insight came to his aid.

To eschew the place beside Miss Whitlow would be to judge her, and for Miss Whitlow to sit on the backward-facing seat with her maid would have been to assume the status of a servant.

What complicated terrain she inhabited, and how tired she must be of never putting a foot wrong on perpetually boggy ground.

"May I?" Michael asked, gesturing to the place beside the lady.

"Of course." She twitched her skirts and cloak aside, and Michael took his seat. At two thumps of his fist on the coach roof, the coach moved off.

The vehicle was warm and the road reasonably free of traffic. One of the advantages of winter travel was a lack of mud, or less mud than during any other season, and thus the horses could keep up a decent pace. Michael's objective was simply to learn where Miss Whitlow would spend the night, so that he could steal a certain object from her, one she might not even value very highly.

He considered asking to purchase the book, but coin carried the potential to insult a former courtesan, particularly one whose decision to depart from propriety had made her wealthy.

Fortunately, Miss Whitlow had failed to notice that the trunks lashed atop Michael's coach were her own.

A soft snore from the opposite bench sounded in rhythm with the horses' hoof beats.

"Poor Lucille is worn out," Miss Whitlow said softly. "She does two things when we travel any distance. Swill hot tea at every opportunity and nap."

"What of the highwaymen?" Michael asked. "Who guards you from them?"

"I guard myself."

Michael mentally translated the words into Latin, because they had the ring of a battle cry. "My barony needs a motto. That might do."

"Better if your family can say, 'We guard each other,'" Miss Whitlow replied. "My grandmother certainly tried to guard me."

Where were her father and brothers when she had needed guarding? "My grandmother was the fiercest woman in County Mayo, excepting perhaps my great-grandmother. Grannie lived to be ninety-two, and not even the earl upon whose land her cottage sat would have gainsaid her. You put me in mind of her."

The coach hit a rut, disturbing the rhythm of Lucille's snores and tossing Miss Whitlow against Michael's shoulder.

"In mind of her, how?"

"She was independent without being needlessly stubborn, and she judged people on their merits, not their trappings. Could quote Scripture by the hour, but also knew poems I doubt have been written down. You and she could have discussed books until the sun came up."

Michael's recitation purposely mentioned no aspect of Miss Whitlow's appearance, though Gran had been ginger-haired in her younger days.

"My grandmother was rumored to be part Rom," Miss Whitlow said. "My father denied it, which only makes me think it more likely to be true."

For a woman who'd been self-supporting for nearly a decade, Miss Whitlow mentioned her father rather a lot. Josiah Whitlow lived in Oxfordshire, not five miles from Michael's property, which was what had given Beltram the idea of sending Michael after the damned book in the first place.

Three months ago, Beltram had invited himself to tea with Henrietta and had seen the tome tucked among some risqué volumes of poetry in her sitting room. With any luck, she'd tossed Beltram's scribblings into the fire when dissolving her household.

"Was your grandmother a lover of books?" Michael asked.

"She was passionate about literature, in part because she taught herself to read after she'd married. She stole out of bed and puzzled over her son's school books, then got the housekeeper to help her. She loved telling me that story."

"I learned by puzzling over my younger brother's books too, then an uncle whose fortunes had improved stepped in and off to public school I went."

Public school had been awful for an Irish upstart with no academic foundation, but Michael had guzzled knowledge like a drover downs ale at the end of a long summer march.

Miss Whitlow studied the snow intensifying beyond the window. "Will you tell me the same lie all titled men tell about public school, and claim you loved it?"

Titled men probably told her worse lies than that. "I learned a lot, and also came to value information in addition to learning. Did you know that James Merton, heir to the Victor family earldom, wet his bed until he was fourteen?"

"Wet his—? Really?" She purely delighted in this tidbit, and who wouldn't? Merton was a handsome, wealthy, horse's arse who fancied himself an arbiter of fashion.

With a glance over at Lucille, Miss Whitlow leaned closer. "He's also afraid of mice. Screams like a banshee at the sight of one and has been known to climb a bedpost if he thinks one is under the—oh dear."

She sat up as straight as she could in a moving coach. "I should not have said that. Not to you, but his mistress told me that herself, and I have no reason… I should not have said such a thing. I do apologize. You must never repeat it, or a woman I consider a friend could lose her livelihood."

Mary Mother of Sorrows, what an impossible life. "I will tell no one, but Henrietta, *you have retired*, and any who hold the occasional humorous reminiscence against you are fools. What sort of man calls himself a woman's protector, then shins up the bedpost at the sight of a wee mouse?"

"He had other shortcomings, so to speak. Gracious,"—she put a gloved hand to her lips as if she'd hiccupped in church—"that didn't come out right."

"One suspected this about Merton," Michael said. "I hope your friend was well compensated for the trials she endured in his company."

"She recounts an amusing tale about him," Miss Whitlow said, her posture relaxing, "but one doesn't joke about disclosing a man's foibles. His friends might make sport of him, his family might ridicule him in public, but a mistress must be loyal, no matter the brevity of the contract."

Not a relationship, a contract.

"So you'd never publish your memoirs?" The question was far from casual.

"Of course not. A naughty auntie might eventually fade from society's view, but not if she memorializes her fall from grace for all the world to read."

"Doubtless, half the House of Lords would be relieved at your conclusion."

Perhaps if Michael conveyed her assurances to Beltram, the viscount might release Michael from the obligation to plunder her luggage in search of a single, stupid book.

"Not half the Lords," she said quietly. "A grand total of six men. We are in the middle of some serious weather."

Six? Only six men in a decade of debauchery? Heathgate had occasionally had six partners in the course of twenty-four hours. Michael considered himself a good, formerly Catholic boy, and even he had enjoyed some notably adventurous house parties.

"I detest serious weather," he said. "The going will be difficult, and the coach will soon acquire a chill. We'd best break out the lap robes now."

Miss Whitlow arranged a soft wool blanket over her maid, then allowed Michael to tuck a blanket over their knees. The progress of the coach slowed, and before Michael could think up another conversational gambit, Miss Whitlow had become a warm weight against his side.

His scintillating company had put the lady to sleep. Within five minutes, her head was on his shoulder, and Michael was more or less alone with his conscience in the middle of a gathering snowstorm.

CHAPTER THREE

Henrietta resisted my lures for weeks—weeks spent cozening her into a parody of friendship. I admired her quiet nature. I begged to sketch her hands—as if a housemaid's hands deserved that honor. I consulted her on my choice of cravat pin and other weighty matters. Never was a mouse stalked with more patience than I stalked Henrietta Whitlow's virtue, and all the while, she was honestly unaware of her peril, such was my skill as a romantic thespian. When I recall my dedication to the task, I truly do marvel at my own tenacity, for once upon a time, Henrietta Whitlow was that bastion of English respectability, the good girl...

In Henrietta's experience, men truly comfortable with their rank and fortune were good company. They neither suffered fools nor put on airs, and the best of them operated under an ethic of *noblesse oblige*. Most were well educated and well informed about the greater world, and thus made interesting conversationalists.

Henrietta had known she was at risk for foolishness with the last man whom she'd granted an arrangement, because His Grace's conversation, his wealth, his grasp of politic affairs, and his generosity hadn't appealed to her half so much as his tacit friendship.

Noah, Duke of Anselm, had truly been a protector, deflecting any disrespect to Henrietta with a lift of his eyebrow. He'd escorted her everywhere with the punctilious courtesy of a suitor, rather than the casual disdain of a lord with his fancy piece.

When he'd informed her that he was embarking on the hunt for a duchess, Henrietta had wished him well and sent him on his way with as much relief as regret. By way of a wedding gift, she'd informed him that his greatest amatory asset was...

His ears.

In the course of their arrangement, Anselm had lingered over breakfast with her, chatting about the news of the day rather than rushing off at first light. He'd never expected her to take him straight from the foyer to the bedroom, as some of his predecessors had, and he'd always approached lovemaking as a conversation. Behind the bedroom door, the taciturn, difficult duke had been affectionate, relaxed, and devilishly patient.

Not quite garrulous, but a good listener. A very, very good listener.

Michael Brenner's willingness to listen eclipsed even the duke's. He never watched Henrietta as if he were waiting for the moment when he could turn the topic to intimacies, and his gaze never strayed even playfully to places a gentleman ought not to look.

Henrietta had lapsed into tired silence mostly because further acquaintance with the baron could go nowhere. She was mulling over that sad fact—also mentally rehearsing Christmas carols with her nephews, Dicken and Zander—when the coach came to a smooth halt.

"That was a fast twelve miles," she said, struggling to sound more awake than she felt.

"Wait a bit," the baron said. "Your hair has tangled with my buttons."

Henrietta was obliged to remain close enough to his lordship to appreciate the soft wool of his cloak beneath her cheek and the scent of lavender clinging to his skin. He extricated her hair from the offending button, and she could sit up.

Lucille stirred as well. "I'll just be having a nice, hot cup of—oh, I must have caught a few winks. Beg your pardon, ma'am. My lord."

"Let's stretch our legs." Anything so Henrietta could put some distance between herself and the man upon whom she'd nearly fallen asleep. She'd shared her bed with a half-dozen partners, which meant she was ruined past all redemption, and yet she was embarrassed to have presumed on the baron's person.

The most highly paid courtesan in London, embarrassed by a catnap.

The baron handed them down from the coach amid steadily falling snow. The coachman clambered off the box, and Lucille disappeared around the side of the inn, doubtless in search of the jakes.

"Please see to accommodations for the ladies, Logan, and a fresh team, unless you're not inclined to press on."

"A bit of snow needn't stop us, my lord," Logan said. "Though you'll be wanting more bricks heated, and we'll have to unload the lady's trunks."

"What are my trunks doing on your coach?" Henrietta asked, counting a half-dozen traveling cases lashed to the roof and boot of the baron's conveyance. "I thought you understood that a valise would be sufficient for my needs." The idea that he'd made free with her possessions or countermanded her orders sat uneasily.

"I gave no order to transfer your belongings," the baron said as his coachman stomped up the steps into the inn. "Perhaps your coachman tried to anticipate your needs. We can unload your bags easily enough and have them sent up to your rooms."

Now that the moment to part was upon her, Henrietta didn't want to lose sight of his lordship. He'd behaved toward her as a gentleman behaved toward a lady, nothing more, and yet his consideration had solved many problems.

"I suppose this is farewell, then," she said.

"If you're biding in Oxfordshire, our paths might well cross again." He'd eschewed a hat, and snow dusted auburn locks that brushed the collar of his cape.

"I generally stay at the Duck and Goose in Amblebank." Henrietta's own father refused to grant her the use of a bedroom, though his manor house boasted eight. She refused to impose on her brothers lest their hospitality to her cause difficulties with Papa.

The baron reached into the coach and produced Henrietta's scarf. "I have the great good fortune to dwell at Inglemere, due east of Amblebank by about five miles. I'd welcome a call from you or your family."

Welcome a call.

His lordship spoke a platitude, but in the past ten years, no one had offered Henrietta that courtesy. She was not welcome to call on old friends and neighbors. They didn't judge her for having wealthy protectors in London, but her own family refused to openly welcome her, and the neighborhood took its cue from that behavior.

If only Papa weren't so stubborn, and if only Henrietta weren't even more stubborn than he.

The grooms led the team around to the carriage yard, where fresh horses would be put to. Abruptly, Henrietta was alone with a man who tempted her to second thoughts and if onlys.

If only she'd met him rather than Beltram when she'd gone in search of employment all those years ago.

If only she'd realized sooner what Beltram had been about.

If only her father had written back to her, even once.

Such thoughts went well with the bitter breeze and the bleak landscape. The falling snow created a hush to complement the white blanketing the steps, bushes, pine roping and the wreath on the inn's door.

The baron studied that wreath as if it bore a Latin inscription. "Will you slap me if I take a small liberty, Miss Whitlow?"

Henrietta wanted to take a liberty or two with him, which came as no little surprise. "Is it a liberty when you ask permission?"

He looped her scarf about her neck and treated her to a smile that crinkled the corners of his eyes. "Excellent point. We'll call it a gesture of thanks for making the miles pass more agreeably."

He bent close and brushed his lips over hers. In that instant, Henrietta regretted her decision to retire from the courtesan's profession. To earn even a semblance of acceptance from any polite quarter, she'd been prepared to give up all kisses, all affection, and certainly all pleasures of the flesh.

She'd thought the absence of masculine attention would be a relief, and she'd been wrong.

The baron tendered a kiss as respectful as it was surprising. His lips were warm, his hand cradling Henrietta's jaw gentle. He didn't *handle* her, he caressed, albeit fleetingly.

He'd be a devastatingly tender lover, and that realization was more sobering than all the arctic breezes in England.

"I'll wish you a Happy Christmas," Henrietta said, stepping away, "and thank you for your many kindnesses."

The door to the inn banged open, and Lucille trudged back around the side of the building. Now—*now*—the chill wind penetrated Henrietta's cloak, and a damnable urge to cry threatened. The baron made matters worse by tucking the ends of Henrietta's scarf about her neck.

"The pleasure was mine, Miss Whitlow. If I can ever be of assistance, you need only send to me at Inglemere, and anything I can do…"

Henrietta's heart was breaking, and over a chance encounter that ought never have happened.

"Godspeed, my lord."

He took out his gloves and pulled them on, and the coach returned from the carriage yard, minus Henrietta's trunks. This team was all gray, their coats already damp and curling from the falling snow.

"Begging your lordship's pardon," said his coachman, who'd emerged from the inn. "I don't think the ladies will want to bide here. There's rooms aplenty, because there's illness in the house. Half the staff is down with influenza, and the innkeeper said the cook was among those afflicted. Shall I have the lady's trunks loaded back onto the coach?"

"Henrietta?" Not Miss Whitlow, and his lordship's familiarity was that of a friend.

Henrietta's relief beggared description. "Lucille catches every illness, and as tired as she is, she'll be afflicted by this time tomorrow if we stay here."

"And then you might well succumb yourself. The next inn is but twelve miles distant, and surely there, you should have better luck."

"Twelve more miles, then," Henrietta said, smiling despite the cold, despite everything. "But no farther."

* * *

"How many more years will we be coming here for a weekly dinner, listening to Papa's pontifications and making our wives and children listen to them as well?" Philip Whitlow kept his voice down, because he stood on the squire's very doorstep.

Thaddeus turned to shield the bundle in his arms from the winter breeze. "I promised Isabel that after the baby came, we'd invite Papa to our table rather than keep trooping over here every Sunday, but the child is nearly six months old, and here we are. Again."

Thaddeus's wife had presented him with a daughter over the summer, and Philip acknowledged a pang of envy. Dicken and Alexander were dear, and he'd gladly give his life for either boy, but Beatrice longed for a daughter.

"Papa gets worse as the holidays approach." As the oldest sibling, Philip expected a certain diplomacy of himself, but at some point, that diplomacy had shaded closer to cowardice.

"Because Henrietta insists on visiting," Thad replied. "She hasn't met her namesake. I expect they'll get on famously."

The infant in Thad's arms was Isabella Henrietta. Her mother called her Izzy. Her father referred to her as his little red hen, owing to her mop of ginger hair.

Unfortunate, that. Both of Philip's boys were red-haired, but they were boys. "Beatrice says we must do more to make Henrietta welcome."

Thad left off fussing with the blankets enveloping his daughter. "Beatrice says? I thought Bea had no patience with straying women."

Bea had no patience with families who couldn't get on with being families. "I might have misread her, somewhat." Or hidden behind her skirts, as it were, or betrayed a sibling for the sake of keeping peace with a parent.

"Isabel said if I ever treat our daughter the way Papa has treated Henrietta, she'll disown me. I do not favor the prospect of being disowned by my dearest spouse."

"If you wrap the child up any more tightly, she'll expire for want of air." How many times had Bea offered Philip the same warning when the boys were small?

Thad rubbed noses with his daughter, which set her to squirming and cooing. "Who looked after Henrietta, Philip? Having a daughter sets a man to wondering. Henrietta was six when Mama died, and my earliest memory is of Henrietta reading to me. I have no memory of our mother, but I can't forget that when Papa was too grief-stricken to recall he had children, Henrietta read to me every night."

Philip came the rest of the way down the steps. "Henrietta was a good girl. That's part of what makes Papa so angry with her."

"He's not angry, he's ashamed. Time he got over it, I say."

Thad was the family optimist, and in part because Henrietta had been such a devoted sister, his recollections of the years following their mother's death were sad but benign. Squire Whitlow's grief had expressed itself in temper and discipline with his two older children.

"People don't get over a hurt because we say so, Thad, but for what it's worth, Beatrice and I agree with you. Henrietta asks nothing of us but some hospitality at Christmas, and she always offers to help if we need it."

Their wives emerged from the manor house, chattering volubly despite being wrapped up in scarves and cloaks.

"I wondered if Henrietta's generosity extended to you as well. I've never had to ask for help, but I'd ask her before I'd ask Papa."

"So would I." Though Philip hadn't realized that truth until he'd spoken it aloud.

"I suppose we'll see you next week," Thad said, taking Isabel's hand. "Unless Henrietta's come to visit."

Beatrice took the place at Philip's side. "Where have the boys got off to?"

"The stable, last I saw them."

"Where they will get their best clothes filthy. Come along, Philip, and prepare to be stern."

"Yes, ma'am."

Thad smirked, Isabel took the baby from him, and Philip wished the holidays weren't bearing down on them all like a runaway team on a muddy road.

* * *

One did not kiss an innocent woman and then steal from her, not if one had any honor.

Michael accounted himself in possession of a modest store of honor, and yet, he'd kissed Henrietta Whitlow, or started to kiss her. That chaste little gesture in the inn yard barely qualified as a kiss, especially when offered to a woman whose affections had been coveted by kings and princes.

And yet that kiss had been enough to set Michael to wondering.

What would kissing Henrietta passionately be like? Holding her through a long and lazy night? Waking to see that red hair in glorious disarray? What would *she* feel like wrapped around him, half mad with desire?

As the coach jostled along the increasingly snowy road, Michael set aside those speculations. He could sleep with any number of women, make love to many more, and hair was hair. What bothered him was that he wanted to know more about *her*, and not simply so he could steal from her with less risk of discovery.

What books did Henrietta Whitlow treasure most dearly?

Did she ever stay up all night reading?

What holiday token would make her smile the way she'd smiled at the serving maid?

How did she *like* to be kissed, if she cared for it at all?

"You've grown quiet," Miss Whitlow said. "You needn't worry for Lucille's slumbers. I've seen her sleep through a gale."

Indeed, the stalwart Lucille had fortified herself with two cups of tea at the last inn and was now wedged against the opposite squabs, a lap blanket tucked beneath her chin, her snoring a counterpoint to the rhythm of the horses' hooves.

"My former employer had the same ability to sleep any time," Michael replied, "though Heathgate limited himself to naps and delighted in making me think he was asleep when he was in truth eavesdropping."

"You miss him."

Michael missed his sisters. Did they ever miss him? "Heathgate and I became a good team. Ten years ago, I was the shy Irish lad willing to do anything to better myself. Heathgate was a fundamentally decent man trying to impersonate a jaded rogue. I had the better classical education and stronger organizational skills, while Heathgate had business intuition and daring. He took a modest fortune and made it enormous, if you'll excuse a vulgar reference to commercial matters."

Miss Whitlow rustled about on the bench beside Michael, tucking the lap robe around her hip.

"Patch leaf," he murmured.

Her fussing paused. "I beg your pardon?"

"The scent you wear. It reminds me of the patch leaf used to keep the moths away from Kashmir shawls. I couldn't place it and have never come across its like on a woman before."

She extended her left arm beneath his nose. "I have it made up specially. At first I was simply storing my clothing with the leaves used to protect the shawls, but then my Parisian perfumer found a way to capture the scent."

Michael turned her wrist and sniffed translucent skin. Blue veins ran from her forearm to her palm, and a single tendon stood out.

"It's different," he said, resisting the urge to taste her pulse. "Unusual."

"I don't care for it. Too exotic, too… loud. I no longer have to be loud or exotic, and what a relief that is." Her fleeting glance asked if her admission offended him, though her idea of loud was probably a healthy man's notion of a seductive whisper.

"What scent do you prefer?" he asked.

"My favorite scents are green tea and freshly scythed grass, but those would hardly do for a fragrance. My mother hung lavender sachets all about the house, from the bedposts, in the linen closets, in the wardrobes, and among the dry-goods pantries. In the new year, I will wear proper English lavender."

On her, that common herb would smell anything but proper. "Why wait until next month?"

"I am determined on an objective, my lord. I expect to fail, but I must try. My success will depend on remaining very much the woman in possession of herself, rather than the meek girl who left Amblebank ten years ago."

The coach lurched sideways, then righted itself. Logan was a first-rate coachman, and thus when he slowed the team to a more cautious pace, Michael didn't countermand his judgment.

And yet, these conversations with Miss Whitlow were driving him barmy. He wanted to kiss her, though his job was to betray her, to the extent purloining one book was a betrayal. To blazes with Beltram, favors owed, and Yuletide travel.

"I find it hard to believe you were ever a meek girl," Michael said, though he well knew she had been. Beltram damned near took pride in "making Henrietta Whitlow what she is today," as if ruining a housemaid was a rare accomplishment rather than a disgrace.

"I was a drudge," Miss Whitlow replied. "A pretty drudge, though I grasped too late how that beauty could affect my fate. I quarreled with my father over his choice of husband for me and decamped for the metropolis, as so many village girls have. The tale is prosaic and my fate not that unusual."

"Your fate is very unusual," Michael countered. "Those village girls often end up plying their trade in the street, felled by the French disease, or behind bars. You had your choice of dukes and, I hazard, are wealthy as a result."

"I am wealthy, and all that coin only makes my father hold me in worse contempt. The wages of sin are to be penury, disease, disfigurement, and bitter remorse, not security and comfort."

Two hours ago, she would not have been that honest.

"Your father's household is the objective you're intent upon?"

She tucked one foot up under her skirts, a very informal pose. "Papa refuses to enter any room I'm in, he will not say my name to other family members, and he's removed every likeness of me from his house."

And to think Michael was pouting because his sisters had declined to join him for Christmas. He did not want to know that Henrietta Whitlow was afflicted with heartaches. He wanted to believe she'd leave her London life, become an intriguing fixture among the lesser gentry of some backwater, and never miss one small volume from among her store of books.

When Christmas angels took up residence at Inglemere, perhaps.

"Why bother with further overtures in your father's direction?" Michael asked. "He deserves to have the cold comfort of his intolerance directed right back at him."

Miss Whitlow peeked beneath the shade rolled down to keep the worst of the cold from leaking through the window.

"I hope your coachman knows this road well. The weather is turning awful."

Was there any change of subject less adroit than the weather? Miss Whitlow hesitated to discuss her family, though she'd numbered her lovers without a hint of a blush.

"I hired Logan when I bought Inglemere. He's driven the route from here to London for years. We can't be far from the next inn, and you are not to worry. Compared to the Norwegian coast in December, compared to the North Sea in a temper, this snowstorm is merely weather."

She continued to gaze out at the snowy landscape, which had acquired the bluish tinge of approaching twilight. Michael was running out of time to plunder her possessions, though tonight, as she slept secure at the next inn, he would surely see his task completed.

"I cannot give up on my father," she said, "because he gave up on me, and that was wrong of him. We are family. I will make one more effort to bridge our differences, and if he remains adamant, then I'll do as you suggest and put him—and my quarrel with him—aside."

Ten years was an infernally long time to quarrel. Mr. Whitlow was a fool to toss away a daughter with that sort of tenacity, but then, Michael was a fool too.

He'd wondered idly about how to concoct some sort of green-tea-and-scythed-grass soap to give Miss Whitlow for a Yuletide token—in a world where he wasn't about to steal more than kisses from her—when what she wanted by Christmas morning was nothing less than a miracle of paternal forgiveness.

* * *

By the time the coach lumbered into the inn yard, Henrietta was tucked against his lordship, all but asleep, and half dreaming of a Christmas dinner with her family—all of her family—gathered around a laden table. Oddly enough, his lordship was present at the feast too.

"I have doubtless snored as loudly as Lucille," Henrietta muttered, righting herself. Her back ached, and her feet were blocks of ice.

The baron retrieved the arm he'd tucked across her shoulders.

"I suspect somebody keeps moving the inns along this stretch of the highway so they recede as we approach. In Ireland, we'd say the fairies have been busy."

The farther the coach traveled from London, the more a soft Irish brogue threaded into his lordship's words. In the dark, his voice would be…

Henrietta nudged Lucille's knee. "We've arrived, my dear. Time to wake up."

Lucille scratched her nose, but otherwise didn't budge.

"Tea, Lucille!" his lordship said. "Hot, strong, sweet, and laced with a dollop of spirits."

Her eyes popped open. "I must have caught a few winks. If you'll excuse me, Miss Henrietta, I'll just be stretching my legs a wee while, and… my gracious, the daylight has all but fled."

Someday, much sooner than Henrietta wanted to admit, Lucille would be old. The maid had a crease across her right cheek, and her cloak had been misbuttoned at the throat. She already had the dowager's habit of falling asleep in company.

Lucille had been in service at Beltram's, the same as Henrietta, and she'd been the first person Henrietta had hired for her own household.

His lordship climbed from the coach to hand the ladies down, and off Lucille went.

"The inn doesn't look like it receives much custom," Henrietta said. The entrance was lighted and the doors sported pine wreaths, but other than a tang of smoke in the air, little suggested the place was open for business.

"I've not had to stay here previously," the baron said. "We're but eight miles from Inglemere. I've seldom even changed teams here, though I will today."

He was traveling on, then. Henrietta hated that notion. As the coach was led away, she wrapped her arms about his lordship's waist.

"I'm taking a liberty with your person," she said. "You will think badly of me, but then, everybody already does. I will miss you."

He drew her closer, though winter clothing prevented the degree of closeness Henrietta sought. He'd been decent to her, and she'd missed decent treatment more than she'd realized.

"I'm rarely in Oxfordshire," he said, "though I will think of you when I travel back this way."

Henrietta knew exactly how to send a man on his way smiling. She usually dropped hints that he'd been the most exciting/passionate/affectionate/inventive lover—something credible, but not too effusive—gave him looks of fondness and regret and a parting exchange of intimacies remarkable for its dullness.

Lest he second-guess his decision to part from her.

In five cases out of six, her paramours had come wandering back around, hinting that a resumption of their arrangement would be welcome. Henrietta never obliged. Anselm had come around as well, and Henrietta had taken fierce joy in the fact that the duke had called simply as a friend, albeit one with marital troubles and a wide protective streak.

She'd not even flirted with Michael, Baron Angelford, and she would miss him.

"You're being kind," she said, stepping back. "Letting me know that some Yuletide chivalry on your part will not develop into anything more. I'm usually the one who must be kind. I suppose we'd best find me accommodations and see about sending word back to MacFergus regarding my whereabouts."

Please argue with me. Please contradict my brisk conclusions, or at least express a hope that we might meet again.

"I've come to Inglemere with an eye toward selling it." His lordship used a gloved finger to brush a wind-whipped lock of hair from Henrietta's cheek. "My sisters bide in Oxford itself, so owning a town house there makes more sense. If you ever have need of me, I can be reached at the home of Clarissa Brenner, Little Doorman Street."

Worse and worse.

"I have brothers in the environs of Amblebank," Henrietta said. "They won't gainsay my father, but neither do they disdain my company. A wealthy sister is allowed a few peccadilloes."

I sound bitter.

Probably because I am bitter.

Henrietta was also tired, cold, and once again a lone female making her way against all sense on a path of her own choosing.

The coachman, Logan, came down the inn's steps. "Ye canna bide here, mistress."

"What do you mean?" the baron snapped. "Miss Whitlow has been traveling all day. She's hungry, chilled, fatigued, and due a respite from my company. You should be unloading her trunks as I speak."

Must he be so ready to get rid of her?

"I'm sorry, guv, but this inn accepts no overnight custom. The innkeeper and his wife are elderly, and they're off to await the arrival of a new grandchild in Oxford. The housekeeper says we can get a fresh team and a hamper, and warm up for a bit in the common, but there are no beds to be had here."

No beds? How ironic that a courtesan, who generally plied her trade in a bed, should be so pleased to find none available.

"What sort of inn stays in business by letting its beds go empty?" his lordship fumed. "I've never heard the like."

"Beds are a lot of work," Henrietta said, which earned her a look of consternation from the baron. "The innkeeper would need maids to change the linens daily, laundresses to do endless washing, heaps and heaps of coal to heat the wash water, more maids to tidy up each room, every day. More coal to keep those rooms warm, and all for not very much coin. The kitchen and the stable generate most of the profit for an establishment like this."

His lordship peered down at her. "How do you know that?"

"I need investments and have considered buying a few coaching inns. Widows often own their late husband's businesses, and thus a female owning an inn isn't that unusual. It's a chancy proposition, though. Very dependent on mail routes, weather, and the whims of the fashionable."

"We can continue this discussion inside," his lordship said. "Get me a fresh team, Logan, and leave Miss Whitlow's bags on the coach. We can push on to Inglemere as soon as the moon rises."

The baron took Henrietta by the hand and tugged her in the direction of the steps, and a good thing that was. Left to her own devices, she might have stood in the snowy yard until nightfall, marveling that his lordship had more or less invited her to spend the night at his own house.

* * *

The storm had obligingly taken an intermission, and in the bright illumination of a full moon on new snow, Michael and his guests continued on their way. Lucille was at least awake, which meant he had more incentive to keep his conversation free of innuendo, overtures, or outright begging.

He wanted time alone with Henrietta Whitlow, he *needed* time alone with her trunks. Having her as an overnight guest at Inglemere would tempt him to arrange the former, when he must limit himself to the latter.

"I do believe it's getting colder," Lucille muttered. "Does that sometimes, when snow lets up. You think it's cold, then winter stops funning about. How much farther, milord?"

Too far. "We're better than halfway," Michael said. "If you'd like to continue to Amblebank, I can have Logan drive you tonight, though I'd suggest you leave your bags with me to make the distance easier for the horses." *Please say you'll go.*

Please stay.

I'm losing my wits.

"Miss Henrietta," Lucille said, "if you make me spend another minute longer than necessary in this coach, I will turn in my notice, so I will."

"You turn in your notice at least once a month," Henrietta said. "In this case, such dramatics won't be necessary. Nobody in Amblebank would be alarmed if my arrival were delayed until next week, though I do want the children to have their presents on Christmas morning."

She'd at least be spending her holiday around children. Michael would have to journey into Oxford for that privilege.

"I never know what to get them," he said. "My nieces and nephews. Two of my sisters are married and between them have a half-dozen children. I'm at something of a loss when it comes to presents. My brothers remain in Ireland, so the issue is less pressing with them." Fine spirits for the menfolk, silk for his sisters, but the children were a puzzle.

Miss Whitlow passed him the flask of tea they'd been sharing, though the contents had grown cold within a mile of the inn.

"You're at a loss because as a child, you never had presents. You had no toys, no books, no pets. My father was of a similar bent, though my mother's influence softened him somewhat."

Michael's diversion had been hard work and harder work. "We had a pig, a grand creature named Bridget Boru. If she had more than ten piglets, my father divided up the proceeds of sale from the extra piglets among us children. The birth of the Christ child was not more warmly anticipated than Bridget's litters."

But how Michael had died a little inside to see those piglets sold off, season after season, and how jealously he'd guarded his "sow bank."

"You had dreams," Miss Whitlow said. "Your nieces and nephews do too. I think of my girlhood dreams when I'm shopping for Christmas tokens."

The question was out before Michael realized how fraught the answer might be: "What were your dreams?"

She took back the flask and capped it. "The same as every other girl's: a home of my own, children, my own tea service."

"Not books?"

"My love of books came later."

When the hope of children and family was beyond her? How odd that

Henrietta and he should share the same dream—a family, in all its prosaic, complex, dear, and exasperating variability. All of his hard work, all of the risks he'd taken, had been so that someday he'd be able to provide for a family, with no fear of potato blight, English prejudice, or hard winters.

"For Christmas, I want never to set my backside upon a coach bench again," Lucille said. "In case anybody should wonder."

"I was consumed with curiosity on that very point," Michael said. "Assuming your wish can be granted temporarily, what else might Father Christmas bring you?"

Lucille's gaze landed on Miss Whitlow. "Peace on earth. It was a fine aspiration back in Bethlehem, though we've yet to achieve it. Peace in Oxfordshire would be a start."

"Lucille." Miss Whitlow's reproof was weary.

"I'll hold my tongue, miss. But his lordship's bound to hear the parish gossip. You haven't done any more than many other country girls do when they're—"

"Perhaps my nieces would like a tea service for their dolls," Michael said, rather than watch the maid's defense further erode her employer's mood. The closer they drew to Amblebank, the quieter Miss Whitlow became.

"That's a lovely idea," she said. "Or a lap desk, for the older children. One with their name carved on the top."

"What about a journal?" Michael mused. "My nieces would memorialize their brothers' every transgression given a chance."

"Not a journal." Miss Whitlow tucked the half-empty flask into her sizable valise—which Michael might also have to search. "Journals can be found and their contents exposed by mischievous siblings at the worst possible moment."

Was no topic of conversation safe with her? "You speak from experience."

"Two brothers' worth. My older brother showed up shortly after my parents married, and I followed less than two years later. My younger brother waited a proper five years to come along. In any case, I learned not to keep a journal. What of you, your lordship? What would you like for Christmas?"

Her question brought an image to mind of Michael in the great hall at Inglemere presiding over a long table shared with sisters, in-laws, children, the occasional cousin, and—truly, he'd been shut up in the coach for too long—Henrietta Whitlow at the far end of the table.

He wanted a holiday full of laughter, warmth, and family.

He'd get a solitary tray in the library and a guilty conscience.

"I hope the coming days will allow me to find some rest," he said, "and peace and quiet. I'll read, catch up on my correspondence, and consider properties in Oxford for possible purchase." His sisters claimed there weren't any, though Michael suspected they'd simply got used to managing without his fraternal interference.

Henrietta was at her customary place beside him, close enough that he could see the fatigue shadowing her eyes, a bleakness in her gaze, and a grimness about her mouth.

"I know it's highly unusual," he said, "and you must feel free to refuse me, but I'd be very grateful if you'd tarry at Inglemere tomorrow. My coachman and grooms deserve to rest, and I daresay you do as well."

He was a cad, a bounder, an idiot, and very good thief. He did not need an extra day to paw through Miss Whitlow's effects.

"I don't—" Miss Whitlow began.

"What a generous offer," Lucille said. "You'll have the rest of your life to wear plain caps, miss, and endure sneers in the churchyard. Might as well get a good night's rest before we embark on your penance, aye?"

"My staff is utterly discreet," Michael said, "and I won't think of you journeying on to Amblebank tomorrow. The roads will be safer in a day or two, and you will be fortified for the challenge of dealing with family."

Didn't he sound like the voice of gentlemanly reason? Miss Whitlow ought to toss him from the coach.

"One day," she said. "One day to rest, get warm, plan my approach, and let MacFergus know what's become of me. One day, but no more."

One day—and two nights—would be more than enough for Michael to trespass against her trust, steal from her, and send her into the arms of the family who presumed to sit in judgment of her. They'd treat her like royalty if she were his baroness, regardless of her past, but he was the last man who deserved to be her baron.

CHAPTER FOUR

Even good girls grow weary of loneliness and poverty. You will realize, of course, that I might have been a tad bit misleading where my comely housemaid was concerned—or perhaps she misunderstood my overtures? Henrietta's education had been neglected in every regard except how to drudge for her menfolk, poor thing.

I didn't go down on bended knee, but I might have alluded to wedded bliss a time or two or twenty. She eventually granted me the prize I'd so diligently sought. For some while, all was not-quite-connubial bliss. Never was my candlestick so well polished, as it were... and I didn't have to spend a penny for my pleasure. I could not boast of my cleverness, trifling with the help being frowned upon, but you must admit, London's bachelors are a happier lot for my having seen to Miss Whitlow's education...

"What the hell are you doing?" Liam Logan kept his voice down lest he upset horses who'd earned a ration of oats for their labors.

"I'm plundering a woman's luggage," the baron replied from the depths of a large, brass-hinged trunk. "What are you doing out and about at this hour?"

The light of the single lantern made the baron look gaunt when he straightened. Gaunt and guilty. He'd served his guests a fine dinner in Inglemere's elegant dining room, and should have been abed himself, not wandering around a darkened stable.

"I'm tucking in the boys," Logan said. "You ought to consider buying these grays. They're a good lot, and they pull well together."

His lordship went back to rummaging in the trunk. "Spare me your analogies. Henrietta Whitlow is no longer for sale. I'm not sure she ever was."

The Quality in a mood were puzzle enough, but Michael Brenner was new to his title, far too solitary, and without much cheer. Liam respected the man and even liked him—the baron was scrupulously fair, hard-working, and devoted to his family—but Liam didn't always understand his employer.

"Miss Whitlow had something on offer," Liam said, tossing another forkful of hay into the nearest stall, "to hear half of London tell it. I don't blame her for that. Dukes and nabobs are as prone to foolishness as the rest of us, and it's ever so entertaining to see a woman from the shires making idiots of them."

The baron straightened, his greatcoat hanging open despite the cold. To Liam, a horse barn would ever be a cozy place, but the baron wasn't a coachman, inured to the elements and dressed to deal with them.

"The damned thing isn't here."

"The only damned thing I see in these stables is you, sir. Care for a nip?"

Two other trunks were open, and the latches were undone on the remaining three. The baron accepted Liam's flask and regarded the luggage with a ferocious scowl.

"I was sure she had it with her. She's closed up her household in London, and these are all the trunks she's brought. Damn and blast."

"Have a wee dram," Liam said. "It'll improve your cursing."

"My cursing skills are excellent, but I try to leave them back in the bogs from whence I trotted. This is good whisky."

"Peat water makes the best, I say. My brother-in-law agrees with me. What are we searching for?"

His lordship sat on one of the closed trunks. "We're searching for foolishness, to use your word. Lord Beltram was Miss Whitlow's first... I can't call him a protector, for he ruined her. He was her first, and in the manner of besotted men the world over, he wanted to immortalize his conquest. Somewhere in Miss Whitlow's effects is a small volume full of bad poetry, competent sketches, and maudlin reminiscences. Can I buy some of this whisky?"

"I'll give you a bottle for Christmas. Miss Whitlow is not in the first blush of youth, if you'll forgive a blunt observation. Why has Lord Beltram waited this long to fret over his stupidity?"

The baron sighed, his breath fogging white in the gloom. "He's decided to find a wife—or cannot afford too many more years of bachelorhood—and this book is a loose end. When they parted, Miss Whitlow asked to have only this book—not jewels, not a bank draft, not an introduction to some other titled fool. All she wanted was this silly journal. Beltram passed it along, thinking himself quite clever for having ended the arrangement without great expense or drama."

Liam tossed a forkful of hay into another stall, working his way down the row. "So Beltram is a fool, but why are you compounding the error with more folly? Miss Whitlow has had years to blackmail the idiot or publish his bad verse. Why must you turn thief on his behalf?"

The baron took up a second fork and began haying the stalls on the opposite side of the aisle. Horses stirred, nickered, and then tucked into their fodder.

"Once long ago," the baron said, "in a land not far enough away, with which we were at war, Beltram's silence saved my life. I promised him any favor he cared to name and only later realized my silence had also saved his life."

"So he took advantage of an innocent maid, and now he's taking advantage of you," Liam said. "And you wonder why the common folk think the Quality are daft. You're not a thief, my lord."

The baron threw hay with the skill of one who'd made his living in a stable once upon a time.

"Unless you've been poor as dirt and twice as hopeless," he said, hanging the fork on a pair of nails when the row was complete, "you don't know how an unfulfilled obligation can weigh on your sense of freedom. Every time I crossed paths with Beltram, I knew, and he knew, that I'd put myself in his debt. I cannot abide being in his debt, cannot abide the thought that ten years hence, he'll ask something of me—something worse than a little larceny—and I'll be bound by honor to agree to it. I gave the man my word."

"Honor, is it? To steal from a woman who's already been wronged?" MacFergus would have a few things to say about that brand of honor, and as usual, this plan gone awry had been his idea.

"I've considered stealing from her, then stealing the book back from Beltram so I can replace it among the lady's belongings."

"Clever," Liam said, wondering what Mary would make of all this nonsense. "Or you might tell Beltram you simply couldn't find the thing. I daresay lying to his lordship won't meet with your lofty idea of honor either."

"If I can't find it, if I honestly can't find it, then I'll tell him that."

"That you wouldn't lie to a nincompoop makes it all better, of course. I'll wish you the joy of your thievery, sir. I'm for bed. Pleasant dreams."

"Go to hell, Logan. If the book isn't here, the only other place it could be is in Miss Whitlow's valise."

Which was doubtless resting at the foot of the lady's cozy bed. "And Happy Christmas to you too, my lord."

* * *

His lordship hadn't come to Henrietta's bed last night.

He'd lighted her up to her room, offered her a kiss on the cheek—the forehead would have provoked her to quoting the Bard's more colorful oaths—and wished her pleasant dreams.

Her dreams had been tormented, featuring an eternity racketing about naked and alone in a coach forever lost in a winter landscape.

"You're already dressed," Lucille said, bustling through the door without knocking. "I bestir myself at a needlessly early hour and find my services aren't required. The baron had chocolate sent up to my room. Fresh scones with butter, and chocolate, kept hot over a warming candle."

Henrietta knew how that chocolate had felt, simmering over the flame. She decided to leave her hair half down, the better to light the baron's candle at breakfast.

"What is wrong with me, Lucille?" She shoved another pin into her hair. "I swore off men more than six months ago and in all that time wished I'd made the decision years earlier." Before she'd met Anselm, in any case. Her memories of him had been a little too fond. "You don't have to make the bed. The baron has an excellent staff."

An excellent, cheerful, discreet staff who appeared genuinely loyal to their employer.

"I cannot abide idleness," Lucille said. "All that feigning sleep in the coach yesterday taxed my gifts to the limit."

Were pearl-tipped hair pins too much at breakfast? "You were feigning sleep? That was a prodigious good imitation of a snore for a sham effort."

"Mostly feigning. You and his lordship got along well. These are the loveliest flannel sheets."

For winter, they were more luxurious than silk, which was difficult to wash. Henrietta had never thought to treat herself to flannel sheets, but she would in the future.

"The baron and I got on so well that after supper he left me for the charms of his library. Perhaps I retired in the nick of time." Was that a wrinkle lurking beside her mouth? A softness developing beneath her chin?

Henrietta had never worried about her appearance before—never—and now… "I have left my wits somewhere along the Oxford Road."

Lucille straightened, a brocade pillow hugged to her middle. "This is what you put the gents through, Miss Henrietta. This uncertainty and vexation. They didn't dare approach you without some sign you'd welcome their advances. Do you fancy his lordship, or merely fancy being fancied?"

"Excellent question." Henrietta began removing the pins she'd so carefully placed. "I fancied being respectable. I know that's not likely to happen for the next twenty years, but I can aspire to being respected. Then his lordship goes and treats me decently, and I'm… I don't care for it as much as I thought I would."

The respect was wonderful. The insecurity it engendered was terrifying.

She cared *for him*, for the boy who'd had no toys, the wealthy baron who didn't know how to entice his sisters to join him for Christmas dinner. She cared for a man who'd not put on airs before a cranky maid, who regarded Henrietta's past as just that—her past.

But she also desired him, which was a fine irony.

"He did invite us to bide here today." Lucille smoothed thick quilts over the sheets. "Have you seen his library?"

"I have not. After supper, he brought me straight up to bed, and I confess I was happy to accompany him. Then off he went, and I'm all in a muddle, Lucille."

"Fallen women get paid for accommodating a man's desire," Lucille said. "Un-fallen women aren't immune to animal spirits. They simply know how to indulge them without being judged for it. I wasn't always a plain-faced, pudgy old maid, you know."

"You are not plain-faced, pudgy, or old. I have it on good authority that men like a substantial woman between the sheets."

Thank God. Though maybe Michael Brenner preferred the golden-haired waifs and blue-eyed princesses of the Mayfair ballrooms, drat their dainty feet. Henrietta's feet were in proportion to the rest of her. Her father had called her a plow horse of a girl, and the baron might see her as such.

"I hate this uncertainty," Henrietta said. "I'm wondering now if men value only the women they must pay for."

Lucille tossed the brocade pillows back onto the bed, achieving a comfy, arranged look with casual aim.

"You have it all wrong, miss, which is understandable given your situation. What the men value, what they respect, is a reflection of what we value in ourselves. You did very well in London because after Lord Beltram played you so false, you never allowed another man to rule your heart or your household. Respect yourself, and devil take the hindmost. You told me that years ago. What are you doing with your hair?"

Henrietta's hair was a bright red abundance she'd refused to cut once she'd arrived in London. She'd also refused to hide it under a cap, and her bonnets had been more feathers than straw.

"I'm braiding it for a coronet. I used to favor a coronet, though my father said that only accentuated my height."

"He didn't like having a daughter nearly as tall as he was," Lucille said. "What will you do about the baron?"

Henrietta finished with her braid, circled the plait about her crown, then secured it with plain pins.

"I'd forgotten my little speech to you all those years ago, but I was right then, and you are right now. I respect myself and will regardless of how the baron regards me. I also respect the baron, though, and hope when we part, that's still the case. With all the other men…"

Professional loyalty to past clients warred with the knowledge that Henrietta was no longer a professional. Society might never note the difference, but Henrietta suspected that six months ago, she would not have given Michael Brenner a second look. A mere baron, merely well-fixed, *merely decent*.

What a sorry creature she'd been.

"With all the others," Lucille said, standing behind Henrietta at the vanity, "your respect was tempered by the knowledge that they paid for your favors. You were compensated for putting up with them, and they knew it, and still sought you out."

The arrangement between man and mistress was as simple on the surface as it was complex beneath. The usual bargain was complex for the mistress and simple for the man. Henrietta finished with her coronet—adding a good two inches to her height—and draped a shawl about her shoulders.

"I know two things," she said, facing the door. "I do not want his lordship paying me for anything, and I'd rather he spent tonight with me than in his library with his books. I'm not sure what that makes me, but breakfast awaits, and I'm hungry."

"Desire for the company of a man you esteem makes you *normal*," Lucille said, tidying up the discarded pearl-tipped pins. "I daresay he's a normal sort of fellow himself. Be off with you, and if you need me, I might be back in bed, munching scones and swilling chocolate. Or I might suggest the staff do a bit of decorating. The holidays are approaching, after all."

Many a day, Henrietta would have regarded lazing about in bed as a fine reward for her exertions the evening before. Today, she wanted to spend as much time with Michael Brenner as she could, either in bed or out of it.

Normal wasn't so very complicated, though neither was it for the faint of heart.

* * *

"I think I'm in love," Miss Whitlow said, taking another book from the stack on the table beside her.

She'd spent most of the day in Michael's library, and he—with a growing sense of exasperation—had sat at his desk, watching her write letters or read. When she looked up, he made a pretense of scribbling away at correspondence or studying some ledger, but mostly, he'd been feasting on the simple sight of her.

When he ought to have been rummaging in her valise.

She wore gold-rimmed spectacles for reading. They gave her a scholarly air and gave him a mad desire to see her wearing only the spectacles while he read *A Midsummer Night's Dream* to her in bed. She favored shortbread and liked to slip off her shoes and tuck her feet beneath her when a book became truly engrossing.

Would she enjoy having her feet rubbed?

The worst part about this day of half torment/half delight was that Michael's interest in the lady was only passingly erotic. He wanted to learn the shape of her feet and the unspoken wishes of her heart. He wanted to introduce her to his horses—which was pathetic—and memorize the names of her family members.

Heathgate would laugh himself to flinders to see his efficient man of business reduced to daydreaming and quill-twiddling.

Michael and his guest had taken a break after lunch, and he'd shown her about the house. Inglemere was a gorgeous Tudor manor, just large enough to be impressive, but small enough to be a home. The grounds were landscaped to show off the house to perfection, though, of course, snow blanketed the gardens and park.

Michael had shown Miss Whitlow his stables, his dairy, his laundry, and even the kitchen pantries, as if all was on offer for her approval.

He wanted to be on offer for her approval, and yet, she never so much as batted her eyes at him. Smart woman.

"You are in love?" he asked, rising from his desk. He probably was too, but could not say for a certainty, never having endured that affliction before.

"You haven't merely collected books for show," she said, hugging his signed copy of *The Italian* to her chest. "You chose books that speak to you, and the result is… I love books. I could grow old reading my way through this library of yours, Michael Brenner."

Not *my lord.* "Have you no collection of your own?"

She set the novel aside and scooted around under the quilt he'd brought her. "I patronized lending libraries. They need the custom, and they never cared what I did for my coin. They cared only that I enjoyed the books and returned them in good condition. Perhaps, when I purchase a home, I'll fill it with books."

While her protectors—Michael was coming to hate that word—had treated her bedroom like a lending library. She'd been well compensated, but he still wished somebody had made her the centerpiece of a treasury that included children, shared memories, and smiles over the breakfast table.

And wedding vows, for heaven's sake.

Michael settled in beside her on the sofa. "You're in the market for a house?" He could help with this, being nothing if not well versed in commercial transactions. He'd searched long and thoroughly before settling on Inglemere for his country retreat.

"I'm in the market for a home," she said. "This is another reason I'm determined to reconcile with my father. All the family I have lives within a few miles of Amblebank, but if he refuses to acknowledge me, then settling elsewhere makes sense."

I'll make him acknowledge you. The only way Michael could do that was by marrying her.

"Give it time," he said, patting her hand. "Family can be vexing, but they'll always be family." Witness his sisters, who had no more time for the brother who dowered them than they did for Fat King George.

Miss Whitlow turned her palm up, so their fingers lay across one another. "You are very kind."

He was a charlatan. "One aspires to behave honorably, though it isn't always possible."

Her fingers closed around his, and Michael felt honor tearing him right down the middle of his chest.

"I have a sense of decency," she said, "as unlikely as that sounds. I've sworn off sharing my favors for coin. I'd like to share my favors with you for the sheer pleasure of it. Lucille has reminded me that the coming years will be…"

She fell silent, her hand cold in Michael's. In another instant, she'd withdraw her hand, the moment would be lost, and he'd be reduced to asking her about Mrs. Radcliffe's prose.

"Lonely," he said. "The coming years will be lonely. The coming night need not be."

Michael drew Henrietta to her feet and wrapped his arms about her. The fit was sublime, and for a moment, he pitied all the men who'd had to pay her to tolerate—much less appear to enjoy—their advances. That she'd offer him intimacies without a thought of reward was more Christmas token than he'd ever deserve.

And in return, what would he offer her?

"I'll take a tray in my room," she said, kissing his cheek. "You can come to me after supper, after I've had a proper soak."

She'd taken a bath the previous evening, as had Michael. He suspected hers had been a good deal warmer than his.

"You don't need to fuss and primp," Michael said. "I don't care if you bear the scent of books, or your hair is less than perfectly arranged. I'd rather be with you as you are."

She drew back enough to peer at him, and they were very nearly eye to eye. "I insist on toothpowder. That's not negotiable."

God, what she'd had to put up with. "I insist on toothpowder too, and I generally don't bother with a nightshirt. Shall we surprise each other with the rest of it?"

"You think you can surprise *me?*"

She'd had a half-dozen lovers, probably not an imaginative bone in the lot, so to speak. "I know I can." Her patch-leaf fragrance was fainter today, as if she'd forgotten to apply it, though the aroma yet lingered on her clothes. Michael bent closer to catch the scent at the join of her neck and shoulder. "Shall we go upstairs now?"

Darkness had fallen, though dinner was at least two hours off. Michael was famished, and food had nothing to do with his hunger. He'd regret this folly, but he'd regret more declining what Henrietta offered.

And if he was lucky, Beltram's damned book had been tossed in the fire years ago.

* * *

Henrietta stepped behind the privacy screen, aware of a vast gap in her feminine vocabulary. No man had sought to share intimacies with her for the simple pleasure of her company. From Beltram onward, all had regarded her as a commodity to be leased, though Beltram had masked his agenda as seduction.

Michael had cast her no speculative glances, assayed no "accidental" touches, offered no smiles that insulted as they inventoried. Any of those, Henrietta could have parried without effort.

His honest regard might have been a foreign language to her.

"Shall I undress for you?" She was tall enough to watch over the privacy screen as Michael added peat to the fire.

"Not unless you'd enjoy that," he said, setting the poker on the hearth stand. "Perhaps you'd like me to undress for you? Can't say as a lady has ever asked that of me."

A lady. To him, she was a lady. "It's a bit chilly to be making a display out of disrobing." Some men had needed that from her, had needed as much anticipation and encouragement as she could produce for them—poor wretches.

"Burning peat is an art, and my staff hasn't the way of it," he said. "I keep the smell about to remind me of the years when a peat fire was the difference between life and death. Your hair is quite long."

Henrietta had undone her coronet, so her braid hung down to her bum. "I might cut it. For years, I didn't." Because long hair, according to Beltram, was seductive. By his reasoning, ridiculously long hair was ridiculously seductive.

Though Beltram's opinion now mattered… *not at all.*

"That is a diabolical smile, Miss Whitlow."

"You inspire me, and if we're to share a bed, you might consider calling me Henrietta."

"I'm Michael." He draped his coat over the back of the chair by the hearth. "After the archangel. Have you other names?"

"Henrietta Eloisa Gaye Whitlow. Is there a warmer to run over the sheets?" Warmed flannel sheets would be a bit of heaven.

"I'll be your warmer."

They shared a smile, adult and friendly. Henrietta decided that her hair could be in a braid for this encounter, and to blazes with the loose cascade most men had expected of her. She'd always spent half the next morning brushing out the snarls, half the night waking because she couldn't turn without pulling her hair loose from her pillow first.

Michael-for-the-archangel removed his clothing in a predictable order, laying each article over the chair in a manner that would minimize wrinkles. He pulled off his own boots, and used the wash water at the hearth with an emphasis on the face, underarms, privities, and feet.

He was thorough about his ablutions, and his soap—hard-milled and lavender scented—was fresh.

"You are not self-conscious," Henrietta said. A surprising number of men were, if the gossip among courtesans was to be believed. Several men might cheerfully aim for the same chamber pot while the port was consumed, but they'd do so without revealing much of their person, or overtly inspecting any other man.

"I was one of eight children sharing a one-room sod hut," Michael said. "Growing up, privacy was a foreign concept."

While hard work had doubtless been his constant companion. Michael had the honed fitness that came from years of physical labor and constant activity. Some wealthy men came by a similar physique by virtue of riding, shooting, archery, and pugilism. Michael had a leanness they lacked, a sleekness that said he eschewed most luxuries still and probably always would.

"Growing up, my modesty was elevated from a virtue to an obsession," Henrietta said. "I like looking at you."

He wrung out the wet flannel over the basin, arm muscles undulating by candlelight. "Does that surprise you?"

"Yes." Henrietta hadn't chosen her partners on the basis of appearance, not after Beltram. He'd been a fine specimen, also selfish, rotten, deceitful, and lazy. She hoped whatever woman he took to wife could match him for self-absorption and hard-heartedness. He'd come by months ago to tell her he'd be wife-hunting, as if his eventual marriage might dash some hope Henrietta had harbored for years.

What a lovely difference time could make in a woman's perspective.

Michael laid the cloth over the edge of the basin and crossed to the bed. "Won't you join me, Henrietta?"

What need did the Irish have of coin when they had charm in such abundance? Michael sat on the edge of the bed wearing not a stitch of clothing, his arm extended in invitation. He was mildly aroused, and his smile balanced invitation with… hope?

Henrietta kept her dressing gown about her. She had no nightgown on underneath—why bother?—but neither did she want to parade about naked, and that too was a surprise.

"I'm all at sea," she said, taking the place beside Michael on the bed. "I know how to be a courtesan. I know what a courtesan wants, how she plies her trade. But this…"

A courtesan never confided in her partner. She managed every encounter to ensure he would be comfortable confiding in her, and what a bloody lot of work that was. The physical intimacies were so much dusting and polishing compared to that heavy labor.

Michael took her hand and kissed her knuckles. "If you're at sea, allow me to row you to shore. This is being lovers. You don't need to impress me, please me, flatter me, or put my needs above your own. We share pleasure, as best we can, and then we share some sweet memories."

"How simple." How uncomplicated, honest, and wonderful—so why did Henrietta feel like crying?

Michael slid his palm along her jaw and kissed the corner of her mouth.

"Simple and lovely. Will you get the candles? I'll start warming up these sheets."

How many times had Henrietta made love with the candles blazing? She couldn't fall asleep that way—lit candles were a terrible fire hazard—though her partners had succumbed to slumber following their exertions with the predictability of horses rolling after a long haul under saddle.

She blew out the candles one by one. Michael had three sheaths soaking in water glasses on the bed table, and he'd already informed Henrietta that she was to notify him of any consequences from their encounter.

She suspected she was infertile, a courtesan's dearest blessing, and for the first time, the idea bothered her. A baron needed an heir, not that Michael's succession was any of her business.

"Come to bed, love," Michael said as candle smoke joined the scent of peat in the night air. "Mind you don't trip over that valise."

Considerate of him. Henrietta hefted her traveling case onto the cedar chest at the foot of the bed, then shed her dressing gown and climbed into bed with… her first lover.

* * *

Hot wax dripped onto Josiah Whitlow's hand and woke him. He'd fallen asleep at his desk for the third time in a week, or possibly the fourth. His housekeeper had given up scolding him for leaving the candles burning.

"Candles cost money," he muttered, sitting up slowly, lest the ache in his back turn to the tearing pain that prevented sleep. The fire in the hearth had burned down—coal cost money too—and the house held the heavy, frigid silence of nighttime after a winter storm.

"You left me on such a night," he muttered, gaze on the portrait over the mantel. Katie had died in March, after a late-season storm that had rattled the windows and made the chimneys moan. Josiah had known he was losing her since she'd failed to rally after a lung fever more than a year earlier. She'd never quite regained her strength after the birth of their younger boy.

"He has a daughter now," Josiah said, draining a serving of brandy he'd poured hours before. "Poor little mite is cursed with your red hair, madam."

He saluted with his glass. "Apologies for that remark. Ungentlemanly of me. Christmas approaches and I… am not at my best."

Every year, Christmas came around, and Henrietta did too. Every year, Josiah found some excuse to lurk in the mercantile across from the inn at Amblebank, until he caught a glimpse of his tall, beautiful daughter.

Henrietta resembled her mother, but every feature that had been pretty on Katie was striking on Henrietta. Katie had had good posture, Henrietta was regal. Katie had been warm-hearted, Henrietta was unforgettably lovely. Katie had known her Book of Common Prayer, and Henrietta—according to her brothers—quoted Shakespeare.

Accurately.

"I kept her from the books," he said, experimentally shifting forward in his chair. "Didn't want her to end up a bluestocking old maid."

Josiah pushed to his feet, though the movement sent discomfort echoing from his back to his hips, knees, and feet. Not gout, except possibly in one toe. Gout was for the elderly.

"Which I shall soon be, God willing."

Katie remained over the dying fire, smiling with the benevolence of perpetual youth. Josiah was glad for the shadows, because his wife's eyes reproached him for the whole business with Henrietta.

Girls fell from grace, Katie had once said, when a man came by intent on tripping them. Lately, Josiah had begun to suspect that Katie's point was not without validity, from a mother's perspective. Henrietta had been sixteen when she'd fled to London, and Josiah had been sure she'd come home within the week, chastened, repentant, and forever cured of her rebellious streak.

Instead, she'd shamed her family, set a bad example for her brothers, and broken her father's heart.

"She made her bed," Josiah said, blowing out the candles on the desk. "She can jolly well lie in it. And—with a damned aching hip—I shall lie in mine. Good night, madam."

The portrait, as always, remained silent, smiling, and trapped in pretty youth, while Josiah steeled himself for the growing challenge of negotiating the main staircase at the end of the day.

* * *

In Michael's wildest imaginings, he could not have anticipated the sheer joy of making love with Henrietta Whitlow. She was like a cat in a roomful of loose canaries, chasing this pleasure, then that one, then sitting fixed while fascinated with a third, until leaping after a fourth.

She wanted to spoon with Michael's arms snug around her, then she demanded to lie face to face and touch every inch of his chest, arms, face, and shoulders. Just as he was having trouble drawing a steady breath—he'd not realized his ribs were ticklish—she'd rolled to her back.

"Now you touch me," she said, and Michael had obliged with hands, mouth, and body.

She gave him the sense that she'd never before permitted herself an agenda in the bedroom other than: Please *him*. Accommodate *him*. Make *him* happy. Her own wishes and dreams hadn't mattered enough to any of the men in her bed—or she'd been that skillful at hiding them—and thus those wishes hadn't been allowed to matter to her.

They mattered to Michael. *Henrietta* mattered.

She liked the sensation of his breath on her nipples, he liked the ferocious grip she took of his hair. Then she wrapped her hand around another part of him, and Michael sat back, the better to watch her face by the firelight as she explored him.

"If women were as proud of their breasts as men are of their cocks…" she muttered, tracing a single fingernail up the length of his shaft.

"There would be more happy women, and happy men," Michael said. "Perhaps more babies too. Would you please do that again?"

She obliged, more slowly. "You ask, you never demand."

"I'll be begging in a moment."

Her mouth closed around him, and for long moments, Michael couldn't *even* beg. He could only give silent thanks for these moments shared with Henrietta, while he tried to ignore the itch of guilt from his conscience.

Her valise sat at the foot of the bed, a reproach every time he opened his eyes. When Henrietta smiled up at him, he shifted over her, so she filled his vision.

"Now?" he asked.

She kissed him, framing his jaw with both hands, wrapping her legs around him. Her movements were languid and—he hoped—self-indulgent.

"I want to be on top," she said. "This time."

Michael subsided to his back, and she straddled him. He used her braid to tug her closer. "Like this?"

With no further ado, Henrietta tied a sheath about him, then sank down over him and joined them intimately. "More like this."

Michael struggled to locate a Shakespeare quote, a snippet, any words to remark the occasion. "Move, Henrietta. Move now."

She smiled down at him. "He demands. At last he demands."

"I'm begging you."

Her smile became tender as she tucked close and *moved*.

CHAPTER FIVE

All good things must end, or at least be paid for, and Henrietta the Housemaid eventually realized that her station in life had changed. I had the sense she might slip back to the shires, given a chance. I was forever finding her in tears over some draft of a letter to her martinet of a papa. No matter how often she wrote to him, he apparently never answered.

Having no recourse, when I offered to put my arrangement with her on professional footing, she accepted, and thus the career of London's greatest courtesan had its origins in my family parlor. Delicious irony, that, but for one small detail, which I must prevail upon you to tidy up...

Michael Brenner had needed a woman.

Or maybe—Henrietta wasn't quite awake, so her thoughts wandered instead of galloped—he'd needed *her*? Somebody with whom to be passionate, tender, funny, and honest. Maybe he'd needed a lover, an intimate friend with whom to be himself, wholly and joyfully.

Henrietta had needed him too. Needed a man who wasn't interested in tricks and feats of sexual athleticism, who wasn't fascinated with the forbidden, or bored with it, but still fascinated with his own gratification. Making love with Michael had been so *easy*, and yet so precious.

She'd been needing him for the past ten years.

To join with Michael had felt intimate, invigorating, and sweet. Surely the Bard had put it better, but Henrietta couldn't summon any literature to mind. The hour was late, and she was abed with a lover.

Her first lover.

She reached beneath the covers and found warmth but no Michael. Her ears told her he wasn't stirring about behind the privacy screen, which meant...

Nothing for it, she must open her eyes.

A page turned, the sound distinctive even when Henrietta's mind was fogged with sleep. Michael had pulled a chair near the hearth and lit a branch of candles. He sat reading a small book, his hair tousled, his dressing gown half open. His expression was beautifully somber, suggesting the prose on the page was serious.

Foreboding uncoiled where contentment had been.

"You'd rather read than cuddle?" Henrietta asked, sitting up. She kept the covers about her, and not because the room was chilly. Michael's expression was anything but loverlike.

"I'd rather cuddle, but I couldn't bear…"

"What?" Couldn't bear to remain in bed with her?

He closed the book and stared at the fire. "I couldn't bear to further deceive you. I have misrepresented myself to you, Miss Whitlow, in part. I've also been honest in part."

Miss Whitlow? *Miss Whitlow?*

"You've been *inside* me, Michael. Several times. Don't call me Miss Whitlow." *And don't remain halfway across the room, looking like a fallen angel on the eve of banishment to the Pit.*

"This book is the reason we met," he said, holding up the little volume. "Lord Beltram wants it back, though legally it is entirely your possession. He's begun searching for a bride and realized what a weapon he'd given you."

No flannel sheets, no cozy quilts, no secure embrace could have comforted Henrietta against the chill Michael's words drove into her heart.

"You *seduced* me to get Beltram's bloody book, and now you're confessing your perfidy?"

"I hope we seduced each other, but yes, my original intention was to steal this book from you." He thumbed through the most maudlin collection of bad verse and inferior artistry Henrietta had ever seen.

She rose from the warmth of the covers, shrugged into her night-robe—and yes, that made her breasts jiggle, and what of it?—and Michael looked away.

"Are you disgusted with the woman you seduced?" she asked, whipping her braid free of the night-robe. "Was bedding me a great imposition, my lord? What hold does Beltram have over you that you'd make a sacrifice of such magnitude with his cast-off mistress?"

"Miss—Henrietta, it's not like that."

Henrietta had a temper, a raging, blazing, vitriolic temper that had sent her from her father's house ten years ago and sustained her when it became apparent that Beltram was exactly the handsome scoundrel every girl was warned against.

She'd learned to marshal that temper in the interests of professional survival, but she was *no longer a professional.*

And she might not survive this insult. "It's never like that," she snapped. "Good God, I thought I knew better. Never again, I promised myself. Never again would a man get the better of me, no matter how handsome, how charming, how sincere…"

Michael rose, tossing the book onto the empty bed. "Henrietta Whitlow, I am not ashamed of you. I could never be ashamed of you. I am ashamed of myself."

"For sleeping with me?" She would kill him if he said yes and then burn his house down, after she'd carted away all of his books.

"I am ashamed of myself," he said, hands fisting at his sides, "for lying to you. For being an idiot."

"Idiot is too kind a term, Michael Brenner. I am Henrietta Whitlow. I turned down the overtures of the sovereign himself and scoffed at carte blanche from countless others, then gave you what they'd have paid a fortune to enjoy. I swore I'd never again… Why am I explaining this to you? Get out and take the damned book with you."

He stayed right where he was. "I should have asked you for the book, straight out. I apologize for not using common sense, but I was too long a thief, a spy, a manipulator of events. I could not simply steal from you, and I've left my honesty too late."

"Which means now you're a scoundrel," Henrietta said, though he seemed to be a contrite scoundrel. "You have exceeded the bounds of my patience, sir. Be off with you."

So she could cry, damn him. Henrietta hadn't cried since her last cat had died two years ago.

"Why have you kept Beltram's book all these years, Henrietta? Are you still in love with him?"

Through her rage, humiliation, and shock, Henrietta's instincts stirred. Michael had what he'd come for—so to speak—and Henrietta's feelings for Beltram ought to be of no interest to him.

At all.

"I kept his awful little book because I didn't want him publishing it and making me the laughingstock of the press and public. Beltram is selfish, unscrupulous, mean, and not to be trusted." And he had clammy hands. "Possession of that book was my only means of ensuring he'd not trouble me after he'd turned me from a housemaid to a whore."

Still, Michael remained before the fire, his expression unreadable. "Why not destroy the book?"

She might have confided that to him an hour ago. How dare he ask for her confidences now? "I will join a nunnery, I swear it, rather than endure the arrogance of the male gender another day."

"You kept that book for a reason. Were you intent on blackmailing him?"

With the room in shadows, Henrietta could believe Michael Brenner had been a spy and a thief. He hid his ruthlessness beneath fine tailoring and polite manners, but his expression suggested he'd do anything necessary to achieve his ends.

He made love with the same determination, and Henrietta had reveled in his passion.

Now, she'd do anything to get him out of her room, even confess further vulnerability.

"I kept the book because I wanted the reminder of what a gullible, arrogant idiot I'd been. Beltram laid out my downfall, page by page. He sketched me in my maid's uniform, adoration and ignorance in my gaze. He sketched me the first night he'd taken down my hair—for artistic purposes only, he assured me. He sketched me after he'd kissed me for the first time. It's all there, in execrable poetry and amateur sketches. My ruin, lest I forget a moment of it."

Michael crossed to the bed, and Henrietta stood her ground. He snatched the book off the bed, and she thought she'd seen the last of him. A convent in Sweden, maybe, or Maryland. If Borneo had convents, she'd consider them, provided they had enough books.

"Henrietta, I am sorry." Michael stood close enough that she could smell his lavender soap. "Beltram did, indeed, have a hold over me. I've fulfilled my part of the bargain and removed the book as a blackmail threat. I have no excuse for insinuating myself into your affections. I'm sorry for deceiving you. My coach will take you to Amblebank in the morning."

"You've insinuated yourself right back out of my affections, my lord. No harm done."

If she'd slapped him, he could not have looked more chagrined. "There's been harm, Henrietta. I know that. I'll do what I can to make it right."

Not more decency, not now when he'd betrayed the trust Henrietta hadn't realized she'd given.

"Comfort yourself with whatever platitudes you please, my lord, but leave me in peace. I'm tired and have earned my rest."

He considered the book, Beltram's exercise in lordly vanity and a testament to feminine vulnerability.

"This book means nothing to you?"

"It's reproach for my folly," Henrietta retorted. "I loathe the damned thing and the man who created it."

Michael threw the book straight into the fireplace, landing it atop the flaming peat.

Henrietta watched her past burn, incredulity warring with loss. As long as that book had been in her hands, she'd had proof—for herself, anyway—that once upon a time, she'd been innocent.

"Did Beltram force you, Henrietta?"

Nobody had asked her that, but Henrietta had asked the question of herself. "He took advantage of my ignorance and inexperience—I'd been chaste before I met him—he misled, he betrayed, he lied and seduced. He did not force. His actions were dishonorable, not quite criminal."

"Then I won't kill him."

Michael stood beside her until the book was a charred heap, its ashes drifting up the flue, and then he stalked from the room.

Henrietta gathered up the pile of fine tailoring Michael had draped over the chair, brought it into bed with her, and watched the flames in the hearth far into the night while her nose was buried in the scent of lavender.

* * *

Michael rose to a house made brilliant by sunshine on freshly fallen snow, though his mood could not have been blacker.

He'd committed two wrongs. First, he'd agreed to thievery to settle his account with Beltram. Stealing was wrong, and neither starvation nor the security of the realm provided Michael any room to forgive himself.

Second, he'd made love with Henrietta Whitlow. Not for all the baronies in Ireland would he regret the hours he'd spent in her bed, but he'd go to his grave regretting that he'd betrayed her trust.

"You will notify me if there are consequences, Henrietta."

He stood with her by the library window, waiting for the coach to be brought around. His house now sported wreaths on the front windows, cloved oranges dangling from curtain rods, red ribbons wrapped about bannisters, and an abundance of strategically placed mistletoe.

The holiday decorations Lucille had inspired were enough to restore Michael's faith in a God of retribution.

"Last night, you called me Miss Whitlow, and I insist on that courtesy today, if you must annoy me with conversation."

Last night, he'd called her his love. "I am annoying you with a demand. If taking me as your lover has consequences, you will inform me, and we will make appropriate accommodations."

Had she grown taller overnight? She certainly seemed taller, while Michael felt once again like that grubby youth clawing his way up from the peat bogs.

She regarded him from blazing green eyes down a magnificent nose. "You must be one of those Irishmen who longs for death. I don't fancy such melodrama myself, but I will cheerfully oblige you with a mortal blow to your cods if you don't cease your nattering."

He leaned closer. She smelled of neroli—orange blossoms—this morning rather than patch leaf, and he was daft for noticing.

"Kick me in the balls, Henrietta, if that will ease any of the hurt I've done you, but we shall marry if you're carrying my child."

She drew in a breath, as if filling her sails for another scathing retort, then her brows twitched down. "Not your child. *Our* child."

The coach came jingling around the drive from the carriage house, for some fool had put harness bells on the conveyance.

"You'd marry me?" Henrietta asked as the vehicle halted at the bottom of the front steps.

"Of course I'd marry you."

"Out of pity? Out of decency? Don't think I'd ever allow you into my bed, Michael."

"I'd marry you in hopes we might put the past behind us, Henrietta. I have wronged you, and I'm sorry for that, but I would not compound my error by also wronging my—our—child. If you closed your bedroom door to me, I'd respect that, for I respect you."

"Perhaps you do," she said, her gaze unbearably sad, "but your version of respect and mine differ significantly. If you'll excuse me, I'll be on my way."

"Henrietta, *I'm sorry.*"

She paused by the door, her hand on the latch. "Would you have stolen from me if I'd been Beltram's sister rather than his ruined housemaid?"

"To get free of that man, I'd have stolen from the bishop of London on Christmas Eve."

Henrietta crossed back to Michael's side, kissed his cheek, and remained for one moment standing next to him. "If there's a child, I'll tell you."

She hadn't agreed to marry him, but Michael was grateful for small mercies.

* * *

"There's no room at the inn," Henrietta said, crossing her fingers behind her back. "I've come home for a visit, and you will either make me welcome, or take yourself off elsewhere."

Papa had aged significantly in ten years. His shoulders were stooped, his hair had thinned, and his clothing hung loosely on his frame. Henrietta steeled her heart against the changes in his appearance, because the jut of his chin and the cold in his eyes promised her no welcome. The housekeeper had tried to show her to the formal parlor, but Henrietta had scoffed at that bit of presumption and let herself into Papa's library.

He stood in the doorway, still apparently unwilling to be in the same room with her. "Madam, you are not welcome in this house." Even his voice had grown weaker.

"Too bad," Henrietta retorted, "because I was born here, and I've nowhere else to go. The least you could do is ring for tea, Papa. Traveling up from London has taken days, all of them cold, and the dratted coaches nearly rattled my teeth from my head."

"Your mother never liked—" He caught himself. "Be gone from this house. Immoral women must fend for themselves."

Stubborn, but then, Henrietta had learned to be stubborn too. "I've given up being immoral. I content myself now with garden-variety wickedness. When I burn my finger, I use bad language. I forgot to say grace before breakfast today, but I was anticipating this joyous reunion. I haven't had a duke in my bed for months, Papa."

"Henrietta!"

Had his lips twitched?

"Well, I haven't." One handsome baron, for a few hours. That hardly mattered. "Unless you intend to scorn me for the rest of my life—or what remains of yours—then you will endure my company over the holidays."

Please, Papa. Please... She'd tried pleading once before, and he'd not bothered to reply to her letter.

His gaze strayed to the portrait over the mantel. Mama's likeness needed a good cleaning, something Henrietta's brothers would never dare to suggest.

"There isn't a single bed available at the inn?"

The inn had never once been full, in Henrietta's experience. "Not that I know of. You're letting out all the heat from the fire."

He took two steps into the room and closed the door behind him. "You have grown bold, Henrietta Eloisa. I do not approve of bold women."

"I do not approve of hard-hearted, cantankerous men." Or thieves or liars.

Papa had always had a leonine quality, and his eyebrows had grown positively fierce. "I'll not tolerate disrespect, Henrietta."

"Then we understand each other, because *neither will I.*"

That earned her a definite twitch of the paternal lips, though she'd never been more serious.

Then Papa drew himself up, into a semblance of the imposing man he'd been in Henrietta's childhood. "Tomorrow, you will find other accommodations. You may stay the night, but no longer."

One night? He'd toss his own daughter out into the snow come morning? Henrietta was tempted to remonstrate with him, to air old grievances and trade recriminations until he admitted his share of responsibility for ten years of rejection.

She was *sorry* she'd disobeyed him and had apologized for her transgressions in writing. She was about to remind her father of those salient facts when she recalled Michael, apologizing with desperate sincerity in the cold morning sunshine.

"Thank you, Papa. I'll have one of my trunks brought in and introduce my maid to your housekeeper."

"You travel with a maid?"

"Of course, and I usually take my own coach and team, though on way up from Town I had a mishap." *I fell in love, but I'll get over it.*

He settled into the chair behind his desk, his movements slow and gingerly. "You have a coach and team. My daughter. Racketing about England in the dead of winter with her own..."

"And a maid too."

"Whom you will see to now," Papa said. "Be off with you, Henrietta. I have much to do, and your brothers will want to know of your arrival. Send them each a note, lest they hear of your visit from some hostler or tavern maid."

Be off with you, not five minutes after he'd stepped into the room. When Henrietta had taken herself away to London, he'd not spoken to her for ten years, now she was to *be off with herself*.

"You can write those notes to my brothers," she said. "My travels have exhausted me, and I'm in need of a hot cup of tea. Shall I have a tray sent to you as well?"

Papa scowled at her as if she'd tripped over a chamber pot. "I prefer coffee."

"Coffee, then. I'll let the maid know." If Henrietta brought him that tray, she might dump it over his head. "It's good to be home, Papa."

She left him in his comfy chair in his cozy study, before she started shouting. For Christmas, she'd longed to have his respect. They were speaking to each other, mostly civilly, and he'd granted her shelter from the elements, albeit temporarily.

That was a start, and more than she'd had from him for the previous decade.

* * *

Five days went by, during which Michael rehearsed enough apologies and grand speeches to fill every stage in Drury Lane. On Friday, he received a holiday greeting from Lord Heathgate that was positively chatty.

Heathgate, once the greatest rogue in Britain, maundered on about his daughters' intrepid horsemanship and his sons' matchless abilities at cricket. The paragraph regarding his lordship's marchioness was so rife with tender sentiment that Michael had nearly pitched it into the rubbish bin.

Instead, he took himself for a long walk and ended up in the stables.

"You again," Liam Logan said. "I'd thought by now you'd be traveling into Oxford to see those sisters of yours."

Michael joined him at a half door to a coach horse's stall. They still had the grays from the last inn Michael had stopped at with Henrietta.

"I thought by now my sisters might see fit to pay their brother a holiday visit," Michael said. "But sitting on my rosy arse amid a bunch of dusty old books hasn't lured my family into the countryside."

"Then you'll want to go into Oxford to purchase tokens for the Christmas baskets," Logan said, reaching a gloved hand to the gelding nosing through a pile of hay.

"My staff has already seen to the baskets. Didn't I give you leave for the holidays, Logan?"

The horse ignored Logan's outstretched hand and instead gave Michael's greatcoat a delicate sniff. Horse breath on the ear tickled, but Michael let the beast continue its investigations.

"That you did, sir, but here I am."

"I won't have much use for—"

The horse got its teeth around the lapel of Michael's collar and tugged, hard. Michael was pulled up against the stall door, and—with a firm, toothy grasp of his coat—the horse merely regarded him. The domestic equine was blessed with large, expressive eyes, and in those eyes, Michael detected the same unimpressed and vaguely challenging sentiment Henrietta had once turned on him.

"Ach, now that's enough," Logan said, waving a hand in the horse's face. "Be off with you."

The same words Henrietta had used.

The horse, however, kept its grip of Michael's greatcoat. If the beast could talk, it might have said, "I weigh nearly ten times what you do, my teeth could snap your arm, and my feet smash your toes. Ignore me at your peril."

I'm to fetch Henrietta home to Inglemere, and to me. For ten years, Henrietta had bided in London, probably longing for her family to fetch her home, because that's what families were supposed to do when one of their number strayed. The idea had not the solid ring of conviction, but the more delicate quality of a hope, a theory, a wish.

Which was a damned sight more encouraging than the cold toes and insomnia Michael had to show for the past week's wanderings.

"Have the team put to," Michael said, scratching the gelding's ear. "We're for Amblebank."

The horse let him go.

"Thank God for that," Logan said. "But you'd best change into some decent finery, my lord. The ladies are none too impressed with muddy boots."

"I'm not calling on a lady," Michael said. "But you're right. The occasion calls for finery."

And some reconnaissance. A comment Henrietta had made about her brothers had lodged in Michael's memory, and the comment wanted further investigation. Henrietta's family was merely gentry, not aristocracy, and life in the shires ran on more practical terms than in Mayfair.

Michael dressed with care, explained the itinerary to Logan, and made only one brief stop on the way to Amblebank. Less than two hours after making the decision to go calling, he was standing in Josiah Whitlow's study, sporting his best Bond Street tailoring and his most lordly air.

Henrietta's father put Michael in mind of an aging eagle, his gaze sharp, the green of his eyes fading, his demeanor brusquely—almost rudely--proper.

"To what do I owe the honor of this call, my lord?" Whitlow asked.

"We're neighbors, at a distance," Michael said. "My estate lies about five miles east of Amblebank, and I've had occasion to meet your daughter."

Whitlow stalked across the room and stood facing a portrait of a lovely young redhead. His gait was uneven, but energetic. "For ten years, I had no daughter."

Whose fault was that? "And now?"

"I've sent her off to her brothers. She tarried here for five days, made lists for the housekeeper, the maids, the footmen, put together menus, hung blasted greenery and mistletoe from—she's no longer here, and I doubt she will be ever again."

Her name is Henrietta. Henrietta Eloisa Gaye Whitlow. "If you've driven her from her only home permanently, then you are a judgmental old fool who deserves to die of loneliness."

Whitlow turned from the portrait, his magnificent scowl ruined by a suspicious glimmer in his eyes. "Do you think I haven't died of loneliness, young man? Do you think I haven't worried for the girl every day for the past ten years? And what business is it of yours? You seek to entice her back to wickedness, no doubt, as if coin can compensate a woman for discarding her honor."

Michael advanced on Whitlow. "Your oldest was born six months after your wedding vows were spoken. Your first grandchild arrived five months after his parents' union. I stopped at the church and leafed through the registries. If I'd had the time, I'd have gathered similar information on half your neighbors. Order a tea tray, Mr. Whitlow, and stop feeling sorry for yourself. You're a hypocrite at best, and possibly a poor father as well."

"You are a very presuming young man."

Stubbornness must be a defining trait of the Whitlows, but the Brenners had clung to life itself on the strength of sheer stubbornness.

"I will not lie—ever again—and say that I've been entirely honorable where Henrietta is concerned, but I promised her I'd do what I could to atone for the wrong I've done. She seeks a rapprochement with her family, and I'll see that she gets one."

Whitlow hobbled over to the desk and dropped into the chair behind it. "I cannot condone immorality, you fool. So she sits down to Christmas dinner with us. If she takes up with the likes of you again, then I want no more to do with her. She deserves better than you strutting young popinjays with your coin and your arrogance. If she can't see that, I'll not stand by and smile while she waltzes with her own ruin."

Michael's father would have understood this version of love. *I'll shame you to your senses,* the argument went. The difficulty was, two people could engage in a mutual contest of wills that had nothing of sense about it.

"Henrietta never wants to see me again," Michael said. "And from everything she's said, she feels similarly about the popinjays, dukes, and even the king."

Whitlow put his head in his hands. "The *king?*"

"Turned him down with a smile. Wouldn't do more than share his theater box for any amount of money."

"Good God. My little hen… and the king." Whitlow's expression suggested he was horrified—and impressed. "She wasn't just making talk about dukes, then?"

"She had her choice of the lot," Michael said. "Dukes, princes, nabobs. She never had dealings with men who were married or engaged. Not ever, and she demanded absolute fidelity from her partners for the duration of any arrangement. The titled bachelors of London will go into a collective decline at her retirement, and she gave up all that power and money just so you could behave like a stubborn ass yet again. I'll not have it."

Whitlow produced a plain square of soft, white linen. "Who are you to *have* anything? Henrietta made choices. She was stubborn. You don't know how stubborn. I had a match all picked out for her. A decent chap, settled, respectable. She flew into hysterics, and then she was gone."

Michael appropriated the chair opposite Whitlow's desk, because the man apparently lacked the manners even to offer a guest a seat.

"You chose one of your widowed friends, I'd guess. A man at least twice Henrietta's age, with children not much younger than she. Her fate would have been to give up drudging for you and her brothers for the great boon of drudging for some middle-aged man and his children. What sixteen-year-old girl with any sense would be flattered by that arrangement?"

Elsewhere in the house, a door slammed, though Whitlow didn't seem to notice. Perhaps he was hard of hearing as well as of heart.

"She was growing too rebellious," he said. "I had to marry her off, or she'd… Sixteen isn't too young to be engaged. I'd talked Charles into waiting until she was eighteen for the wedding, and that would have been in the agreements. Henrietta said in two years the damned man would probably have lost the last of his teeth. She cursed at me. My own daughter, cursing."

"And because even cursing didn't get your attention, she ran away rather than bow to a scheme that would only make her miserable. What else was she to do?"

Whitlow had had ten years to convince himself that he was the wronged party, and yet, Michael still saw a hint of guilt in his eyes.

"In time, she would have been a well-fixed widow," Whitlow said. "Many women would have envied her that fate."

"In twenty or thirty years? Assuming your friend and his children didn't spend his every last groat first? You are blind, Whitlow, and Henrietta was too. She went to London, a complete innocent, a young girl who thought men were selfish, irascible, and high-handed, but not her enemies. She went into service, glad to have employment in the house of a titled family, prepared to work hard for a pittance.

"She had no inkling that her virtue was at risk. She'd been trained to wait on the men of her family, to see to their every need, to put their welfare before her own, and by God, you trained her well. She had no grasp of her own beauty, no sense of what men might do to possess it, or how to defend herself from them. That is your fault as well, and no other's."

Whitlow erupted from his chair, bracing his hands on his desk blotter. "How dare you lecture me about the daughter I raised in this very house? How dare you presume to make excuses for a girl who knew right from wrong as clearly as I know noon from midnight?"

"Better you should ask how dare her employer ruin her and suffer no consequences for his venery," Michael said. "Read this."

He tossed Beltram's letter onto the desk, where it sat like a glove thrown down to mark a challenge.

"What is it?"

"A letter to me from the man who destroyed your daughter's good name, but not, fortunately, her self-respect. He plotted, he schemed, he lied, he charmed, and he made empty promises of matrimony. He behaved without a shred of honor and left Henrietta broken-hearted, ruined, and alone at the age of sixteen. She took the same risk her mother did—granted favors to a man promising matrimony. Her mother is enshrined over your mantel for that decision, while Henrietta was banished from your household."

This was not the speech Michael had rehearsed, but he should have, for the recitation nearly broke his heart, while Whitlow appeared entirely unmoved.

"Henrietta's failing was that she trusted the wrong man," Michael went on more softly. "*She trusted you* to forgive her for straying into the wrong pair of arms, and in that, she erred. I'd guess she wrote to you, asking permission to come home, and you denied her. Read that letter, Whitlow."

Whitlow subsided into his chair, regarding Beltram's letter like the foul excrescence it was.

Michael rose and leaned across the desk. "Read it, or I'll read it to you loudly enough that the whole house will hear me. Then I'll read it in the tavern. I'll read it to her brothers. I'll read it in the church if I must, or the village square. I'll read the damned thing in the House of Lords, and then all will know of your shame. Not hers. Beltram's—*and yours*."

Whitlow read the letter, then sat unmoving, his gaze on the portrait over the mantel.

"Will you apologize to your daughter, Whitlow?"

He nodded once, a tear trickling unchecked down his weathered cheek.

"Then I'll wish you the joy of the season and take my leave."

CHAPTER SIX

I don't regret a moment of the time I spent making Henrietta Whitlow what she is today, though she's never thanked me for the effort I put forth, peeling her grip from the dust mop and rags of propriety. When our paths cross now, she adopts an air of subtly injured dignity, though I can't imagine she'd ever want to go back to dreams of wedded contentment, or a quiet life in the shires.

She's had the pleasure of my protection, after all, and I'm nearly certain when I ended our affair, her heart was broken for all time. I did her a very great favor, if so, for what woman plying the oldest trade has any need for tender sentiment or permanent attachments?

"She has your hair, Henrietta," Isabel said, taking a seat across the kitchen table. "I think Thad is pleased by that. Philip's two got it as well."

Henrietta stroked the downy head pillowed on her shoulder. "The little ones all have Mama's hair. I hope the children got Mama's sweet nature too."

Isabel searched through a bowl of whole cloves. "You have a sweet nature."

"You're being kind." Both brothers, and their wives, and even Alexander and Dicken were being kind, treating Henrietta with the unfailing cheer of those on nursing duty in a sickroom. She was sick—at heart—but her family need not know that.

"I'm being honest," Isabel said, jabbing a clove into an orange. "If you'd been less sweet, the squire would never have been so daft as to think he could marry you off to Charles Sampson. Those oldest three sons of his have gambled away half his fortune, and the second Mrs. Sampson is rarely out of childbed."

The kitchen was perfumed with cloves and oranges, and the baby was a warm bundle of joy in Henrietta's arms. Isabel's words were an odd sort of comfort too.

Henrietta *had* been sweet, far too sweet. "I didn't know Mr. Sampson had remarried."

"Mrs. Sampson got a procession of runny noses and lazy housemaids. You got London and the company of dukes, from what I hear."

Isabel selected another clove from the dish, her focus overly intent.

"Only two dukes, Isabel, and they're much like any other man. One of them snored a bit and had a cold nose, which he delighted in nuzzling against my neck. The other fretted endlessly over his three sisters and had a fondness for chocolate."

Isabel popped the clove into her mouth. "No orgies, then?"

"Not a one. I would have sent any man who suggested such foolishness on his way with a flea in his ear."

"And they would have departed on your whim," Isabel said. "You're not sweet, biddable Hen anymore. Has that child gone to sleep?"

A quiet slurping near Henrietta's ear suggested otherwise. "Not quite. How many cloves will you stick into that poor orange?"

The hapless fruit resembled a beribboned mace from days of old. Isabel set it aside and plucked another orange from a bowl on the table and measured off a length of red ribbon.

"So what now, Hen? You've made your fortune, turned your back on Sodom, and here you are. The whole shire knows you bided with the squire for most of this week, and we'll drag you to services on Sunday if you like. If you were here to make a point, you've made it."

"I am here to enjoy my family's company over the holidays," Henrietta said, though also, apparently, to make a point. "Attending services needn't be part of the bargain. Papa allowed me to bide with him, but he might as well have been billeting a French prisoner of war for all the hospitality he extended."

The squire had barely spoken to her, had barely acknowledged her at meals. Henrietta had been tolerated under her father's roof because to toss her out would have created more scandal than to allow her a few days at her childhood home.

And that tolerance had been more hurtful than all his years of distance, oddly enough.

Isabel cut the red ribbon with a single snip of the shears. "Do you believe that if you attend services, then you can't go back to your old life? Is waking up in the middle of the night to a duke's cold nose pressed to your neck that thrilling? I can suggest a few dogs who'd be as obliging, though they might not pay you in any coin but loyalty and devotion."

The baby sighed, and no exhalation was ever softer than a baby's sigh.

"She might be falling asleep now," Henrietta said.

"Good. I suspect the poor thing is getting ready to present us with a few teeth, and that's always an occasion for misery."

Isabel wrapped the ribbon about the orange with an expert flip and a twist, such that the fruit could be tied to any handy rafter or curtain rod. Henrietta had dealt with her partners in much the same way.

Flattery, affection, an interest in the man's welfare, a semblance of friendship always bounded by pragmatism. When the gentleman grew too demanding or restless, a subtle cooling from Henrietta was all it took to nudge him out the door and add another diamond necklace to her collection.

The oranges Isabel decorated would shrivel and turn brown, then be tossed to the hogs, no matter how pleasing their fragrance now.

"I don't want to go back to what I was," Henrietta said, "but I'm not sure in what direction I should move next."

Michael Brenner's image came to mind as Henrietta had last seen him. He'd followed her out to the drive at Inglemere, bowed over her hand in parting, and remained bare-headed at the foot of his front steps, his hair whipping in the winter breeze as the coach had taken off down the drive.

He'd looked lonely. Papa had looked lonely when Henrietta had packed up her coach and taken herself to Thad's house. Her next stop would be Philip's, after Christmas, but then…

Would Michael still be at Inglemere when the new year came?

"Has Thad ever broken your heart?" Henrietta asked.

Visiting with Isabel wasn't so different from visiting with other courtesans. Henrietta had somehow concluded that decent women sat about discussing the weather or recipes for tisanes rather than men and teething babies.

Courtesans had all too many babies, and all too many men.

"He came close," Isabel said, impaling the second orange with its first clove. "The year after we were married, I thought I was carrying, though it came to nothing, and that unnerved him. He got a bit too close to Penelope Dortmund, who'd been widowed the year before. She had the knack of grieving ever so prettily."

Henrietta had not been invited to her younger brother's wedding or any of the christenings. "What happened?"

Isabel jabbed three more cloves into the orange. "I saw them in the livery, literally rolling in the hay, though Thad hadn't got under her skirts yet. When he came home, I plucked a bit of hay from his hair and told him only a very foolish man would sleep beside one woman while playing her false with another. He barely tipped his hat to the widow after that."

"You *forgave* him?"

Isabel set the orange aside and took another from the bowl, a perfectly ripe fruit. She tore a section of peel off, then another.

"Have you seen Izzy's cradle, Henrietta?"

"It's gorgeous." The cradle was made of polished oak—a heavy, durable wood that wasn't easy to work with. The oak was carved with flowers, a rabbit, a kitten, and the words *Mama and Papa Will Always Love You.*

Henrietta couldn't stand to touch it. Another one very much like it lay in the squire's attics.

"Thad made that cradle. Stayed up late, worked on Sundays. He said it wasn't labor, it was love for the child I carried that sent him out to his woodshop. He built this house for us. He puts food on my table and coal in my hearth. He's not perfect, but neither am I. The widow wanted a stolen moment, but Thad asked me for my entire future. For better or for worse means for better or for worse."

She passed Henrietta a section of orange, then took one for herself.

"You love each other." The words hurt.

"Mostly. We used to argue more than we do now. Izzy helps. Thad adores that child."

The baby was fast asleep, an innocent, endlessly lovable little being who years from now might roll in the hay with the wrong man, or disappoint her papa in a fit of indignation. Henrietta hugged the baby close, and that, of course, woke the child.

"She'll be hungry," Isabel said, wiping her fingers on a towel. "Give her to me, and you can finish this orange. So will you go to services with us on Sunday?"

Isabel put the child to the breast while Henrietta took up stabbing cloves into the thick rind of the orange.

"I don't know about attending services. I think so. I'll scandalize the entire congregation."

"If they can't muster a bit of warm-heartedness at Christmas, then they're not much of a congregation, are they?"

"I wasn't much of a courtesan," Henrietta said, wondering why she'd taken ten years to realize this. "Papa never bade me come home, I was ruined, and I simply didn't know what else to do." And there Beltram had been, just full of suggestions and bank drafts, when it was clear that a life in service would mean more Beltrams who wouldn't bother to pay for the favors they sought.

Henrietta was abruptly glad Michael had pitched the bloody book into the fire.

"You're home now," Isabel said. "That's a start. I didn't realize Thad had taken the sleigh over to Philip's."

Henrietta went to the window, because the rhythmic jingle of bells heralded a conveyance coming up the drive.

Not Michael.

"It's Papa, driving himself, and both Thad and Philip are with him. He'll catch his death if he doesn't wear a scarf in this weather."

Papa was coming to call at a house where Henrietta dwelled. She did not know what to feel, and now, unlike the past ten years, her feelings mattered. Did she want to see her father when he was being such a pestilential old curmudgeon?

Did she care that he'd come to call on a house where she dwelled just days after waving her on her way?

"You'll have to see to him," Isabel said with a glance at the baby. "Izzy does not care for the company of her grandpapa, and the squire doesn't think to lower his voice around a small child. He walks into the room and she fusses. I'll join you as soon as I can."

Voices and heavy footsteps sounded in the hall above.

"Henrietta Eloisa! I know you're here because your coach yet sits in the carriage house at the livery. Show yourself this instant and prepare to go calling with your family!"

"Has he been drinking?" Henrietta muttered, gathering up her shawl. "I cannot tolerate an intemperate man."

"He never drinks to excess. Go see what he wants, and recall that it's Christmas, Henrietta. Dredge up some charity for a lonely old man, because when you leave here, the rest of us have to put up with his moods and demands."

"You don't have to, actually," Henrietta said, taking a moment to arrange her shawl before starting for the stairs at a decorous pace. "You never did."

* * *

Michael closeted himself in the library—the last place Henrietta had kissed him—but he couldn't focus on work. He'd written to Beltram, one sentence informing his lordship that the book had been destroyed by fire before Michael's very eyes.

Had Michael's future with Henrietta been destroyed as well?

The door opened, revealing Michael's butler. "You have callers, my lord. Squire Josiah Whitlow and company. I put them in the family parlor because it's the only one with a fire."

Wright's words held reproach, for a proper lord would expect callers at the holidays and keep the formal parlor heated for the vicar and the second parlor toasty for the neighbors.

"Thank you, Wright," Michael said, turning down his cuffs and shrugging into his coat. "Please send up a tray on our best everyday service with a few biscuits or some shortbread. Did the squire bring his sons?"

"He did, sir." Wright bowed and withdrew on a soft click of the door latch. Wright would have made a good spy, except a palpable air of consequence enveloped him whether he was polishing the silver or lining the staff up to welcome Michael home.

Back to Inglemere—not home.

Perhaps Squire Whitlow was visiting for the purpose of calling Michael out, which occasion would necessitate the presence of the sons, who'd serve as seconds. Hardly a holiday sentiment, calling on a man on Christmas Eve to announce an intent to end his days.

Would Henrietta care? Other duels had been fought over her, but she was retired, and the last thing Michael wanted was to give her more cause for upset.

Then too, Michael was a baron now, and strictly speaking, a titled man did not duel with his social inferiors. He paused for one fortifying moment outside the parlor, then made a brisk entrance and stopped short.

"Mr. Whit... low."

Michael remained in the doorway, gawping like an idiot, for Henrietta graced his family parlor. She was resplendent in yards of purple velvet with red trim. Her father and brothers were so many drab grouse compared to her, none of them looking particularly comfortable to be paying this call.

Michael was pleased. Cautiously pleased.

"Welcome to you all," he said. "Squire, introductions are in order."

The squire cleared his throat, harrumphed, then stood very tall. "Henrietta, may I make known to you Michael, Lord Angelford, who has taken possession of Inglemere since last you bided in Amblebank. His lordship paid a call on me yesterday, hence our neighborly reciprocity of his gesture. My lord, I make known to you my daughter, Henrietta, and her two brothers, Philip and Thaddeus Whitlow. You can thank the mighty powers that my grandchildren did not accompany us, else they'd be climbing your curtains and breaking yonder porcelain vase by now."

Whitlow had introduced her with all appropriate decorum, even knowing Michael was not a stranger to Henrietta.

The strategy was brilliant, did Whitlow but know it.

"Miss Whitlow," Michael said, taking the lady's hand and bowing. "I am honored by your company." He bowed in turn to Philip and Thad, who were younger versions of the squire. The tray soon arrived, and much to Michael's surprise, the squire carried the conversation.

He inquired regarding crops and tenants, drainage—ever a fascinating subject to the English gentry—and game. Henrietta presided over the tea tray with perfect grace but added little to the conversation.

What did it mean that she'd come to call? Was her family treating her well, and how could Michael find five minutes alone to ask her if she'd forgiven him?

He'd watched every crumb of shortbread disappear down the gullets of the Whitlow menfolk and was about to embark on a discourse regarding the construction of a ha-ha bordering a hayfield—about which he knew not one damned thing—when Wright interrupted again.

"More callers, my lord, and I hesitate to bring bad tidings, but they've children with them. Noisy children."

"Healthy lungs on a child are always a cause for rejoicing," Squire Whitlow said. "Well, don't just stand there," he went on, waving a hand at Wright. "Get us another tea tray with plenty of biscuits and show the visitors in. You're in the household of a baron, and company will be a constant plague."

"Wright," Michael said, rising. "Who are these callers?"

"Your sisters, my lord. All of them. With all of their children, and a husband or two, if I'm not mistaken. Cook will have an apoplexy."

His sisters? *All of them?* And the children and the husbands?

The cautious joy blooming in Michael's heart lurched upward to lodge in his throat. "Make them welcome, Wright, or I'll sack you on Christmas Day. You will make my family welcome, no matter how much noise they bring, or how many vases they break."

Wright bowed very low—though not quite low enough to hide a smile—and withdrew.

"Shall we be going?" Philip Whitlow asked, rising. "Your lordship's apparently quite busy with visitors today, and we wouldn't want to overstay our welcome."

"My friends are always welcome here," Michael said, and he was smiling too, because now—finally—Henrietta was looking straight at him and appearing very pleased with herself.

Or possibly, with him?

* * *

Michael did not look well-rested, but neither was he being the unapproachable lord. As Papa bleated on about ditches and boggy ground, Henrietta considered that Michael Brenner might be a shy man. She liked the idea and, as she watched Michael draw both Thad and Philip into the discussion, admitted that she liked Michael as well.

What's more, Papa liked him.

"I'll suggest we remove across the hall to the library," Michael said, "lest the size of the company exceed the capacity of the parlor. My nephews can be rambunctious."

"So can mine," Henrietta said, offering Michael her hand. Her brothers looked surprised, but then, her brothers had been indulged by wives who'd let manners lapse amid the exigencies of domestic bliss.

Michael's grasp was firm, but fleeting. "You'll find the library a little lacking in warmth," he said, aiming his comments at Henrietta. "But the room could be gracious with a little attention."

His library was lovely, though his desk was a bit untidy, as if he'd tried and failed a number of times to write a difficult letter. Henrietta was wandering about, trying to casually work her way to the desk when a herd of small children galloped into the library.

"I get the ladder!" one boy yelled.

"First on the bannister!" another cried.

"I get the bannister," a small girl called, elbowing one of the boys in the ribs.

"Reminds me of you lot," Papa said, taking some book or other from Henrietta's hands, while Michael went to the front door to greet his sisters. "That man is in love with you, Henrietta. Properly head over ears. I had to see it for myself, and he did not disappoint. If you show him the least favor, he'll make you his baroness."

Papa's words were offered beneath the pounding of a dozen small feet up the spiral staircase in the corner of Michael's library. His lordship rejoined the group in the library, bringing four laughing, chattering sisters with him and two much quieter men.

Pandemonium ensued, with children sliding down the spiral bannister, mamas and papas clucking and scolding, Philip and Thad putting a boy each on their shoulders to reach the higher shelves, and Papa—Papa?—presiding over the bowl of rum punch on the sideboard.

"You come with me," Henrietta said, taking Michael by the hand. "We're seeing to more refreshments."

He came along docilely—brilliant man—while one of the girls snatched Henrietta's serving of punch and nipped up the steps with it.

"My sisters have come to call," Michael said. "I've been hinting and suggesting for weeks, but they never acknowledged my overtures. Now they're here, and all I want is to see them off so I can have more time with you."

"Where's the formal parlor?" Henrietta asked.

"Two doors down, to the right. My staff has doubtless lit the fire there, because they're certain the vicar will soon be joining the riot that passes for my household at present."

Henrietta escorted Michael to the formal parlor, a lovely room full of gilt chairs upholstered in pink velvet, thick carpets, an elegant white pianoforte, and a pink marble fireplace.

"The quiet," Michael said as Henrietta closed the door. "Just listen to the quiet."

The only sound was the fire crackling in the hearth, though Henrietta could feel her heart pounding against her ribs too.

"Listen to me," she said. "I don't like that you stole my book, Michael Brenner. You should have asked me for it."

He stuck his hands in his pockets, though the parlor was cozy. "Would you have given it to me? I was a stranger to you, a man you had no reason to trust."

"Then you should have taken the time to earn my trust."

"I should have, and I am profoundly sorry I didn't. I behaved badly, but Henrietta…"

From the library came the happy shrieks of children loose for the first time in their uncle's home. The sound nearly broke Henrietta's heart, though at least Michael's family had come, however dubious their timing.

"But what, Michael?"

He put his hands behind his back and approached her. "I do not regret the intimacies I shared with you. I can't, and I never will. If I'd approached you as Beltram's negotiator, bargaining that book away from you with coin, charm, or threats, would you ever have allowed me close enough to become your lover?"

She'd wondered the same thing. "I don't know."

He stepped away, and the silence grew to encompass Christmases past, future, and all the years in between. Without Michael, those Christmases would be terribly lonely, even if Henrietta became the doting aunt and spinster daughter her family now invited her to be.

A revelation, that.

"I do know," Henrietta said, "that I treasure those moments shared with you too. I should have thrown that book in the fire years ago, but hadn't the courage. I wouldn't be here, calling on you, if my father hadn't kidnapped me and demanded I accompany him on a holiday call, as a proper daughter ought. He's gone daft."

"He's apologizing, in his way. He and I had a frank talk the day after you left his household. Will you accept his apology, Henrietta?"

"You and Papa had a frank talk? What did you and he have to talk about?"

One corner of Michael's mouth lifted. "I wanted to ask him if I could pay you my addresses, but the topic didn't come up. I was too busy lecturing him."

Henrietta sat on the nearest reliable surface—a tufted sofa. "There's too much pink in this room."

"Then redecorate it," Michael said. "May I sit with you?"

"You wanted to ask Papa if you could *court* me? You're a baron, and I'm a…" A woman in love, among other things. Henrietta patted the place beside her. "This is all very sudden."

"This is all ten years too late." Michael came down beside her and took her hand. "Can you forgive me, Henrietta? I have wronged you, but I also hope I've nudged things with your family in a better direction. I couldn't think what else to do."

Michael had *had a talk* with Papa. Henrietta shuddered to think what that conversation had entailed, but Papa had introduced her not an hour past as a proper young miss, which she most assuredly would never be again.

"Whatever you said," Henrietta replied, "it opened a door that all of my wrenching and wrestling couldn't budge. Papa and I will never get back the last ten years, but you've given us the years to come, and that's miracle enough."

Michael's grip on her hand was loose and warm. "You'll allow me to court you?"

Henrietta didn't fly into giddy raptures, though she was tempted to. Ten years ago, she might have. Michael apparently didn't expect giddy raptures, and that made up her mind.

"Papa has the right of it," she said. "You will court me, right down to asking his permission before he leaves here today. You'll walk out with me, when the weather moderates."

"And join your family for Sunday dinner," Michael said. "Sunday dinners are very important."

"I'll get to know your sisters—I wrote to them, by the way."

He kissed her knuckles. "You put them up to this invasion?"

"You looked so lonely and they hadn't had a formal invitation, only hints and suggestions. They were waiting for the great baron to do the pretty, never having had a great baron in the family before."

"Thank goodness you came along to translate the brother into the baron, then. Will we cry the banns?"

This discussion was so odd, and so right. This was two people discussing a shared future, not an arrangement. This was solving problems, forgiving, loving, and moving forward, not choosing jewelry or signing a lease on a love nest.

This was what a happily ever after in the making looked like.

"We'll decide whether to cry the banns or use a special license if you propose," Henrietta said. "First, you must have permission to court me."

"No," Michael said, taking her in his arms. "First, I must kiss you, then I must gain permission to court you—provided you're willing?"

Henrietta kissed him with all the willingness in her, and not a little stubbornness, along with heaps of gratitude and bundles of hope. Desire was making the list just as the door flew open, and a small red-haired girl pelted into the room.

"Can I hide in here?"

"You may," Michael said. "But only for a short while. I'll need this room for a private chat with Miss Whitlow's father."

The child darted behind the sofa. "Good! Don't tell anybody I'm here."

So it came to pass that Michael asked Squire Whitlow for permission to court Henrietta while one of Michael's nieces giggled and fidgeted behind the sofa. Henrietta fidgeted in the library—but did not giggle—until her Papa returned from the formal parlor to offer her a cup of punch from the nearly empty bowl on the sideboard.

"He'll do, Henrietta," Papa said. "The fellow's besotted, worse even than I was with your mama. Don't make him wait too long, please. A man's dignity matters to him."

"So does a woman's," Henrietta said. "I want to be married in spring, with my family all around me, and Michael's family too. You'll give me away?"

Michael returned to the library, a little girl carried piggyback. "Nobody found me!" she cried. "I won!"

Michael found me, and I won too.

"Of course I won't give you away," Papa replied. "I'll walk you up the church aisle, but don't ever expect me to let you go again."

He passed Henrietta his serving of punch so she held two nearly full cups, kissed her cheek, then crossed the library to pluck the child from Michael's back.

Michael joined Henrietta and took one of the cups of punch from her. "If the squire made you cry, I'll thrash him, and I will not apologize for it."

"He made me cry, but don't you thrash him, not for that."

The children were thundering out of the library, every bit as loudly as they'd arrived, and mamas and papas were calling for wraps and finishing servings of punch. A game of fox and geese was being organized, and nothing would do but Uncle Michael must referee.

"Shall I return you to your family, Henrietta? Your father was most insistent that all proprieties be observed."

"You already did return me to my family, and we'll observe the proprieties only when privacy is denied us. I'll marry you, Michael, gladly, but I'd like some courtship first. Not for my sake, but for—"

"Your family's," Michael said. "You'll go from your father's household to this one. I understand."

His kiss said he did understand and confirmed for Henrietta that early spring would do for a wedding date, possibly even late winter.

Uncle Michael presided over the holiday game of fox and geese, which became a tradition that grew into a family tournament. Michael and Henrietta's own brood joined the hunt, along with cousins, aunts, uncles, and—when the snow wasn't too deep—the squire himself.

Then all would repair inside to enjoy the Christmas punch and listen to a version of the story of how Michael and Henrietta had found each other—and happiness—in the midst of winter's chill. Some of the details were edited, but Christmas after Christmas, the ending was always the same, a happily ever after, forever in progress.

Patience for Christmas

GRACE BURROWES

To those who must work when the rest of the world frolics.

CHAPTER ONE

"Professor Pennypacker is wise, kind, cheerful, and witty. Why shouldn't I loathe him?" Patience Friendly's honest question met with smirks from her dearest friends in all the world, though she'd spoken the plain, seasonally inappropriate truth.

"You don't loathe the professor," Elizabeth Windham said. "You have a genteel difference of opinion with him from time to time, such as educated people occasionally do. More tea?"

Patience paid regular visits to the four Windham sisters because they were excellent company, though their lavish tea tray figured prominently in her affections as well.

"Half a cup, and then I must be going."

Elizabeth obliged, her idea of a half portion coming nearly to the cup's brim.

"It's the first Monday of the month. Does Dreadful Dougal demand your time, again?" Charlotte Windham asked around a mouthful of stollen.

"Mr. MacHugh is my publisher. I ought not call him that." In her thoughts, Patience called him much worse. "He might be lacking in polish, but Dougal P. MacHugh ensures my little scribblings find their way into many hands."

Dougal referred to Patience's advice columns as little scribblings, but the coin her writing earned was not so little to a spinster without means.

"Your advice to that boy who bashed his sister's dolly was lovely," Megan Windham said. Unlike her sisters, she wasn't embroidering (Elizabeth), knitting (Anwen), or devouring tea cakes (Charlotte). Megan had a quiet about her that soothed, though Patience suspected that quiet hid a lively imagination.

All four sisters shared Patience's red hair, but they were from a ducal family. If they'd gone swimming in the Serpentine, that would have become the latest rage. Their red hair made them striking, while Patience's earned her frequent admonitions from her publisher to control her temper.

"I'll take you up with me in the carriage," Anwen said. "I'm to read to the boys this afternoon, and one wants to be punctual when setting an example for children."

"You're passionate about that orphanage," Patience said. "I wish Dread— Mr. MacHugh permitted me to write about the plight of poor children in winter, instead of limiting me to an advice column."

Nothing in all of creation compared to the pleasure of a good, strong cup of black tea on a cold December day, unless it was the same cup of tea shared with friends. Without the company of these four young women, Patience would likely have been reduced to rash acts.

Marriage to the curate, for example.

As Anwen put away her knitting and Charlotte wrapped up the stollen— most of the loaf for the orphans, but two slices for Patience—snow flurries danced outside the parlor window. A brisk breeze pushed them in all directions, and the gray sky threatened a proper snowfall.

Mr. MacHugh would call it a braw, bonnie day, but he was Scottish, and his view of life paid little heed to tea cakes, cozy parlors, or mornings spent with friends. He was all business all the time, the opposite of the company Patience treasured most dearly.

"You'll come by the Wednesday before Christmas to see how we're progressing with our holiday baking, won't you?" Elizabeth asked as Patience accepted a cloak and scarf from the Windham butler. "We still use your mama's recipe for lemon cake."

A woman who lived alone didn't bother with the expense of holiday baking. "I'll see you on baking day, just as I do every year, and I'll try to get Mr. MacHugh to publish a piece on Anwen's urchins. If people won't contribute to charity at Yuletide, then we've become a hopeless species indeed."

The prospect of persuading Mr. MacHugh to do an article on Anwen's favorite orphanage was daunting, and as Patience bundled into the Windham coach, a predictable melancholy settled over her, as heavy and familiar as the woolen lap robes.

How many more years would pass in this same pattern? Writing at all hours, battling with Dougal MacHugh over the content of the columns, envying friends their holiday luxuries, and hoping the winter was mild?

The problem wasn't entirely poverty. Many families with little means found joy in one another's company and celebrated the holidays cheerfully.

The problem was Patience's life, and no advice columnist in the realm—not even her kindly, wise, dratted competitor, Professor Pennypacker—could tell her how to repair an existence that felt as bleak and barren as the winter sky.

* * *

"I have never met a female more inappropriately named than Patience Friendly," Dougal MacHugh muttered. "If I ask her to meet me on the hour, she's fifteen minutes early, and if our meeting requires an hour of her time, she's pacing my office thirty minutes on. Send her in."

"Shall I put the kettle on, Dougal?"

Harry MacHugh was a good lad, but he was a cousin—most of Dougal's employees were cousins of some sort—and thus he presumed from time to time where prudent men would not.

"She'll not take tea with me, Harry. Ours is a business relationship." A lucrative one too. But for that signal fact, Miss Friendly would doubtless have ejected Dougal from her life as briskly as she dispatched her readers' problems.

"Even business associates can share a cup in honor of the season," Harry said. "I'll just—"

"You'll just show the lady in, and then dash off a note to your mum and da. It's Monday."

"Aye, Dougal."

Oh, the martyrdom a fifteen-year-old could put into two words and a heavy sigh. Over the past year, as Harry had shot up several inches in height, his penmanship had improved, as had his vocabulary and grammar. Dougal had the boy review the ledgers too, and purposely made the occasional error to test Harry's skill with figures.

Harry clomped out of Dougal's office as the clock on the mantel struck a quarter till the hour. Miss Patience Un-Friendly whisked through the open door a moment later.

Once a month, Dougal endured the disruption of her presence in his office. Discontent accompanied her everywhere, a discontent she channeled into repairing the lives of readers without the sense to solve their own problems—bless their troubled hearts. Even the rhythm of her footfalls—rapid, percussive, confident—spoke of a woman determined on her own ends.

And the damned female had the audacity to be lovely. She wasn't simply pretty—pretty was for daffodils and landscapes—she was... all wrong.

A woman dispensing advice as the practical, blunt Mrs. Horner ought not to have a full mouth made for kisses and smiles. She ought not to have features that bore the serene grace of a Christmas angel, and she had no business having a figure that put Dougal in mind of cozy Highland winters and a wee dram shared before bed.

He'd hoisted an occasional wee dram to Miss Friendly's beauty, and many more to her blazing intelligence and nimble pen.

"Miss Friendly, good day. Perhaps your watch is running a bit fast."

"Mr. MacHugh, greetings." She pulled off her gloves and tossed them onto the mantel. "Sooner begun is sooner done. Shall we get to work?"

She usually remarked on how much Harry was growing, and how fat the office cat—King George—had become.

"Are you in a hurry, madam? We can reschedule this meeting if you'd like, but I've a special project to discuss with you."

"No time like the present, Mr. MacHugh. Let's be about it." She took her customary seat at Dougal's worktable, a battered, scarred article that had been in the MacHugh family since Robert the Bruce had been in nappies.

"Shall I build up the fire, Miss Friendly?"

"Why would you do that? Coal is dear, Mr. MacHugh, as you well know."

From her twitchy movements and the bleak quality in her gaze, Dougal knew something was bothering her—more than the usual weight of the world she carried on behalf of her readers. The daft woman took her job seriously, considering her replies to each letter as if the fate of entire neighborhoods might rest on whether she could solve the reader's dilemma.

Dougal added half a scoop of coal to the fire in the hearth. "You're still wearing your cloak. I thought you might be cold."

She shot to her feet and plucked at the buttons marching down the front of her cape. "You're absolutely right. How silly of me. My mind is on this month's stack of letters, and—"

Miss Friendly fell silent, her expression disgruntled as she fussed with the fastenings at her throat. In the clerk's office, she would have had a mirror to aid her, but Dougal had no need to examine his own features.

"Allow me," he said, brushing her hands aside. She'd knotted the strings more tightly rather than loosening the bow, and Dougal took a small eternity to get her free. In those moments, Miss Friendly stared over his shoulder as if he were a physician taking medically necessary liberties, while Dougal tormented himself with stolen impressions.

She smelled of damp wool, for the day had turned snowy, but also of lemons and spice. Clove, cinnamon, he wasn't sure what all went into her fragrance, but it put him in mind of Christmas cakes, cloved oranges, and blazing Yule logs.

The backs of his fingers brushed against her skin, which was surprisingly warm, given the inclement weather. Also soft. For a moment, her pulse beat against his knuckles, and then the strings came free.

"There ye go." His burr showed up at the worst moments, when he was angry or tense.

Or drunk.

"My thanks." Miss Friendly stepped away to draw the cloak from her own shoulders. She hung it over a hook on the back of the door and started fishing in the pockets.

Her hems were damp, and her boots were likely soaked. Dougal discreetly moved her chair closer to the fire and waited for the lady to take her seat.

"Are you looking for something?" he asked when she'd searched both pockets thoroughly.

"I've misplaced my glasses, or forgotten them. Without them—"

"Use mine," he said, plucking the spectacles from his nose. "You'll be able to see halfway to the Highlands with them."

Her gaze went from the eyeglasses in his hand—plain gold wire and a bit of curved glass—to his face, back to the glasses.

"I couldn't take your spectacles, Mr. MacHugh."

Because he'd worn them on his person? "We'll get nothing done if you can't see the letters to read them. I have a spare pair."

He retrieved the second pair from his desk and donned them, though the earpieces were a trifle snug and the magnification wasn't as great.

"So you do. Well." Miss Friendly was practical, if nothing else. She put the glasses on and took her seat. "Let's get to it. The holidays bring all manner of problems, and I'm sure I can offer some useful advice in at least a few instances."

"You'll have to do better than that," Dougal said, settling into the chair across from her.

Always across from her, for two reasons. First, so he could torment himself with the sight of her, sorting and considering, losing herself in her work; and second, so no accidental brush of hands, arms, or shoulders occurred.

"I do not care for your tone, Mr. MacHugh," she said, taking off the spectacles and polishing them on her sleeve. "I always do my best for my readers. If you imply something to the contrary, we shall have words."

"I'm a-tremble with dread, Miss Friendly," he said, passing her a wrinkled handkerchief. He loved having words with her. She hurled arguments like thunderbolts, didn't give an inch, and was very often right—and proud of it.

"What is this?" she asked, peering at the embroidery in the corner. "Is this a unicorn?"

"Wreathed in thistles. My cousins Edana and Rhona MacHugh do them for me. Winters are long in Perthshire, and Edana and Rhona like to stay busy."

Eddie and Ronnie had a small business, about which their brothers probably knew nothing. They and the ladies of their Perthshire neighborhood embroidered various Scottish themes on handkerchiefs, gloves, bonnet ribbons and so forth, and shipped them to Dougal. He distributed the merchandise to London shops and fetched much higher prices for the goods than the women could have earned in Scotland.

"It's quite pretty," Miss Friendly said, passing the handkerchief back. "More of a lady's article than a gentleman's though, don't you think?"

"Perhaps, but it reminds me of home and family, and fashion is hardly foremost in my mind."

"One could surmise as much." She gave him a perusal that said his plain attire was not among the problems she was motivated to solve, then picked up the first letter in the stack.

This was Dougal's favorite part of the meeting, when he could simply watch Patience at work. She read each letter, word for word, considered each person's problems and woes as if they were her own, then listed and discarded various possible solutions to the challenge at hand. By the time she left, she'd have a month's worth of worries put at ease, a month's worth of difficulties made manageable for some poor souls she'd never meet.

"We'll have to work quickly today," Dougal said before she'd reached the end of the first letter.

"Because of the weather?"

The snow was coming down in earnest now, though it could easily let up in the next five minutes.

"Because I've got wind of a scheme Pennypacker's publisher has devised to take advantage of the holidays. You said it yourself: The holidays bring problems, and old Pennypacker isn't about to leave his readers without solutions."

"It's unchristian of me, but I dislike that man."

"No, you do not." Dougal hoped she did not or the poor professor was doomed to a very bad end.

"The professor takes issue with my advice at least once a month, and directs people into the most inane situations. Why he's become so popular is beyond me, though I'll grant you, the man can write."

Ever fair, that was Miss Friendly. "He can make you a good deal of coin too." Dougal rose to retrieve a ledger from the blotter on his desk. "These are your circulation figures from last November and from this November."

She studied the numbers, which Dougal had checked three times. "We're doing better. We're doing appreciably better."

That news ought to have earned Dougal a smile at least, but the lady looked puzzled. "I'm not doing anything differently," she said. "Mrs. Horner's Corner dispenses kindly, commonsense advice and responds to reader pleas for assistance with domestic problems. What's changed?"

Exactly the question a shrewd woman should ask. Dougal passed her another sheaf of figures.

"Take a look at August and then September. The numbers begin to climb, and the trend continues into October and then last month. The increase isn't great between any two months, but the direction is encouraging."

The rims of Dougal's spectacles glinted in the firelight as Miss Friendly ran a slender, ink-stained finger down a column of figures. The picture she made was intelligent, studious, and damnably adorable.

"That man, that dreadful awful man," she murmured, setting the papers aside. "Pennypacker began writing his column in August. You think the readers are comparing my advice to his?"

"I'm nearly certain of it," Dougal said. "All too often, Pennypacker deals with at least one situation that's remarkably similar to the situations you address, and his advice is often contrary to yours. In the next column, you'll elaborate on your previous suggestions, annihilate his maunderings, and further explicate your own wisdom. He returns similar fire, and in a few weeks, we have a bare-knuckle match over the proper method for quieting a querulous child at Sunday services."

"Gracious, I'm a pugilist in the arena of domestic common sense."

Now she smiled. Now she beamed at the flames dancing in the hearth as if Dougal had handed her the Freedom of the City and a pair of fur-lined boots.

"Pugilists have to defend their titles, Miss Friendly, and if we let this opportunity slip by us, the crown will go to Pennypacker."

She glowered over the spectacles. "He's a posing, prosy, pontificating *man*, Mr. MacHugh. Why on earth his opinions of household management should signify, I do not know. The professor has likely never rocked a baby to sleep or kneaded a loaf of bread, if he's even a professor."

Had the prim Miss Friendly ever tended a baby? Did she long for an infant of her own, or even a family complete with adoring husband? Self-preservation suggested Dougal ask that question at another time.

"You might think gender alone disqualifies Pennypacker from having anything useful to say," Dougal replied, removing his spare glasses before they gave him a headache. "But his publisher intends to let him natter on for twelve consecutive days as we lead up to Christmas. Yuletide special editions they're calling them, the publisher's holiday gift to the masses, though the gift won't be free."

Miss Friendly drew off the spectacles and covered her face with her hands. The gesture was weary, but when she dropped her hands, sat back, and squared her shoulders, the light of battle shone in her blue eyes.

"Twelve consecutive days? That means answering dozens of letters."

"Sundays off, I'm assuming, but yes. At least three dozen letters answered in less than two weeks. I know it's a challenge when your friends will be expecting you to socialize and exchange calls."

Her shoulders slumped. "They will. It's baking season. Drat."

When Dougal had opened his publishing house three years ago, he'd faced enormous odds. London had a thriving, highly competitive publishing industry with each house specializing in certain products—herbals, sermons, animal husbandry, memoirs, and so forth. A readership took time to develop, and Dougal's inheritance was all he'd had to sink into his business.

He'd teetered on the brink of ruin until Patience Friendly had shown up in his office, full of ideas, pen at the ready.

Mrs. Horner's Corner had rescued an entire publishing house—women were avid readers, it turned out—and when Dougal had moved her column to the top of the front page, the entire business had found solid footing. He was on his way to becoming the domestic advice publisher, and Patience Friendly was his flagship author.

Dougal could not afford—literally—to either coddle her or earn her disfavor. "I know the timing is poor," he said. "I'm sure you don't want to spend your holidays ignoring friends and family—but this is an opportunity. If we don't step into the ring with the professor now, we'll lose ground when we could take ownership of it. You have the better advice, and the ladies who buy my paper know it."

"My readers are very astute," she said, worrying a nail. Her readers, not the customers, not *the* readers. *Hers*, just as Dougal had referred to the paper as *his*. "And yet, they depend on me. Do you know, my laundress discusses my column with my housekeeper, and they both say that at the baker's, the ladies talk of little else."

Yes, Dougal knew, because he frequented taverns, coffee shops, booksellers, churchyards, street corners, all in an effort to aim his business where the public's interest was most likely to travel.

Dougal kept his peace. Twelve special broadsheet editions in fourteen days was an enormous undertaking, but he was determined that his business thrive, and that Miss Patience Friendly thrive too.

He owed this woman.

And he always paid his debts.

* * *

Heavenly choruses, a dozen columns in two weeks!

The part of Patience that loved to be of use, to write, to feel a sense of having made a contribution leaped at the prospect. The part of her who'd had enough of Professor Pontifical was ready to answer every letter in Mr. MacHugh's stack.

But other parts of her…

Across the table, Dougal MacHugh waited. He was deucedly good at waiting, arguing, persisting—at anything necessary to further his business interests. Patience admitted to grudging admiration for his tenacity, because at one time MacHugh's determination to build a business had been all that stood between her and a life in service, or worse, dependence on a spouse.

She didn't *like* his tenacity. Didn't like much of anything about him, though he had a rather impressive nose.

He'd taken off his spare glasses, and thus good looks entirely wasted on a Scottish publisher were more evident. Untidy dark hair gave him a tousled look that made Patience want to put him to rights.

He'd probably bite off her hand if she attempted to straighten his hair.

His eyes were a lovely emerald color, fringed with unfairly thick lashes, and his mouth—Patience had no business noticing a man's mouth. Anybody would notice Mr. MacHugh's broad shoulders and his height. He was a fine specimen, which mattered not at all, and a finer businessman.

That mattered a great deal.

"You think we can do this, Mr. MacHugh? Put out twelve special editions in two weeks?"

His regard was steady. Patience liked to think of it as a man-to-man gaze, because not even her dear friends regarded her as directly.

"I think *you* can do this, Miss Friendly."

Did Mr. MacHugh but know it, his confidence in her was worth more than all of the pence and quid he paid her—and he did pay her, to the penny and on time.

"My compensation will have to reflect the effort involved."

"Madam, if this goes well, your compensation will result in a very fine Christmas for some years to come."

Patience longed to pick up the next letter and lose herself in the worries and quandaries of her readers, but she'd yet to agree to take on Mr. MacHugh's project.

"What do you mean, a very fine Christmas for some years to come?"

He came around to her side of the table, bringing pencil and paper with him. He moved with an economy of motion that Patience associated with cats and wolves, not that she'd ever seen a wolf.

Mr. MacHugh took the chair beside her. "Look at the numbers, Miss Friendly."

Who would have thought a publisher would smell of apples and pine? That scent distracted Patience as Mr. MacHugh explained about the printer's pricing scheme, the potential market for broadsheets in London, the publishing houses that had recently closed, and the magnitude of the opportunity awaiting Mrs. Horner's Corner.

"So the professor has chosen an excellent time to cast a wider net," Mr. MacHugh concluded. "I'd suspect him of being a Scotsman, his maneuver is so exquisitely timed."

Patience picked up the page, half covered with numbers and tallies. Impressive tallies. "Not all keen minds are Scottish, sir."

Patience wasn't feeling very keen. Her earnings had crept up, true, but she'd used the monthly windfall to pay off debts and set aside a bit for leaner times. What would it be like to know she had enough when those lean times came around?

For they inevitably did.

"You hesitate to spoil your holiday season with too big an assignment." Mr. MacHugh stuck his pencil behind his ear. "I can't blame you for that, it being *baking season* and all."

He lowered his lashes in a manner intended to make Patience shriek, his tone implying that crumpets would of course hold a woman's attention more readily than coin.

"Without a steady income, Mr. MacHugh, there can be no crumpets. My concern is that the work you put before me must meet the standard I've set over the past two years. Perhaps the professor can churn out his drivel at a great rate, but my efforts are more thoughtful."

"Your efforts are very thoughtful."

Mr. MacHugh knew how to deliver a compliment that was part contradiction, part goad. Rather than toss his own spectacles at him—they were fine eyeglasses—Patience got up to pace.

"Christmas falls on a Saturday this year," she said. "If we're to publish twelve editions, the last on Christmas Eve, that means—"

"The first edition should come out this Saturday, December eleventh. The twelfth and the nineteenth being the Sabbath, that means—"

"This Saturday! That means we go to the printer's four days from now."

"Aye. Glad to see your command of the calendar is the equal of your ability with words. Can you do it?"

Could she give up the baking, the buying last-minute tokens for Elizabeth, Charlotte, Megan, and Anwen? Hustle past the glee clubs singing in the holidays on London's street corners when she longed to linger and bask in the music? Give up sitting quietly at church just to hear the choir rehearse the holiday services?

Upon reflection, yes, she could. Putting aside holiday folderol for two weeks to secure a nest egg was the practical choice.

"You hesitate," Mr. MacHugh said, tossing his pencil onto the table. "This is a once-in-a-lifetime opportunity to build Mrs. Horner's Corner into an institution, and you hesitate. What are you afraid of, Miss Friendly?"

Of all Dougal MacHugh's objectionable qualities, his perceptivity ranked at the top of the list. Were he not also unflinchingly, inconveniently, relentlessly honest, Patience could not have endured his acuity.

When her writing was weak, he told her. When the solution she proposed was poorly thought out, he told her. When she was repeating herself, preaching, making light of a problem, or otherwise missing the mark, he told her.

And worst of all, when he was wrong—a maddeningly infrequent occurrence—he admitted it.

Patience took her seat beside him, where the fire threw out the most warmth. "What if I can't do this?"

"Failure is always a possibility, but we minimize it with planning and hard work."

"You haven't left me any time to plan."

"Opportunity looks like inconvenience to the indolent."

She wanted to stick her tongue out at him. "Must you be so Scottish?"

"*I am Scottish.*"

"You needn't make it sound as if that's the most wonderful status a man could boast of. Back to the matter at hand, please. If I attempt this twelve-edition madness and fail, it's worse than if I'd let the professor bore everybody for two weeks straight. The readers will say I've exceeded my limits and overtaxed my dim female brain."

"Your brain, while admittedly female, is anything but dim. Think like a general. What do you need for your campaign to succeed?"

Generals were not female... except *some of them were*. Patience had learned from the same tutors hired to instruct her brother—Papa had seen no reason to also pay governesses—and throughout history, some generals had been female.

There were female deities, female saints, and female monarchs. All the best tribulations in mythology had been female too. The Medusa, the sirens, the furies.

"I'll need help," she said. "I'll need immediate editorial reviews, somebody to run errands for me, and *crumpets*. Lots and lots of crumpets."

She'd surprised him. How Patience loved that she'd surprised the canny, competent, *Scottish* Mr. MacHugh.

"There's a bakery on the corner for your crumpets. Detwiler will be happy to edit material as you complete it, and I will be your personal errand boy. Shall we begin?"

Gracious warbling cherubim. Patience knew the bakery well—she walked past it every time she dropped off her columns. Mr. Detwiler was as fast as he was competent, but as for that other item...

Apparently, Mr. MacHugh could surprise her too.

"We begin now, and your first assignment as my errand boy is to fetch me a batch of crumpets."

CHAPTER TWO

Dougal set a package of warm crumpets on the worktable. "I had a thought."

"You had a thought." Miss Friendly lifted the parcel to her nose and inhaled without even untying the bow. "Does that unprecedented development require a broadsheet alerting the masses to your good fortune? Perhaps we might refer to it as a seasonal miracle."

"You're quite on your mettle, Miss Friendly." Surrounded by letters, with the cat napping on the mantel behind her, she looked a little less wan, a bit less weary than she had when she'd arrived for the monthly meeting more than an hour ago.

"You brought me warm cinnamon crumpets." She tossed the string toward the hearth, though it caught on the screen. "How could I not be inspired?"

"I'm inspired too," Dougal said, unwrapping his scarf and hanging it over the hook on the back of the door. "The professor is printing twelve special editions, and that means he'll have to start on Saturday if he wants to get them all out before Christmas."

"Why Mr. MacHugh, you've learned the days of the week by heart. Perhaps Harry has been tutoring you. Such a dear boy, though somebody needs to let down the hems on his trousers."

Dougal shook his greatcoat then hung it over his scarf. "The professor's twelve days begin on Saturday. Ours ought to begin Friday."

She'd lifted a crumpet halfway to her mouth, and it remained there, poised before her. "*Friday?* Have you misplaced what few wits you claim, Mr. MacHugh? That means we have to have the first column to the printer on Thursday morning."

"Which means if you have it written by tomorrow evening, we can edit it Wednesday, and beat the professor at his game."

She took a dainty nibble of her sweet as cinnamon perfumed the office. The cat woke, stretched, and nearly fell off the mantel before re-situating himself more comfortably.

"You want me to write a column of insightful, kind, articulate advice." She took another bite of crumpet. "We haven't even chosen all of the letters yet, Mr. MacHugh. I can't conjure solutions without time to think them up."

"We'll argue them up." Dougal took the chair beside her, because the day was bitter and his backside craved the warmth of the fire.

"We're good at that," she said, nudging the crumpets toward him. "Take more than your share, and you'll get no columns from me."

Dougal used his penknife to slice one of the four crumpets in half, took a bite, then gestured with the remaining portion.

"Are these the letters you're considering?"

"Yes. Don't get crumbs on them."

He picked up the first one and scanned it. "The old *my sister is making eyes at my husband.* Husband's holiday token ought to be a month of slumber on the sofa, or a stern warning from sister's husband—and his brothers."

"Don't be such a man."

"*I am a man.*"

"Don't be such a crude man. We don't know if husband is making eyes back at the sister. If he is, there's a problem. If he's not, then the sister is simply making a fool of herself. We don't know if the sister is married, which also matters. The issue, though, is loneliness."

The issue was lust.

Dougal spoke around a mouthful of crumpet. "How do you figure that?"

"If the sister were content with her lot, she'd not be trying to attract the attention of her brother-in-law, which efforts are doomed to misery, no matter where they lead."

"True enough." Though Dougal had yet to have an entirely miserable time sharing a bed—as best he recalled those few and distant occasions—and a shared bed was the logical conclusion to this domestic drama.

"If the wife were secure in husband's affections," Miss Friendly went on, "she would not be troubled by her sister's behavior."

"Some women are born troubled."

Sharing that eternal verity with Miss Friendly earned Dougal the same look George gave him when the cat had been put out first thing on a snowy day.

She paused before starting on a second crumpet. "If the husband were entirely secure in his wife's affections, he wouldn't strike the sister as a man who could be tempted."

"Some men like to be tempted. They aren't interested in the sin itself, they just like to know they could be naughty if they wanted to."

She frowned at her half crumpet. "Like some women keep men dangling after them. There are names for women like that, but when a man is flirtatious, we call him a gallant."

The last of her crumpet met its fate, and an unhappy silence grew.

"Whoever he was," Dougal said, pushing to his feet, "he was an idiot, and you're better off without him. I need some tea."

He left the office not to see to the teapot—the clerks always had one going on the parlor stove in cold weather—but to put distance between himself, Miss Friendly, and thoughts of shared beds. Dougal had no business *speculating* where Patience Friendly was concerned, but he'd long ago given up lecturing his imagination on that score.

As he brought a tea tray back into his office, it struck him that for Miss Friendly, being closeted alone with a man under the age of eighty must be an unusual occurrence. If she'd had a flirtatious swain in tow at some point—a gallant—she wasn't the daughter of a merchant, schoolteacher, or yeoman.

"Will you answer the letter about the flirting sister?" he asked.

"I can use the letter as a point of departure regarding holiday loneliness and remind the readers that problems admit of solutions when we're in possession of all the relevant facts. Shall you eat that last half crumpet?"

Dougal set the tray down and regarded the sweet. The part he'd eaten had been delicious. Perfectly baked, between cake and pudding in the center, sweet, spicy, delightful.

"No."

Miss Friendly reached for it, and Dougal grabbed her wrist. "You've had three, madam."

"It shouldn't go to waste."

Someday, Dougal wanted her to look at him the way she regarded that last half crumpet.

"It won't. Harry!" he called. "Come clear up this mess, please."

Harry trotted into the office, wrapped the paper around the last half crumpet, and swept the table free of crumbs.

"Anything else, Dougal?"

Before non-family, Harry was supposed to call his employer Mr. MacHugh. "Aye. Send 'round to the chophouse for two plates at half four. The usual portions, and tell the lads they can go home an hour early if the snow keeps up. Fill up the coal buckets before you go and sweep off the steps."

"Right, Dougal."

The instant Harry had gone, Miss Friendly was on her feet, hands at her hips. "I can't believe you just threw away a perfectly good half of a delicious..." Her eyes narrowed. "You saved it for the boy."

"Nothing edible goes to waste when Harry's on the premises. Now, about this letter?"

She flounced back to her seat, and then the real arguments began.

* * *

Patience had never spent most of a day at her publisher's office. The insights gained were fascinating. The pace of the work never let up, with clerks coming and going, errand boys and printer's assistants adding to the traffic, and packages coming in by the hour.

The bustle was distracting at first, but then it became a sort of music, like a string quartet playing in the background at a Venetian breakfast. Several hours of choosing and discarding letters with Mr. MacHugh also revealed that clerks did not always use refined language, and most of Mr. MacHugh's staff spoke with thick Highland burrs.

As for MacHugh himself, he was the biggest revelation of all. He was gruff, demanding, tireless, and devoted to his staff.

"You sent your clerks home early," Patience said, getting up to fetch a cushion from the sofa. "Will you dock their pay?"

"Of course not. They're paid little enough as it is, and they'd work late if I asked it of them. We should finish up here. We've chosen enough letters to last you the first six days, and it's dark out."

Patience tossed the cushion onto her chair, then resumed her seat. To blazes with decorum when her backside ached.

"The food was surprisingly good," she said, surveying the remains of their meal. The chophouse had sent around a hot sandwich, ham and cheese, the cheddar almost melting but not quite, a perfect dash of mustard turning good food into a feast.

At home, dinner would have been soup made from the leftovers of the Sunday joint, but mostly broth, potatoes, and carrots.

"We're faithful customers at the chophouse," Mr. MacHugh said, moving the empty plates to the desk. "Shall we be on our way?"

"You needn't walk me home, Mr. MacHugh."

He leaned back against the desk, arms folded across his chest. At some point, he'd taken off his coat, and Patience had taken off her boots.

A far cry from the propriety with which she'd been raised, but propriety did not keep the coal bins full.

"Miss Friendly, I conceded to you on the matter of the child who'd pinched horehound candy from the sweet shop. I capitulated regarding the mother-in-law's awful bread pudding. I compromised regarding the best way to scent tapers without spending a fortune, but I will not allow a woman in my employ to walk alone on the streets of London at night."

The snow had stopped, but slippery footing was not the worst that could befall a solitary woman on London's streets, especially at night. Poor women took their chances, while wealthy women never went anywhere unescorted.

Patience would never be wealthy again. "Can't you send Harry with me?"

"Can't you accept my company for the distance of a few streets? You've spent the better part of a day with me, and we didn't come to blows."

"A near thing, and only because I disapprove of violence."

"You disapprove of me," he said, pushing away from the desk. "Get your boots on, and I'll see to it you're home safe in a half hour. I'll send Harry around to fetch the first column from you tomorrow afternoon."

He passed her the boots, which needed new heels, but kept her feet reasonably dry over short distances. The temptation to argue was strong, also unwise. Patience put her boots on, then wrapped herself in her cloak and scarf and let Mr. MacHugh accompany her to the front stoop.

Down near the corner, some elderly soul shuffled along, bent against the bitter breeze, but the thoroughfare was otherwise deserted.

"Let's be off," Mr. MacHugh said. "A bit of fresh air is all well and good, but I don't fancy a lung fever when the work is piling up." He tucked Patience's hand around his arm and set off at a surprisingly considerate pace, given the difference in their heights.

Fatigue descended as they walked along, and in the privacy of her thoughts, Patience was grateful for Mr. MacHugh's presence. The streets were unsafe for a woman traveling by herself at this hour.

And they were lonely.

After all the bickering, discussing, arguing, and debating, the silence of the December night was profound. The new snow muffled even church bells, and the smell—coal smoke on a frigid breeze—was desolate.

They had turned onto Patience's street when she broke the silence.

"I don't disapprove of you."

Mr. MacHugh made a disparaging noise between a snort and a huff.

"I don't," Patience went on. "I might not… That is to say, I don't know what to *do* with you. I was not raised to be in anybody's employment. I don't care for it, but I don't care to rely on charity either."

"You'd rather be idle?"

His curiosity was genuine, not a taunt aimed at a class of society for which Mr. MacHugh had little respect. At least he hadn't asked if she'd rather be married.

"I'd rather be the employer, if you must know. I cannot abide somebody telling me what to do, presuming to know what's best for me, or how I ought to go on."

"Especially not a man?"

"Not anybody."

Patience braced herself for a lecture on the way of the world, the dictates of the Almighty, nature's laws, and other masculine flights of self-importance. If men were so infernally smart, competent, and ideally suited to ordering creation, then why was most of the Continent constantly at war, and why hadn't men been chosen to endure the agony of childbirth?

"I don't care for being told what to do myself," Mr. MacHugh said. "There are sheep and there are shepherds. I'm not a sheep, and I'm not convinced gender matters the way the preacher claims it does, but that's just a former schoolteacher's point of view."

They'd reached Patience's doorstep, the only one on her side of the street with a lamp lit.

"You were a schoolteacher, Mr. MacHugh?"

"Aye, and still would be, except my grandfather left me some means. In the schoolroom, I saw what a difference knowledge could make to a receptive mind. I must admit small boys are not always ideal students, while little girls on the whole struck me as cleverer than the boys, more eager for knowledge. I had hoped that as a publisher, I might be able to do more to make knowledge available to receptive minds."

Mr. MacHugh's high-crowned hat gave him extra height in addition to what nature had bestowed, and yet, a hint of the small boy remained in his gaze as he studied the lamp post.

"Have you given up so easily on that dream of sharing knowledge, Mr. MacHugh? Your publishing house is not quite three years old."

He took off his hat and dusted a few snowflakes from the brim. "I'd planned to be the publisher who brought enlightenment to the masses, you see. Science, languages, tales of faraway lands, all for a reasonable price. No Gothic novels, scandal sheets, or fashionable nonsense for me. It hasn't worked out that way."

Half the elderly women who dwelled across the street were probably peering out their parlor windows, horrified that Patience was having discourse with a man on her very doorstep.

Warmth blossomed in her heart nonetheless, because Dougal MacHugh was not quite the pinchpenny taskmaster she'd thought him to be. He had dreams, he'd known disappointment. He'd not been above instructing little girls or noticing their intelligence.

"If this project goes well," Patience said, "you'll have some latitude, some room to put a bit of knowledge before the masses and see if they like it. That will be my holiday wish for you, Mr. MacHugh, that your dream can come closer to reality."

He tapped his hat back onto his head. "Give the professor a sound drubbing, Miss Friendly. That's all I ask. I'll bid you good evening."

Patience made her way up the steps, while, like a suitor, Mr. MacHugh waited for her to safely enter her home. She closed the door behind her and, before she undid her cloak and scarf, peered out the window.

Mr. MacHugh was already in motion, his stride confident, his dark cloak flapping against his boots. He hadn't scoffed at Patience's dreams, and he had dreams of his own. Watching him make his solitary way down the street, Patience considered she might have something else in common with Mr. Dougal MacHugh.

Perhaps he was lonely too.

* * *

"You canna tell the woman to leave her husband," Dougal shouted. "You'll put me oot t' business, ye daft woman. I'll have preachers six deep on m' doorstep citing Scripture, and a bunch of harpies quoting that Wollstonecraft woman in response."

For the space of a day, Dougal had pondered his walk through the snowy evening with Patience Friendly. From his perspective, their dealings had subtly shifted as a result of that walk, the shared meal, and the long afternoon spent shaping the details of their holiday project.

He'd given her a piece of his past, something none of his competitors knew. The schoolteacher from Perthshire aspired to commercial success, and Patience Friendly had not mocked his ambition.

Now, he aspired to turn her over his knee.

"The poor woman's husband is gambling and drinking away coin needed to feed her child," Miss Friendly retorted, marching across the office. "If she stays with him, she and the child will die, or worse."

"Such drama over a man enjoying a wee dram or two. What could be worse than death?"

She aimed a glower at him, magnificent in its ferocity. Up close, her eyes were storm gray rather than their customary blue, though she still bore the fragrance of lemons and spices.

"Must I spell it out for you, Mr. MacHugh? You've lived three years in London. Are you still in ignorance of the Magdalene houses and foundling homes?"

"Don't insult me, Patience Friendly."

"Don't ignore a woman whose child's life is imperiled, Mr. MacHugh. I say my reply to the letter stands. If a man is fonder of his pint than he is of his own child, he's a menace to the child. A father's first obligation is to protect his young."

"Find me Scripture to back up that position, and I'll let you quote it, but that's as far as I'll go."

"You arrogant varlet." Miss Friendly's voice cracked like a tree trunk sundered by gale-force winds. "Scripture is *written by men, interpreted by men, translated by men, and preached by men.* What would a man know of a lady's plight in this situation? The mother—a countrywoman from your benighted Scotland—didn't write to the all-knowing professor, she wrote to *me.*"

The staff was accustomed to Dougal raising his voice, and heated arguments among the clerks were not unusual. Dougal wasn't above dressing down a printer who failed to deliver on time, and some of the other authors—the male authors—could be colorful in their choice of words.

To have provoked Miss Patience Friendly to shouting felt like both an accomplishment and a disgrace. A violation of some natural order that stood above even Scripture.

"She's right," Harry said, sauntering through the open door with a bag of crumpets. "'Let the women keep silent in the church,' for example. Why wouldn't God want to hear from half his children? Doesn't make any sense to me, and yer auld mum would agree, Dougal."

"There you have it," Miss Friendly snapped, snatching the bag of crumpets from Harry. "From the mouths of babes, or in this case, strapping youths coming into the full glory of their intellectual powers." She tore open the bag and passed Harry a crumpet.

Harry accepted the sweet, bowed, and smirked his way out the door.

"We'll set the letter aside for now," Dougal said. "Plenty of others remain, and we needn't tackle that one first."

Miss Friendly held her crumpet as if she were considering pitching it at him. "We can set the letter aside for now, but the misery of poor children ought to be a suitable topic for the holiday season. You will not convince me otherwise."

For them, this was a compromise. A show of diplomacy was in order. "Convince you to change your mind once you've formed an opinion? Daft I might be, but I've no desire to end my days prematurely. Enjoy your crumpets."

Dougal tried for a dignified exit, but Miss Friendly tore off a bite of cinnamon heaven and popped it into her mouth as he passed her.

"You don't care for a crumpet, Mr. MacHugh? They're very tasty."

"I'll have a half."

The rest of the afternoon went the same way, bickering and sweets, then the occasional philosophical argument, followed by a heated difference of opinion over the placement of a comma.

All quite invigorating, and yet the disagreement over the gin widow's letter left a sour taste in Dougal's mouth.

"Has Miss Friendly driven you from your own office?" Harry asked as the clerks began packing up. "I can still make a run to the chophouse if you're going to demand more work from her."

Dougal eyed the closed door to his office, which sported his name—Dougal P. MacHugh, Publisher—in shiny brass letters. An hour ago, that door had opened enough for a disgruntled King George to be shoved into the clerk's room, but Miss Friendly hadn't emerged or demanded more crumpets.

"She's working," Dougal said. "You lot go get the greenery, and mind you, don't overspend. We've a budget in this office."

"We've a budget even for a frolic," Harry retorted. "Is it any wonder the Scotsman has a dour, miserly reputation?"

"Hear, hear," old Detwiler chorused from his desk.

"Traitor." Dougal pushed a few coins into Harry's hand. "Stand the lads to a pint when you're finished outside. Detwiler must buy his own, though."

The office emptied, save for Dougal, King George, and the literary force of nature who'd taken over Dougal's office.

Miss Friendly had said she wanted to be the employer, an unusual ambition for a woman her age. Widows could own entire networks of coaching inns, breweries, and all manner of establishments, but a single woman of Miss Friendly's age—a spinster—could dream of managing only her own household.

"Rrrlf."

George stropped himself against Dougal's boot. Dougal considered shoving the cat back through the door, a sort of reconnaissance maneuver, but decided on safety in numbers instead. He picked up George, did not knock on his own door, and entered the office.

He faced a writer's version of a battlefield. A dictionary lay open on the table. The remains of a bag of crumpets sat beside it. Foolscap had been crumpled and tossed toward the hearth, and more sheets covered with scrawling penmanship were scattered over the table.

Miss Friendly sat at Dougal's desk, her arms crossed on the blotter, her cheek pillowed on her forearm. Dougal set the cat on the mantel and crept closer, for his most popular author was apparently fast asleep.

"Miss Friendly?"

Her breathing continued in the slow, mesmerizing rhythm of exhausted sleep. A quill pen lay beneath her right hand. At rest, her features were more elegant, more delicate than when animated with her endless opinions.

Dougal slid the quill from beneath her grasp, and still she remained asleep. George paced back and forth on the mantel, as if waiting for a laggard minion to build up the fire.

Instead, Dougal lit a candle from a spill and took the candle to the desk. Better light didn't change what he'd observed when he'd first approached his sleeping beauty.

Miss Friendly was tired—her eyes were shadowed with fatigue, and her sleep was sound. She had also been upset, apparently, for in her left hand she clutched a lace-edged handkerchief, and her cheeks were stained with tears.

* * *

Patience dozed in that half-dreaming state where sounds from the waking world had no significance and thoughts drifted freely.

At least she hadn't cried in front of Dougal MacHugh. He wasn't exactly dreadful anymore, but he was disappointing, which was worse. On Monday, he'd acknowledged that even a young female might have a nimble mind. Today, he'd gone right back to parroting hidebound attitudes merely because they'd keep his business from offending the good clergy of London.

Let the women keep silent in the church, indeed.

"Miss Friendly."

Patience wasn't feeling very friendly. Other snippets of Scripture floated past, none of them useful when a child's belly was empty. The cat rustled about the office, and Patience had the odd thought that she liked having George underfoot.

"Madam, wake up. The lads will say I worked you to exhaustion."

That growling burr was familiar, and not.

Somebody gently shook Patience's shoulder. "Woman, ye canna be sleeping in my very office. We'll stop at the bakery and get some tarts, for I'm certain you've eaten every crumpet in Bloomsbury."

The word *crumpet* had Patience opening her eyes. "I adore a fresh lemon tart."

Dougal MacHugh knelt beside the desk, his emerald eyes full of concern—for her?

"I'll buy ye a dozen. Why were ye cryin', Patience?"

Patience. He avoided using her given name, but she liked the way he said it.

"How did you know I was crying?" For she had been, and dissembling would simply make her look foolish. More foolish. She sat back, knowing her sleeve had left a crease on her cheek, and her hair needed tidying.

She'd taken a break to read the morning paper and seen an engagement announced. Not just any engagement, but the one that ten years ago should have been hers.

A callused male thumb stroked her cheek. "I see the evidence of your tears. If somebody needs a beating, I'll gladly do the honors." In his way, Dougal MacHugh claimed a certain rough charm.

"He's a viscount now. He'd see you put out of business and laugh about it with his friends."

Mr. MacHugh brushed an errant lock of hair back from Patience's brow. "I liked teaching little children their letters, sums, and history. I'd like teaching a viscount his manners more. I take it your papa wasn't in a position to hold the bastard accountable."

Bastard was such a vulgar, *appropriate* word. "Papa was the reason the viscount went on his way, even though the engagement had been all but announced."

This was ancient, entirely irrelevant history. The Windhams knew all the details and had stood by Patience through it all, though the rest of her acquaintances had dropped her flat. Used goods. A jilt. A jade. Patience was no stranger to vulgar words, though she had denied herself use of them regarding the viscount.

"Was there a disagreement, lass?"

Small children had likely confessed all of their troubles to Dougal MacHugh when he put questions to them so gently.

"There was a predictable melodrama," Patience said, "though I was the only one not given the script. Papa, like many younger sons, lived beyond his means. He had a falling out with his older brother, and the debts began to pile up. Papa realized that he couldn't afford more than one Season for me, but for that one

Season, he spared no expense."

Mr. MacHugh turned and perched with his back to the desk drawers. "And when the viscount realized you were not an heiress, not even in possession of good settlements or on good terms with the head of your family, away he went. He broke his word, and he broke your heart."

"Well put." The first mattered more than the second, in hindsight.

"Your uncle was no help?"

"My uncle was determined to teach my father a lesson, my father was intent on the same exercise where the baron was concerned, the title has since gone to a cousin I've never met. I think Scottish families must be different."

"Scottish families are poorer, for the most part. We can't afford such meanness to one another."

Meanness, another appropriate word. "The viscount proposed to me. Not down on bended knee, but sitting in the pergola. He proposed, and I accepted. I know now why a young man is left alone to propose to his lady."

"Because men can't bear to have witnesses when they're rejected?"

"That too, but also so they don't have witnesses when their proposal is accepted. He later claimed I'd misconstrued his words, I'd read into friendship a regard that hadn't been tendered."

Mr. MacHugh rose straight to his full height. "Patience Friendly, if ever a woman had a fine command of the language, and the many subtleties thereof, you are that woman. You misconstrued nothing, and the viscount was never your friend."

He tugged Patience to her feet, and because she'd been sitting so long— surely that was the reason—she wobbled and clutched at the nearest stable object.

Her arms found their way around Mr. MacHugh's waist, and—later was time enough to wonder why—his enfolded her.

"Nobody has ever said that to me." She gave him her weight, and he obliged with a genuine embrace. "My parents questioned me endlessly. What had he said? Was I sure? Could I have misheard him? What words did he use? It's as if they wanted him to be right and me to be a witless ninny."

"You were right, they were wrong. You are not a witless ninny. Your parents' first responsibility is to protect their young—I have this on the best authority— and they failed you."

A queer feeling came over Patience, part sadness, because her parents had failed her spectacularly, but also part relief. No witnesses could verify the harm done to her by a faithless young man, and thus doubt had assailed her, even from within.

Had she misheard? *Was* she exaggerating? *Did* she misconstrue words intended to convey only general esteem?

"Papa said I must have misunderstood. I didn't misunderstand the viscount's hands under my skirts. Only a fiancé or a cad takes such liberties."

She buried her face against Mr. MacHugh's shoulder, appalled at her own honesty, and even more appalled at how ignorant she'd been ten years ago.

"Losing our innocence is painful, but it's how we find out what sort of person we are."

The desk and the chair prevented Patience from stepping back, and yet, she wanted to see Mr. MacHugh's eyes, wanted to assure herself he brought no judgment of her to this discussion.

Because if he did not judge her, perhaps she might cease judging herself. She'd accused herself of ignorance, while Mr. MacHugh pronounced her guilty only of trusting the wrong man.

She scooted onto the desk, and Mr. MacHugh remained where he was—close enough to hug, his hands at his sides.

"You could have gone into a decline," he said. "Thrown yourself on your uncle's charity, embroiled the viscount and your family in worse scandal than a simple reversal of fortune. You didn't. You soldiered on. You are still soldiering on, and God pity the fool who thinks to take advantage of you ever again."

Dougal MacHugh's approval made Patience want to cry all over again, also to smile. To beam, to laugh, to hug him again.

How odd.

"I could not allow my brother to suffer as a result of my situation. Mama pawned her jewels to buy him a commission and found work tutoring bankers' daughters in elocution, deportment, and French. She wrote pamphlets on the same subjects, and then I took up that occupation when she died."

Please don't ask about Papa. She could see the question in Mr. MacHugh's eyes, could feel it bearing down on her.

"And your father. Did he drink, Patience?"

"Sometimes. Mama said he expired of shame. We moved in with her mother, and that's the only reason I have a roof over my head. Grandmama left everything she had to me. You mustn't think my circumstances are pathetic."

Precarious, yes. Never pathetic. Not as long as Patience had friends and meaningful, paying work.

"I think you are resourceful, resilient, and brilliant at what you do, but it's time I got you home, Miss Friendly."

Patience didn't want to leave, and she didn't want to be *Miss Friendly*. She wanted to sort through the remaining letters, eat more of the hot, delicious food from the chophouse, and argue with Dougal until full darkness had fallen.

Except it already had. "Is my first column ready for the printer?"

"We'll send it over bright and early tomorrow. Three letters, all answered with your signature good sense. Come Friday, the professor will have an apoplexy."

"Good," Patience said, scooting off the desk. "He's certainly given me a few bad moments. The man is insufferable. Thinks he knows everything, and what he lacks in pragmatism he makes up for in long-windedness."

She was wrapped in her cloak and at the front door when it occurred to her that something about the office had changed. The scent was different, for one thing. Beneath the coal smoke, ink, and paper smell lay the fragrance of pine.

"You decorate for the holidays? Doesn't that cost a bit of coin, Mr. MacHugh?" The windows were swagged with pine roping, a wreath of pine and holly graced each of the double doors, and cloved oranges hung from the unlit wall sconces.

"The clerks enjoy decorating, the patrons like it, and my competitors do it, so I make a few gestures. It's in the budget, though I'll have a word with Harry tomorrow regarding fiscal restraint."

He pointed a gloved hand upward, to a sheaf of greenery dangling by a red ribbon from the chandelier.

Every spinster's worst holiday nightmare hung overhead—mistletoe, and plenty of it.

"Come along," Patience said, wrapping her arm through Mr. MacHugh's. "Tomorrow will be another demanding day, and we've tarried long enough."

She nearly shoved Mr. MacHugh through the door, and then engaged him in a discourse on the writings of Mrs. Wollstonecraft. Patience wasn't familiar with the author's philosophies, but if they had earned Mr. MacHugh's notice, she'd remedy that oversight posthaste.

CHAPTER THREE

The previous evening, Dougal had prosed on for the duration of three quiet snowy streets, regaling Patience with the writings of a woman either ahead of her time or bent on destroying the social order, depending on the critic's perspective. All the while, Dougal had been rearranging his emotional budget where Patience Friendly was concerned.

She was, indeed, a lady fallen on hard times. Very hard times, very much a lady, and her contrariness was a result of betrayed trust rather than arrogance. No wonder she argued every comma, demanded a say in which letters she answered, and had thrown herself into this project.

On Thursday morning, the office was tidy and neat—unlike Dougal's thoughts—thanks to Harry's efforts, though Dougal had enjoyed seeing the battlefield where Patience had thrashed her next deadline into submission.

"Shall I buy more crumpets?" Harry asked, shuffling through the door. "I can take them with me when I fetch Miss Friendly's column for tomorrow."

"I'll fetch her column," Dougal said. "You can take down the mistletoe, my lad. This is a respectable establishment."

"I'm not tall enough to take it down—yet. Mind you don't be pinchin' the lady's sweets, Dougal. I'd hate to have to peach on you to Cousin Hamish."

Cousin Hamish was head of the Perthshire branch of the family, a former colonel who owned two breweries and considerable acreage. His brother, Cousin Colin, owned a distillery, while their sisters, Rhona and Edana had yet to settle on a single enterprise. In England, the ladies might be discouraged from commercial ventures. In Scotland...

Family supported one another. Hamish had been the one to talk Dougal into trying his hand at publishing, for example.

"Cousin Hamish is hundreds of miles to the north," Dougal said, "and he likes it up in Perthshire. Be gone with ye, and don't be telling tales that reflect on a good woman's name."

Harry folded himself into one of the chairs facing Dougal's desk. "Are you thinking of offering for her?"

"Are *you*, Harold Bruce Sylvester MacHugh?"

Harry's ears turned red, but his grin was pure MacHugh. "I haven't sown my wild oats yet, or she'd succumb to my legendary charm in a thrice, and you'd have no one to write Mrs. Horner's Corner. Speaking of writing, what's that you're working on?"

Dougal picked up the page and poured the sand from it back into the tray. "None of your business, but it's almost ready for the printer. Fetch Miss Friendly's completed column from Detwiler, give it a final read, and you can take this with you when you make the morning run to the printer."

"I don't fancy running anywhere today, Dougal," Harry said, rising and holding his hands out toward the hearth. "That sky is getting ready to snow from now until Christmas. Mr. Detwiler's sacroiliac is acting twinge-ish, and you know what that means."

"It means when we need him most, Detwiler will take a day off, claiming his back has laid him low. It's winter, Harry. The sky looks like a winter sky. See to Miss Friendly's column, please."

Harry left off petting King George and went about his assignment. He was indeed growing out of his trousers—again—and would need new boots before too long as well.

Dougal read over the page he'd written, looking for mistakes or even a comma out of place. In his dreams, he'd give this piece to Patience to tear apart, edit, and refine, but that way lay a war Dougal wasn't prepared to fight.

Not yet, possibly not ever.

* * *

"That scoundrel!" Miss Friendly cried, boots thumping on the office floorboards as she stalked about like King George in a taking. "That dastardly, underhanded, pestilential, infernal—oh, I wish I were more proficient with foul language."

"Scurrilous dog?" Mr. MacHugh offered. "Varlet?"

"Too trite, but certainly in the right direction. How did he know, Mr. MacHugh? How did the professor know we were starting a day early?"

Patience stood at the front window, one floor above a familiar scene. On the nearest corner, Jake, the newsboy with the loudest voice, hawked the MacHugh and Sons broadsheets to the Friday morning crowd.

"Mrs. Horner solves all your holiday woes! Family squabbles, lack of funds, stains on the tablecloth—no problem for our Mrs. Horner! Disaster avoided, and a happy Christmas from MacHugh and Sons!"

On the opposite corner, a slightly older boy offered the competing product. "Professor Pennypacker packs all the advice you'll need into one column. Why listen to a nattering old woman when the learned professor has all the answers?"

This had been going on for half the morning, with each newsboy obligingly falling silent when his opponent held forth. A strolling fiddler played holiday tunes on the third corner, and a meat-pie vendor occupied the fourth.

"I have my sources in the offices of the other publishers," Mr. MacHugh said. "I'm sure Pennypacker's newsboy occasionally chats with my lads over a pint. I've Harry keeping an eye out, but where's the harm in some friendly competition?"

Mr. MacHugh stood behind Patience at the window, close enough to remind her that they'd embraced, even held each other, for a few moments. The sky hadn't fallen, King George hadn't abdicated his place on the mantel, but Patience's opinion of Mr. MacHugh had shifted—a bit.

He wasn't ambitious for his own sake. He employed a dozen relations and had sunk his last groat into his business. That took courage, daring, and determination, all of which were admirable qualities.

In a man.

Necessary qualities in a woman without means.

"Is Jake the best choice?" Patience asked. "He's smaller than Pennypacker's boy. Younger. The cold might be harder on him."

"Because his family is from Jamaica? Jake was born in London—he knows our winters—and he's good at what he does. I thought we might move him to Oxford Street when he sells out this lot."

"Oxford Street?" Patience turned from the window. "The great houses of Mayfair don't need Mrs. Horner's advice."

Mr. MacHugh perched against his desk and folded his arms. That gesture usually signaled an opinion cast in granite. It also accentuated the breadth of his shoulders.

"Think about it, Miss Friendly. The great houses of Mayfair sit in Mayfair, but the day help, the merchants, the clerks, shopgirls, and not-so-great all come and go between Mayfair and the rest of London. Oxford Street sees much of that traffic, and the professor's not distributing his wares there."

A week ago, Patience might have spent half an hour arguing: Jake would waste at least thirty minutes getting to Oxford Street, but he could sell a few copies along the way. Pennypacker's boy might simply follow Jake and stand him to one of those pints Mr. MacHugh had mentioned. The entire lot of papers might end up in the ditch if young Jake took a tumble on the snowy streets.

Courage, daring, and determination were not the exclusive province of a man in business.

"Oxford Street," Patience said. "A different block every day, so Pennypacker has to chase us. One of the other boys can bring Jake a fresh lot on the hour, so Jake doesn't have to waste time coming and going from here every time he runs out. If it's a war Pennypacker wants, it's a war he shall get."

"We'll have Harry take Jake's place out front, and send Jake out the back."

"Oh, that is diabolical, Mr. MacHugh. I take back everything I ever said about you—well, some things. The parts about being—"

He took off his glasses and polished them on his sleeve. "Time for crumpets?"

Patience was tired of crumpets. The treat that had loomed beyond her means had lost its appeal in a few short days.

"Lemon tarts. This calls for lemon tarts, and then I must apply myself to the next set of letters."

"Harry!" Mr. MacHugh called. "To the bakery, and tell Jake to come in when he's sold the last of his stack. Lemon tarts for Miss Friendly today."

"And a lemon tart for Jake if he sells out in fifteen minutes!" Patience called.

A cheer went up from the clerks, along with promises to take newsboy duty for the next week, for the next year, if *fresh tarts* were part of the compensation.

Patience not only understood the ribaldry, she delighted in it. "What are you smiling at, Mr. MacHugh?"

His smile transformed him, from a sober and somewhat ruthless man of commerce, to a buccaneer of business, a pirate prince of the publishing world. A quantity of alliterative excesses occurred to Patience, but they all came down to the fact that when Mr. MacHugh smiled at her, he was as attractive as a plate of fresh lemon tarts.

Delicious, complicated, spicy, tart, with just the right amount of sweetness too.

"I'm smiling at a general forging of a path to victory. Pennypacker is no match for you, Patience Friendly, and I think his good fortune has turned against him."

"What do you mean?"

"You're selling more copies because he came out a day early, just as you did."

The newsboys called back and forth to each other, exchanging taunts and jibes. "So is Pennypacker."

"He won't be on Oxford Street." The smile came again, along with a lifted eyebrow that promised doom to the presuming professor.

Patience smiled back and got to work on the next column.

* * *

Patience Friendly was gorgeous when she smiled. Full of mischief, plans, and energy. When she smiled, she sparkled like moonlight on snow. To see her illuminated with joy was like imbibing a fine dram on a cold night. Every particle of Dougal's soul was warmed and cheered by the sight, just as he delighted to watch her hurling thunderbolts of advice in active voice.

Friday had been lemon tart day. Today she'd had Dougal send for stollen and divided the loaf among all of the clerks, then disappeared back into Dougal's office.

"So you've put out two editions now." Detwiler tossed half a scoop of coal into the parlor stove, then straightened on an old man's sigh. "How's your plan working, lad?"

"You're wasting coal, Aloysius Detwiler. The lads have left for the day." Dougal remained perched on Harry's stool, for it was closest to the fire. Only Detwiler, as the senior editor, merited his own desk.

"But Mrs. Horner remains in your corner, scribbling away." Detwiler moved about the room, tidying up. Good editors were born to tidy and fuss, and Detwiler was the best. Fortunately, he was married to a MacHugh and had some notion of family loyalty.

"Time I walked the lady home, then," Dougal said. "She'll be pleased with today's sales."

The clerks came in an hour later on Saturday morning and left at midafternoon, though there had been plenty of time for Jake and Harry to sell out their supplies of broadsheets.

"Miss Friendly wasn't pleased that the professor followed us to Oxford Street." Detwiler went around the room, putting all the quill pens at the same angle in their standishes. "She'll be furious to learn she's been working for the professor himself."

"You promised you'd not breathe a word."

"The door is closed, and as much time as you spend in there with Miss Friendly, I'll not find you any more alone than you are now. You're playing a dangerous game, Dougal. What's to stop Mrs. Horner from going into business for herself? Ladies write entire books when the need for coin is great enough."

"Patience hasn't the coin to compete with me." Not to mention, she was female, of marriageable age, unwed, and without male relations who might mitigate those unfair realities.

"You should tell her, Dougal."

He should. A woman who'd been played false regarding her entire future would not take kindly to being manipulated, even in the interests of securing greater income.

"I'll tell her when we've put out the remaining editions. She works wonderfully under pressure and has an instinct for battle. She should have been a barrister."

Detwiler settled onto the cushion in his chair and withdrew a pipe and nail from a pocket. "That, my boy, will be twelve editions too late. For Christmas, you will reveal to Miss Friendly that she's been lied to, played for a fool, taken advantage of, and exploited without mercy. All to put coin in your pocket."

"Yours too, and hers." Especially hers. "I've increased the print runs for next week, we're doing so well."

The nail scratched across the bowl of the pipe. "If you say so, professor."

"She might never find out."

Scratch, scratch, scratch… The world of London newsprint journalism was about the size of a Highland village, and twice as prone to gossip.

She'd find out. "Take yourself off, Aloysius, and my regards to Cousin Avery."

Detwiler tapped his pipe against his palm and tossed the ash into the bin beside the stove. "You and Harry joining us for Christmas dinner this year?"

For the past three years, Dougal had been the bachelor relation taken in over the holidays as a kindness on the part of his relatives. Where would Patience spend Christmas? With whom? As far as Dougal could tell, she hadn't even a cat to share her household.

"I'm sure Harry will devour half your goose, but I've other plans, thanks very much."

"More for Harry, then. See you Monday." Detwiler pushed to his feet, got his coat and scarf, and shuffled out into the gray afternoon. London winters weren't as dark as their Perthshire counterparts, but an overcast December day was still a glum undertaking.

When a man had a guilty conscience.

"Has Harry left for the day?" Miss Friendly stood in the doorway to Dougal's office, his glasses perched on her nose, a folded broadsheet in her hand.

"Aye, but we can stop at the bakery when I walk you home."

Her brows twitched down. "I'm in the middle of a reply, but did you see the professor's column for today, Mr. MacHugh?"

He'd written it. "What transgression has the old boy committed now?"

Patience stomped across the clerk's office. "You have remarked that he and I often deal with similar situations, and a general discourse follows regarding who had the better advice."

A general donnybrook followed, of the literary sort, and the readers loved it. "I've wondered if people don't write to you both, just to see whose advice is superior."

She paused at Harry's table and nudged his pen around in a circle. "You think the readers are playing us off each other? Making up situations to pit the professor against me?"

"I hope they are. That tells me the readers are invested in your column, like a sweepstakes, or a cricket match they've bet money on."

She clambered onto Harry's stool. "My advice column isn't a sporting match, Mr. MacHugh. I care about my readers. I genuinely want to help them with life's more vexing challenges. I'm not writing to entertain, I'm writing to educate, to commiserate."

Why did she have to turn up philosophical now? "You're writing to earn coin, Patience." Dougal stalked into his office and busied himself banking the fire, but a familiar tattoo of feminine boot heels followed him through the door.

"I earn coin for helping people sort out their difficulties," Patience said, a strident note creeping into her voice. "I'm not a dancing bear, writing farce for the masses. A woman who'd poach on her own sister's marital preserves is not a joke, Mr. MacHugh."

Dougal straightened and found himself face-to-face with King George lounging on the mantel. The cat's expression was superior, even smug. *Tell her, laddie. Tell her now.*

"I should put George out," Dougal said, scratching the idiot cat's head.

"*Mr. MacHugh.* You posit that my advice is not even addressed to real problems. You will please assure me that the letters I diligently sort through and consider each week are received from the post?"

"They are."

"Since when has petting that beast become such a fascinating undertaking that you can't face me as we have this discussion?"

Dougal turned. "The letters you respond to are received from the post, Miss Friendly. I can assure you of that. I suspect some might be fabricated."

That much truth filled her with consternation. If Dougal had told her the bakery had closed up shop, or he was canceling her column, her expression could not have been more perplexed.

"How do you deduce such a thing?"

Because Dougal saw every word of every letter, not only the redactions and paraphrases printed in the broadsheets. "You dealt with a sister making calf's eyes, and he addresses a brother engaged in the same sort of flirtation."

"Exactly!" Patience said, brandishing the broadsheet. "Do you know what his advice was?"

Yes, Dougal knew. "Tell me."

"To ignore the whole situation! To do nothing, to pretend obvious displays aren't taking place, and a marriage at risk for serious damage is fine, fine, just fine. The professor counsels dignity and forbearance."

Dougal took the broadsheet from Patience and laid it on his desk. "While you said without a command of all the facts, devising a course of action was difficult. Sound advice." Which Dougal had not thought to offer.

"Boring advice," she retorted. "I should have told that good woman to accost some handsome man under the mistletoe while her husband looks on. The professor would never have come up with such a bold approach to the situation as that, and the readers would have been impressed with the novelty of a woman taking action."

Dougal had gone all day without arguing, but that... that... *pronouncement* required a response.

"The professor would never have been so daft. Kissing some callow swain to provoke jealousy is the stuff of the very farce you seek to avoid."

She pushed her glasses up her nose, marched up to him, and jabbed at his chest with one finger. "A passing indulgence in a venerable holiday tradition, in which you yourself apparently see no harm, is not a farce."

"I told Harry to take that damned stuff down."

She smiled, looking very much like King George when Dougal had spilled the cream pot all over the desk blotter.

"Language, Mr. MacHugh."

Dougal might have yet salvaged a respectable argument from the moment, but Patience smoothed ink-stained fingers over his neckcloth, turning victory into a rout.

"Profanity is the crutch of the linguistically uninspired," she went on, quoting from one of Mrs. Horner's most popular articles.

Dougal was inspired—to sheer foolishness. "You think a kiss under the mistletoe is a harmless holiday tradition?" He took Patience by the wrist and led her from the office. "A mere gesture, of no significance? A quaint tradition, nothing more?"

"A venerable tradition, but quaint, yes. Mr. MacHugh? What are you—Mr. MacHugh?"

Dougal led her to the front door, to a spot beneath the offending greenery hanging from its red ribbon.

He yanked both shades down, gave her the space of two heartbeats to register a protest—which he would have heeded, had any been forthcoming—and then he kissed her.

* * *

The heavenly choruses that had appeared to the shepherds in Bethlehem might have inspired the same upwelling of joy Patience experienced under the mistletoe with Mr. MacHugh.

She'd braced herself for an admonitory lecture of a kiss, having every intention of lecturing Mr. MacHugh right back. Instead of that figurative lump of coal, Mr. MacHugh's kiss was full of sweetness, tenderness, and delicacy.

He offered her a cinnamon biscuit of a kiss—he even tasted of cinnamon—offer being the operative verb. His attentions were beguilingly gentle and his palms cupping Patience's cheeks warm and cherishing.

"I don't know how—" She didn't know how to kiss, where to put her hands, *what to do*, and her ignorance was a terrible burden.

Mr. MacHugh solved those dilemmas by putting Patience's hands at his neck and stepping closer.

"There's no wrong way to kiss, Patience. A kiss doesn't have to be constructed with consistent tenses and agreement of gender, number and case. Kissing is for moments beyond words."

Mr. MacHugh gave her a treasure trove of such moments when he stroked the backs of his fingers against her cheek, when he cradled her head against his palm, when he traced his tongue over the seam of her lips.

She retaliated—reciprocated, rather—and his lips parted.

Oh, gracious. Oh, Happy Christmas, Happy New Year. Where to put a comma—a most excellent premise for a discussion—had nothing, *nothing* on the complexities of how to turn a kiss into a conversation.

Patience shifted and accidently trod on Mr. MacHugh's toes. She stepped back, horrified to have put an end to such a rare delight, and found Mr. MacHugh beaming down at her in the dim foyer. He held out his hand, an invitation, and the festivities recommenced next to the unlit sconce.

Mr. MacHugh braced his back against the wall, and Patience bundled in for another round of affection, exploration, and—heavenly choruses in the happiest of keys—arousal.

This was what it felt like to be intimately interested in a man, to desire *him*, not the secure future his proposal offered, not the protection of his name, or the dream of children to love, but *him*.

Patience smoothed her hand over broad shoulders and a muscular back, then sank her fingers into thick, dark hair. Mr. MacHugh's flavor was spicy, sweet holiday treat, his textures were varied—silky hair, whiskery cheeks, lean angles, soft lips, hard…

Patience had inspired Mr. MacHugh to arousal as well, to the heat in the blood, the catch in the breath, that signaled two adults susceptible to passion for each other.

The joy of that, the startling, gleeful satisfaction of it, had Patience leaning against him, all her attention centered where his arousal pressed unapologetically against her belly.

"Tell me, Patience. D'ye still think advising a kiss beneath the mistletoe is in keeping with Mrs. Horner's signature common sense?"

She wiggled, and he sighed. The cloved orange bobbed against her elbow, and Patience could not recall a time when she'd been so utterly, completely, unexpectedly happy—or glad to be wrong.

* * *

Dougal could not recall a time when he'd been so utterly, completely, inexcusably dunderheaded—though happily dunderheaded.

He'd stolen a kiss, and Patience Friendly had stolen his every good intention, not that the lady was accountable for his actions. She was untutored in the art of kissing, but a damned fast learner. Her kisses were as eager as they were inexpert.

And God above, the passion in her. As dedicated as she was to her writing, as exacting and demanding as she was about the written word, her kisses were ten times more… *more*.

"I have an idea," she said, her hand trailing over Dougal's chest.

Perhaps this idea would involve the sofa in his office, in which case Dougal would have to pitch himself out the window into the nearest snowdrift.

"I've always admired your nimble mind, Patience." And her ink-stained hands, which Dougal wanted to kiss. Her curves were delightful too, as was her vocabulary and her ability to reduce a complex problem to its simplest form.

"I'll write holiday couplets for Jake to sing when selling the broadsheets."

Dougal made himself focus on assembling her words into a sentence he could comprehend, for the weight of her against him was perdition personified.

"Holiday couplets?"

"Yes! The clerks can help with them." She whirled away, back into the clerk's office. "You know, 'God rest ye merry, gentlemen, here's a broadsheet you can read/Mrs. Horner has a clever solution to your every single need.'"

"That sounds naughty." Memorable, though. Very memorable.

She stopped short and patted Dougal's cheek. "You've been disporting under the mistletoe, Mr. MacHugh. Try to focus on the issue at hand."

As he trailed Patience into his office, all Dougal could focus on was the twitch of her skirts. "Couplets aren't a bad idea, but a whole chorus would be better."

"One aimed mostly at the women." She ensconced herself behind Dougal desk. "Let the professor sing to the men. I also think we should collect up the holiday columns and publish them as a pamphlet, Mrs. Horner's Help for the Holidays. Has a nice ring to it. Let the printer know now, so ours will be ready to go days ahead of the professor's feeble reprise. Toss in a bonus column on difficulties surrounding celebration of the new year."

One kiss, and the woman was on fire.

One kiss, and Dougal had made a delicate situation impossible. "Patience, we're alone here."

She extracted a penknife from one of the desk drawers. "I know, else I shouldn't have kissed you." She pared a fresh point on his best quill pen, her movements economical and practiced.

"*You* kissed *me*, did you?"

The penknife paused. "I thought I did a passably good job, for being out of practice." A hint of vulnerability infused her words. She put the knife away and took a fresh sheet of foolscap.

Dougal banked the fire, though George's tail dangled about his head all the while. "If that's your idea of a passably good kiss, then heaven defend the man who's on the receiving end of your polished efforts. I'm walking you home, Patience. Now."

She brushed the quill across her mouth, and Dougal had to look away.

"I believe your nerves are overset, Mr. MacHugh. Perhaps it's best if we do take some air. Based on your discourse regarding Mrs. Wollstonecraft, I've arrived at a few insights regarding the dictates of propriety."

Yes. Frigid, fresh air. Just the thing. "Mrs. Woll—? Oh, her."

"Does George go out?"

"I'll come by on my way to services tomorrow and put him out for a bit. He guards the castle at night, or that's the theory. Mice can do a lot of damage to paper and glue. Your cloak, madam."

How could she do this? Maintain an animated focus on literary affairs while Dougal wanted to toss Mrs. Horner's Corner, the professor, and the entire yuletide problem into the nearest bowl of Christmas punch.

So he could resume kissing Patience.

She prattled on for the length of three London streets about how the rules of propriety were a subtle scheme to protect not the young lady, but the fortune that accompanied her hand in marriage. Women of lesser station received much less protection, but their relative poverty also gave them more freedom.

This theory was just outlandish—and logical—enough that Dougal could pay some attention to it. Not as much attention as he gave to the way Patience spoke with her hands when impassioned by a topic, or to the memory of those hands smoothing down his back.

Next time, she might venture a bit farther south.

God help me. There must be no *next times.*

"You're not inclined to argue with me?" she demanded as they turned onto her street.

"I'll consider your theories as we take our day of rest tomorrow." Dougal would spend that day furiously drafting the professor's last few columns, with apologies to the good Presbyterian pastor in Perthshire, who'd be horrified at such industry on the Sabbath. "Why has nobody lit a single lamp yet on your entire street?" London homeowners were subject to regulations requiring porch lights.

"We're thrifty in this neighborhood," Miss Friendly said as they approached her doorstep. Her building was fashioned so the first floor overhung the doorstep, creating an alcove protected from the elements and, at this gloomy hour, from the view of prying neighbors.

Dougal wrestled with the realization that he could kiss her again.

"I'll wish you a peaceful Sunday," Patience said, "and look forward to an industrious and lucrative two weeks."

Industrious and lucrative. Dougal MacHugh, proprietor of MacHugh and Sons, Publishers, should have applauded those sentiments. They were exactly what he'd envisioned when he'd concocted this ludicrous twelve days of competing broadsheets.

Patience offered her hand, and Dougal bowed over it. "A peaceful Sabbath to you too. Miss Friendly."

Before he could tug her closer, gaze longingly into her eyes, or otherwise make an ass of himself, she ducked through the door and left him alone in the freezing air. Dougal took himself back in the direction of the office, the wind stinging his cheeks and his toes going numb.

Which did nothing—not one thing—to get his mind off the question that had plagued him the whole way to Patience's doorstep.

If one kiss sent the woman off into flights of cleverness—God rest ye merry, gentlemen, indeed—then Dougal marveled to think what a bout of passionate lovemaking might do for her creativity.

CHAPTER FOUR

The yuletide season was bringing Patience all manner of insights, about herself, about life, about Mr. MacHugh. She occasionally slipped and referred to him as Dougal in her thoughts, because Mr. MacHugh might be a penny-pinching, ambitious merchant, but only Dougal could acquit himself so impressively beneath the mistletoe.

Only Dougal escorted her home, giving her companionship as she left the hum and bustle of the office for the near silence of her home. Only Dougal lent her his copy of Mrs. Wollstonecraft and told her to keep it.

Wednesday morning, though, he was very much Mr. MacHugh.

"If the professor has followed us to Oxford Street, then we should remove to Piccadilly," Patience said. "He'll take up at least part of a day finding Jake, and in that time we'll sell to throngs of holiday shoppers the professor will miss entirely."

Dougal—Mr. MacHugh, rather—plucked away the pencil Patience had tucked behind her ear and tossed it among the foolscap, pen trimmings, sand, and crumbs on the table.

"Madam, you do not understand. What sells so many copies is the very competition between you and Pennypacker. You and he are putting on a prize fight for the literate. Piccadilly is that much farther from Bloomsbury for Jake to travel, and next you'll be telling us we should sell in Haymarket."

Mr. MacHugh looked tired, as if even the effort to explain—his term for denigrating Patience's logic—wearied him.

"We should do both" Patience said. "Sell in Haymarket and Piccadilly. They're crowded locations, and we'll be a novelty. We should do a special edition, one that's out the previous evening, and give away a few copies so that by morning—"

Mr. MacHugh rose, pinching the bridge of his nose in a gesture reminiscent of a longsuffering governess Patience recalled from nearly a quarter century past.

"Need I remind you, Miss Friendly, we are doing twelve special editions, and to compensate the printer for an evening run would be costly, if he could do it at all with virtually no notice. You'd have Jake shivering in the dark, wasting his health, your time, and my money, all to prove to some gold-plated pompous ass of a professor that you can sell more copies of a broadsheet than he can."

Patience liked that Mr. MacHugh would raise his voice when a point mattered to him. That was one of the revelations this holiday project had brought.

"Mr. MacHugh—Dougal—sit down, please. The professor and I often disagree about how a problem ought to be solved, but he's not pompous. He's erudite, compared to me. Far better read than I am, as is obvious from the literature he quotes. I'm better at Scripture, but that's because my mother inclined toward the Dissenters."

Mr. MacHugh didn't sit so much as he collapsed into his chair. "You defend Pennypacker now?"

Patience fished among the detritus on the table for her pencil. "The professor, as you've pointed out, has made me a significant sum of money, and you as well. I doubt he's a gold-plated anything. I know how hard we're working to get these columns. He has to be putting in comparable effort. Shall we order from the chophouse?"

"I don't want to order from the blasted chophouse."

Something was troubling Mr. MacHugh, which made no sense. He was never happier than when the business thrived and he could pit his wits against his competitors. The clerks and newsboys were in a fine humor of late, and the printer had sent around a basket of holiday fruit. Even King George seemed less cranky.

"You are worried this whole scheme will collapse," Patience said, thinking out loud. "You anticipate that because all is unfolding exactly according to your plan—you've increased the print run twice already—disaster will soon strike. This is the thinking of a jilted debutante, sir, and I'll thank you to put it behind you."

He ran his hand through his hair, then sat back in one of the poses Patience found most fetching. His ankle crossed over his knee, one arm hooked over the back of the chair. A gentleman would never sit thus before a lady, and a dandy's breeches would have been too tight to even attempt such a position.

"I'm a jilted debutante? Madam, were you up too late reading that drivel from Mrs. Wollstonecraft?"

Patience had devoured the entire treatise in a single sitting on Monday night.

"You can't bait me that easily, Mr. MacHugh. I'm speaking from experience. When I realized the viscount had been in love with my settlements, not me, I saw betrayal everywhere. If the coal man made a mistake on his bill, if the pastor failed to greet me personally on the church steps, I was certain they intended thievery and insult."

He sat forward and organized the loose papers into a stack, then swept the crumbs and trimmings into his palm. "How do you know the coal man wasn't trying to cheat you, or the pastor trying to cut his association with you?"

"The coal man had never cheated us previously, not in years of service. The pastor was a busy man. They hadn't changed, I had. You planned on modest success, you didn't plan on this scheme making you the talk of the town."

The orts and leavings from the table went into the dustbin. "I'm not a problem to be solved, Patience. What will you do about the lady who's overspent her holiday shopping budget?"

"Why won't you let me answer the woman whose husband is drinking away the rent money?"

He lifted the cat off the mantel and resettled in his chair. "I'm working on that one. Give me some time. You can't suborn petit treason and expect this publishing house to stand."

A week ago, Patience would have argued this issue too, but since then, she'd seen the publishing house from the inside. Most of the staff was young, just starting out, and if the business failed, they'd face a long, expensive journey home to Scotland. Some of them wouldn't have the means to make that journey.

Jake was the oldest of six, with another on the way. His father was a groom at a coaching house, his mother took in mending.

Harry aspired to become a man of business.

Mr. Detwiler was old and slow and couldn't work the long hours the youngsters could, but he knew everything about London publishing and the English language.

"I'll give you a week to decide how I can help that woman, but she deserves an answer," Patience said, petting the cat. King George's purr was the small thunder of feline contentment, though more than she wanted to pet the cat, Patience wanted to touch Dougal.

Running a business was a burdensome ambition. What she'd realized in the past week was that she enjoyed seeing how Dougal met that burden. Instead of penning her columns in solitude on Tuesday and Thursday afternoons, the twelve-edition project meant she was at the publishing house daily, ruminating on columns by night and monitoring sales with an enthusiasm she hadn't previously.

Having a job could give the day purpose. Having people who shared that job meant forming bonds of a sort. Trade, in other words, could be exciting.

How the other debutantes who'd come out with Patience ten years ago would have swooned at such a notion.

"What are you planning now?" Mr. MacHugh asked. "You're absorbed with some thought."

"Do you know how boring it is to be wealthy?"

The cat extricated himself from Mr. MacHugh's arms and strolled across the table.

"I have no firsthand experience with the condition. My cousins are quite well-to-do, and they don't strike me as bored."

"They aren't pretty little debutantes whose signature accomplishments are parlor French, a sonata or two, and embroidery. How did I stand it, Dougal?"

Mrs. Wollstonecraft bore some of the blame for Patience's changed perspective, but so did the realization that Mrs. Horner mattered, she made a difference, not only to Patience's financial situation, but to others.

Did a waltzing debutante know what it was to *matter* in any regard except as breeding stock for some titled nincompoop? What could she look forward to, other than a remote sort of maternal involvement in the lives of children raised by nurses, governesses, and tutors?

"I'm guessing you dealt with your boredom by reading a great deal," Mr. MacHugh said. "I certainly did."

The cat flopped down among the papers, his front half covering the page of the dictionary beginning with *evince*. A companionable moment sprang up as Patience stroked George's furry head.

"I read my papa's entire library, several times over, and then we sold the bound books. Will you kiss me again, Mr. MacHugh?"

Patience hadn't intended to ask such a question—a proper lady wouldn't. But a woman who made her living with words, and presumed to solve problems for others, needn't be such a ninnyhammer.

"That kiss was by way of argument, Miss Friendly. Not well done of me."

"I thought it was very well done of you."

Mr. MacHugh was on his feet and shrugging into his greatcoat. "Back to the profligate holiday shopper with you, madam. I'm for the chophouse."

Patience scooped the cat into her arms. "Coward." What a delight to be so honest in her discourse with another, much less with a man whom she'd kissed. But how lowering too, that she couldn't tempt him to kiss her again.

"Not a coward, but a gentleman," Mr. MacHugh countered, "in my bumbling fashion. A gentleman making a tactical retreat. I don't regret kissing you, Patience, but you might one day soon regret kissing me. Shall I stop by the bakery?"

"No more sweets for me. I'll feast on the knowledge that we're outselling even your most optimistic projections. I'll also counsel the holiday shopper to forgive herself for yielding to generous impulses where friends and family are concerned."

Mr. MacHugh took his leave, though he forgot to don his scarf—a cheerful, bold green and blue plaid.

Patience put George on the mantel and tried to focus on crafting her reply to the shopper who'd disrespected the budget set by her husband. The reply was slow to come and required much revision, for Patience was preoccupied with a question.

Why on earth would she ever, ever regret sharing a wondrous kiss under the mistletoe with Dougal P. MacHugh?

*   *   *

"You sent Harry along home with your lady?" Detwiler asked, settling on the side of the table nearest the hearth. "Was that wise, Dougal? The boy's growing, true, but he's not much protection against thieves or pickpockets."

"There's still plenty of light," Dougal countered, except in his soul, night was falling. Patience wanted more kisses—a fine notion, but for the fact that Dougal wasn't the man she thought him to be. He was Professor Pennypacker, a braying, useless old nodcock who spouted platitudes and quotes and generally sounded like the retired schoolteacher he was.

"Dougal,"—Detwiler glanced at the closed office door—"you have to tell her."

"I can't tell her now. She's enjoying herself too much." As the week had progressed, Patience had thrown herself into her work with an energy that put the youthful clerks to shame. The entire office was more cheerful, more productive, and *better*. The lads competed to come up with the cleverest holiday rhymes, Detwiler arrived on time most mornings, and even George was friendlier.

Patience blossomed more gloriously with every hour she spent at MacHugh and Sons, while Dougal watched the earnings increase along with his sense of guilt.

"Did you notice Jake has started smiling?" Dougal murmured, propping his feet on a corner of the desk. "The boy has a beautiful smile." And a smiling newsboy sold more copies, earned more coin, and had more reason to smile.

Patience had done that, with her rhymes, her roving newsboys, her clever wit on the page.

"Any boy enjoying a steady diet of holiday sweets has cause to smile," Detwiler said, "while you have become positively glum."

"I'm Scottish. I'm allowed to be glum."

"You're a Scotsman whose coin is multiplying," Detwiler replied, shifting in his chair. "You enjoy good health, and in Patience Friendly, you've found a gold mine. What's more, she has a gold mine in you. Very few other publishers would have seen her potential, Dougal, much less given her a chance to shine like this. All over London, people are quoting Mrs. Horner and saving their broadsheets to pass on to their friends and neighbors."

"They're quoting old Pennypacker too. That was the plan. She'll hate me if I tell her now, Aloysius." Dougal nearly hated himself.

"What's the worst that could happen? You have a rousing spat, and then she sees what a fine scheme you've concocted. She'll settle her feathers and come up with more ways to increase the readership. That woman respects coin of the realm. I suspect there's some Scots in her, a generation or three back."

Dougal rose, because he could not stand to be in his office another moment. A subterfuge was in progress on his premises, and every day that went by, the dishonesty he perpetrated bothered him more.

"Patience respects me," he said, getting into his coat. "I'd like to keep it that way."

"Where are you off to? I thought you wanted to discuss this letter from the gin widow?" Detwiler brandished a thin, much-folded piece of a paper.

Dougal studied the direction on the letter, jammed his hat on his head, and grabbed his scarf. "Before it starts to damned snow again, I'm going for a walk."

"Away with you, then, and George and I will manage the lads in your absence."

"Fire the professor, why don't you? He's a pontificating old bore who's served his purpose."

Detwiler snorted, and Dougal went on his way. The clerks were enjoying a heated argument about which of the nearby taverns had the best recipe for rum buns, and the printer's lad was helping himself to an apple from the basket in the window. From the street below, an impromptu glee club had borrowed some of Mrs. Horner's lyrics for a bit of holiday Handel, and brilliant afternoon sunshine poured in the windows.

All was merry and bright, and Dougal had never dreaded the yuletide season more.

* * *

"How do you endure this?" Patience muttered. "Detwiler claims to be ill, the dratted cat has shredded two days' worth of work, it's pouring ice outside, and nobody will buy anything until the weather improves."

"The lads go from pub to tavern to coaching inn, and they'll sell a fair amount, despite the weather," Mr. MacHugh said. "I can buy you some crumpets, if that will help."

The cat, who'd spent an evening scratching three of Patience's columns to bits, was draped like so much holiday greenery on the mantel.

"Throwing George out the window might help."

Mr. MacHugh went to the window and raised the sash. Bitter, coal-smoke air wafted in, though the cold at least revived Patience's flagging energy.

"Stop being literal, sir."

He lowered the sash. "I am a publisher. Of course I'll be literal. George would simply land on the roof of the awning, scramble down the trellis, and come in the back way. He's a Scottish cat and not as decorative as you might think."

George's owner was very decorative. Since kissing Mr. MacHugh more than a week ago, Patience had done little else but notice how thick his lashes were, how lovely his burr, and how the muscles of his forearms flexed when he sat at his desk and wrote. Before the clerks and the trades, he always had his coat on and his neckcloth neatly tied, but in the privacy of his office, he could be less proper.

He was kind to Detwiler, strict but fair with the boys, and scrupulously honest with the printers, authors, and merchants upon whom a publishing house depended.

"I thought a publisher was an idler," Patience said. "A man who sat about all day, smoking noisome cigars and joining gentleman's clubs."

One corner of Mr. MacHugh's mouth quirked up. "Like a debutante tatting lace? Virtually indolent, but for some light reading?"

"I imagined you could engage in political discourse, which a debutante would never do. Be glad you weren't consigned to studying fashion plates by the hour, or memorizing Debrett's."

What bleak years those had been, what meaningless, empty years. This past week had given Patience the words to describe those years. For nearly a decade, she'd thought the problem had been her failure to secure a husband. The problem was that finding a husband was all young ladies from good families were allowed to do.

"Temperature's dropping," Mr. MacHugh said. "We should get you home, Miss Friendly."

The sky had been delivering a combination of rain, ice, sleet, and snow all day. Ice clicked against the window, though sunset was still a good two hours off.

"If I go home, I'll be behind. The professor will have the street corners to himself come Thursday, and I cannot possibly allow him to have the last word."

Christmas fell on Saturday, and Patience had already decided to spend the entire day in bed, swilling tea, and not eating crumpets, or tarts, or stollen. With fresh, free sweets available in quantity, Patience had lost her taste for them. She still sent the boys out for parcels from the bakery, but her consumption was more for form's sake than out of any craving.

She did fancy another kiss with Mr. MacHugh though.

"So let the professor have Thursday," Mr. MacHugh said, "and you can put out your final column on Christmas Eve. It's not the Sabbath, and people will be on the streets visiting back and forth and calling on family."

Patience rose because her back ached. Her eyes ached, and her head ached, but she had three columns to replace before she'd quit the premises.

Her conscience ached too, truth be told.

"I like that—having the last word," she said. "I'll re-create my three columns and then I'll go. If you need me after today, send Harry 'round to fetch me. You never did let me offer that gin widow any advice."

And Dougal MacHugh would not have lost track of the letter. He was relentless about details, and that letter was not a detail.

"I'm off to fetch a cab for Detwiler," he said. "If that old man walks home in this mess, Cousin Avery will report me to the authorities for disrespecting my elders."

Mr. MacHugh departed, and the silence in his wake was bewildering. He no longer argued with Patience, didn't contradict her, didn't instruct her on the finer points of managing a competitive enterprise. She caught him watching her, peering at her over his glasses, leaning against the doorway of the office when she looked up from her writing.

By the time he came back—soaked to the skin—Patience was busily rewriting one of the columns George had destroyed. Mr. MacHugh shook out his greatcoat, droplets of melting snow dotting the floorboards.

One of them hit her on the cheek. She swiped it away and got back to work.

"Patience, the weather is truly foul. Let me get you a cab."

"I have one more column to go. The rain will let up, and then you won't need to call me a cab."

"It's not raining now. It's snowing like it means business."

"Ah! I need another word for business."

A great sigh gusted from across the room. "Commerce, enterprise, trade, mercantile endeavor."

Patience considered the walking thesaurus grousing at her from across the room. "I like that last one, mercantile endeavor. I have a question, though, about your own mercantile endeavor. Why name it MacHugh and Sons? You're not a fundamentally dishonest person, but you are in want of progeny."

He shook his scarf out next. Some of the shower hit the cat on the mantel. George woke up, glowered at his owner, then went back to napping.

"MacHugh and Sons is poetic license," Mr. MacHugh said. "If I make a go of this place, then I'll be free to marry, and the sons might well follow. One wants to sound successful while one is trying to be successful."

Patience sprinkled sand on the page she'd completed. "Just as I'm Mrs. Horner, a staid, respectable matron with years of domestic experience. Do you suppose Pennypacker is a professor?"

Every time she brought up the professor, Mr. MacHugh's eyes went bleak. "He knows his books. He's no match for you when it comes to domestic issues. I'm for some tea. Would you like a cup?"

She rose and came around the desk. "You haven't been getting enough rest. Is that why you're so surly lately?"

"I'm no' surly."

Mr. MacHugh's hair had a tendency to curl when damp, and it was a touch longish at the back. Patience liked it longish. She liked *him*, and she did not like that he was troubled when, for the most part, all was going well. Rather than kiss him, she slid her arms about his waist and leaned close.

"Patience, you mustn't…"

"This is a hug. H-u-g. Detwiler says we don't know where the word comes from, but Shakespeare used it, so it has to be good old English. You mustn't worry, Dougal. Your plan is going brilliantly, and all will be well. Do you miss Scotland?"

Patience had missed *this*, the feel of him close and solid in her arms, the rhythm of his heart beneath her ear, the fragrance of his heathery soap blending with the ink-and-starch scent of a publisher at his trade.

"I'll miss you, lass." His arms came around her on that cryptic admission, and for a long moment, Patience remained in his embrace. To be held like this was fortifying, a boon most couples probably took for granted after the first few weeks of courting.

And yet, holding Dougal was frustrating too. He made no move to kiss her and no move to leave her embrace.

Was he humoring her? On that horrifying thought, Patience drew back. "Fetch your tea, and I'll finish up these last paragraphs. I won't know what to do with myself, now that—what day is this?"

Now he smiled. An indulgent, understanding smile. "Tuesday, December 21, in the year of our Lord, eighteen hundred and—"

"I forgot *baking* day. I've made nothing to contribute to baking day and I can't arrive empty-handed. The Windham ladies will be wroth with me."

"Heaven forbid you lost track of baking day. Shall I send Harry off with a note conveying your apologies?"

Beyond the window, a proper snow squall was in progress. "Not in this weather. I'll send an apology tomorrow."

He kissed her forehead. "Don't fret. At the pace you've been working, it's not unusual to become absorbed in the task. The instant you're finished with your last column, I'm walking you home."

And then he was gone, yelling for Harry to shovel the walkway and steps, lest the lord mayor of London fall on his bum and on their very doorstep.

"I like working here," Patience informed the cat. "I like working here all too well, and Mr. MacHugh kissed me. Not much of a kiss, but something. How am I supposed to concentrate after that?"

George yawned, stretched, flicked his tail a few times, and commenced washing his paws.

CHAPTER FIVE

If one thing held Patience Friendly back as an author, it was self-doubt. She quibbled over words, commas, responses, and revisions. Some of that dithering was the writer's delight in every detail of her craft, but much of it was what happened when nobody appreciated a natural talent, obvious though that talent might be.

"Have I ever thanked you for how much you encourage Harry and the other lads?" Dougal asked as Detwiler bundled into a coat.

"I'm the editor," Detwiler said. "My job is to correct, improve, and admire. The boys are loyal to MacHugh's, and they are a bright lot."

Unlike the publisher. The words hung in the air as Detwiler went about putting the quill pens in order.

"Be off with you, Aloysius. The cab is waiting at the door." Dougal slid into the seat behind Detwiler's desk, opened a drawer, and withdrew the professor's final two columns.

At the top of the first page, the overspending housewife—a newlywed in this version of the letter—silently reproached him.

"You tell that poor woman to throw herself on her husband's mercy," Detwiler said, tossing a scarf around his neck. "But when it comes to confessing your own transgressions, you're not half so forthcoming, *professor.*"

"You have the correcting part off by heart, old man. The cab driver's horse is standing out in this weather while you sermonize at me."

"I do admire you, Dougal, and I fancy Miss Friendly does too. Start there—with all that mutual admiration—and the transgressing takes on a different perspective. If a housewife can admit she's bought a few too many holiday tokens for her loved ones, can't you admit that your ambitions for a talented author got away from you?"

Dougal's ambitions for Patience hadn't merely got away from him. They'd gone completely to Bedlam.

"That's the problem," Dougal said, staring at the words marching across the page. Schoolteacher words, very articulate, but lacking the warmth Patience brought to her advice. "Patience will think all I admire is her writing ability. She'll think I've engaged her affections merely to use her talent for my own ends."

Detwiler jammed a newsboy's cap on his head. "You are thinking too hard, being too much the academic fellow and not enough the callow swain. There's a flask in the bottom drawer. May it bring you the comfort and joy my common sense cannot."

A gust of cold air wafted in as Detwiler shuffled through the door.

Somewhere in Detwiler's haranguing, Dougal sensed a kernel of wisdom.

A schoolteacher learned the value of judiciously praising ability and honest effort. He also saw the nearly irreparable harm done when both were ignored for too long. How was a woman to have confidence in her abilities when for her entire upbringing she was trained not to bring notice to herself?

Dougal hurt for Patience and promised himself he'd remedy the harm done to her self-confidence, assuming she spoke to him, wrote for his publications, and gave him the time of day once she learned that the entire Christmas project had been based on a lie.

He read over his columns one last time and put them back in the drawer, then put his feet up on the corner of the desk and indulged in a pastime from his youth: reading the dictionary. For each letter, he read the entry for the first word his gaze landed on.

Admire. Patience was a gifted author, and she had a keen instinct for the publishing business. Dougal admired that about her.

Besotted. Dougal was, in fact, besotted with her energy, her intellect, her kisses, and her determination. She'd made the best of a trying situation, when she might have thrown herself on the charity of distant family, or accepted the proposal of any doddering opportunist who came along.

That thought gave him a very bad moment, indeed.

Callow. Patience would have no interest in the attentions of a naïve, unfledged boy. She deserved a man who'd stand toe-to-toe with her, give as good as he got, and yet, grasp that fostering her confidence would be a delicate undertaking.

Dougal had made it past o-is-for-obligation and onto p-is-for-passion, when a signal truth beamed up at him from the pages of the lexicon.

He owed Patience Friendly for giving him the foundation upon which he could grow his business.

He also loved her.

The realization put something fundamentally right with him, because love was the word that encompassed all he felt for Patience. Affection, desire, respect, protectiveness, friendship, all tied up with a bow defined as *love*.

And with that realization, he grasped as well how to unravel the problem he'd created with the fictional Professor Pennypacker.

For Christmas, Dougal would offer Patience all that had been tendered to her previously—a future, a husband, a lover, security, a family of her own. At some point, years and several babies hence, Dougal would find a casual, merry moment over breakfast and mention that he might have penned a column or two as Professor Pennypacker.

Patience would be surprised and amused, and tell him she'd speculated as much—might he please pass the teapot?—and they'd share a laugh as they recalled how well the whole plan had worked.

Dougal continued to leaf through the dictionary, pleased with the reply he'd fashioned to the conundrum of his situation with Patience. He didn't read any more words, he simply enjoyed the feel of the lexicon in his hands, the sound of each page turning.

Marriage. Good old, traditional, happily-ever-after marriage. The notion, worthy of the learned Pennypacker himself, left Dougal feeling so rosy and replete, he started humming Christmas carols.

* * *

A rough, warm sensation against Patience's wrist woke her.

"George."

The cat paused in his licking, squinted, then resumed taking liberties with Patience's person. In the darkness, the beast's eyes glowed like nacre, giving him a predatory beauty he lacked when lounging above the hearth.

The fire had burned down to little more than coals, and outside, all was darkness.

"Oh dear. I suppose I must thank you. The columns are complete." Very good columns they were too. Patience put them in Dougal's top drawer, King George having proven himself a menace to paper, if not to mice.

The next challenge was extricating herself from Dougal's chair. Her back protested, her feet were cold, and her eyes gritty. She detected neither light nor sound from beyond the office door. Dougal would never have left her alone on the premises, and yet, business hours had apparently ended.

Patience lit a carrying candle and went to the clerk's office. The air was noticeably cooler, and because the heat source was a parlor stove, the room was without illumination other than her candle. Dougal sat at Detwiler's desk, his feet propped on one corner, a book open in his lap. His arms were folded, and his chin rested on his chest.

"Oh, you poor dear." Patience took a moment to memorize the sight of him, the ambitious publisher asleep amid the trappings of his empire. His weapons were the quill pens and foolscap neatly stacked on each clerk's high table, his mission to relieve ignorance and boredom at a reasonable price.

She gently lifted the book from his lap—a dictionary, of course—and then unhooked his spectacles from his ears.

As a younger woman, she would have pitied the lady whose lot was to be courted by a man in trade. A merchant or professional was all very well for those born to that strata, her papa had claimed, but better families could look higher.

"What higher purpose is there," she murmured, "than to enlighten and enliven the lives of those who do the actual work in this life?"

Dougal's eyes opened. "Is that a quote?"

Patience handed him his spectacles. "We can make it the MacHugh and Sons business motto." His gaze was tired—this project had demanded quite a bit from him too—but even weary, he was attractive.

He sat up and rubbed his eyes, then put his glasses back on. "Patience, why didn't you wake me? It's dark out."

"I fell asleep too. George woke me, probably to tend his personal fire. Are we alone here, Dougal?"

He rose and stretched, hands braced on his lower back. "But for George, I suppose we are." He flipped open a pocket watch, the gold case gleaming by the light of the single candle. "God in heaven, Patience, it's nearly nine o'clock."

Patience rummaged around in her emotions for dismay, alarm, some vestige of the young lady's fear of ruin, and found only anticipation. Ruin lay ten years in her past, but to be alone with Dougal at such an hour inspired all manner of fancies.

He was at the window, scowling down at the street. "There's two feet of snow on the ground and more coming down. It will take ages to get you home in this mess."

"Dougal, don't be daft. Nobody has shoveled the walkways at this hour, and the only people abroad are those preying on the unwary. I wouldn't let you walk me home tonight for all the crumpets in London."

"You've grown bored with crumpets," he said, letting the curtain drop. "This is not a good situation, Patience. If anybody learns that we've been alone for this long, under these conditions, your good name is compromised beyond recall, and so is mine."

"Your safety matters more to me than my good name, Dougal, and so does my own welfare."

She expected him to argue, and looked forward to it, in fact. Lately Dougal had passed up every opportunity for confrontation, and she'd missed his logic and his unshakable confidence in his own perspective. He was a worthy opponent and thus a worthy ally.

"Your safety matters to me more than my own," he countered. "I haven't seen a storm like this since coming to London. After this much snow, the temperature can plunge drastically. The Thames will likely be frozen by morning, or very nearly."

While Patience's heart was melting. Tired, worried, and rumpled, Dougal was ten times the man the viscount had ever aspired to be. Happy Christmas, Happy New Year, happy rest of her life.

"You're often the last one here at night, aren't you, Dougal?"

"Aye. I own the place. If it fails, I own that too. Are you hungry?"

Starving. "A bit, also chilly. I should keep a shawl here."

He looked at her, a direct, considering gaze, the first in many days. "I can get you warm. Let me see to the fire in the office, and we'll asses our situation over a pot of tea."

"For a cup of strong, hot tea, I would write you an entire column at no charge, Mr. MacHugh."

"You've grown light-headed with fatigue," he said, moving into his office. "Don't jest about giving your work away, Patience. When your labor is your sole means of earning coin, then nobody should expect you to part with it in the absence of compensation."

"Are you sure you were a schoolteacher, Dougal? You sound like a preacher."

He stopped before the hearth. "You are very calm for a woman who's in the process of being compromised. This situation is serious, Patience."

Patience went up on her toes and kissed him. Not a buss to the cheek, but not a declaration of unending passion either. He had a point: Her words were valuable.

So were her affections.

"When the viscount tossed me aside, my name went into the ditch along with my prospects. I don't know if he saw to that, or if polite society—notice nobody refers to them as compassionate, kind, or tolerant society—did me that favor. My true friends stood by me, Dougal, and they won't quibble because I had the sense to stay out of a dangerous storm."

"The lads won't breathe a word," Dougal said, tucking a lock of Patience's hair behind her ear. "Detwiler's discretion is absolute. I only wish…"

In all of Patience's dealings with Dougal MacHugh, she'd never heard him use the verb *wish*. "What do you wish, Dougal? My last columns are complete. Your project has earned MacHugh's the notice of half of London, and the new year promises success to us both. I wish you'd thought to pit me against Pennypacker like this two years ago."

He took her hand and led her to the sofa. "The time wasn't right. You were still finding your balance, and there wasn't a Pennypacker to pit you against."

They sat side by side, and Dougal kept her hand in both of his. The moment might have been awkward—last week's kiss was but a memory, and Dougal had been anything but amorous since—and yet, Patience was at peace.

Hard work had won her a measure of security, and though her feelings might not be requited, she'd found a man she could esteem greatly. Dougal was capable of desiring her, for all he seemed reticent to take any further liberties, and that reassured the part of her rejected so long ago.

The problem wasn't her—the problem had never been her.

"Patience, I account myself an articulate man, but some words elude capture when I need them most. You know I respect you."

What was this? "You argue with me." Nobody else did. Nobody else took her opinions seriously enough to differ with her.

"Arguing with you is a certain sign of my esteem. I think you enjoyed our kiss under the mistletoe."

"I can barely recall our kiss under the mistletoe, Mr. MacHugh, and you've shown no inclination to refresh my memory."

He kissed her knuckles. "I'm glad you're making me work for this. The prize is worth every effort."

"I'm not a prize. I'm a talented writer who has a lot to offer her readers, and—" Patience heard the battle cry in her words, heard how easily she'd taken up the cudgels, even in the absence of any threat. "Dougal, what are you trying to say?"

"I'm bungling this. I'd planned to wait, to see how the finances for the year closed, to have more to offer you, so I could take the next steps when it was prudent to do so, but circumstances have changed, and—"

He slid off the sofa, down to one knee. "Patience Friendly, will you do me the great honor of becoming my wife?"

Gracious heavens. Perhaps fatigue had made him light-headed. "Dougal, get up. You'll get cat hair on your trousers."

He resumed his place beside her, keeping her hand in his all the while. "Is that a yes?"

Douglas was proposing—proposing *marriage* to her. As the wind howled outside, and the fire danced in the chimney drafts, Patience savored the moment, and the clasp of Dougal's hand. This was how a proposal ought to be offered, clearly, calmly, *sincerely*. Bless Dougal forever, because he'd thrown into high relief the disrespect done Patience by her titled former suitor.

She wanted to say yes, to Dougal, to a future that included love and meaningful work both, to a busy life far from what she'd been raised to expect. The thought that stopped her from giving him the response he sought was: *If I marry, I lose my house.*

Her grandmama's legacy, all that had preserved Patience from a dreadful marriage or a life of drudgery. If Patience married, that house became her husband's. If she married, she gave up even the right to spend her own wages. If she married... if she became Mrs. Horner in truth, then she ceased to be Patience Friendly in any meaningful sense.

"I've surprised you," Dougal said.

Ambushed her, more like. She should have known that his brooding looks and odd distance were symptoms of a scheme afoot.

"I care for you, Dougal P. MacHugh. So much. I hope that's not a surprise, but I don't even know where you live. I've never met your family, and two weeks ago…"

"Come," he said, rising and bringing Patience to her feet. "I can show you where I live, and we can talk about the rest."

He grabbed the candle and led her to a door that Patience had assumed was a closet. A stairwell rose up into darkness, the air frigid.

"It's not much," he said, "but it's mine and quite convenient."

A merchant family often lived above or behind the shop. Why shouldn't Dougal do likewise? His apartment was at the top of the stairs, his sitting room cozy, much like the one Patience had inherited. A velvet sofa sat before a brick hearth. A dry sink held china and glassware—also a pair of decanters.

"I didn't realize you had quarters up here."

"This apartment is part of the reason I bought the place," Dougal said, kneeling before the cold hearth. "Starting a business calls for long hours, and the less time spent gadding about the streets, the more time spent on productive labor."

The distinguishing feature of the room was the number of books. Shelves along one wall included classics, novels, atlases, histories, poetry, and herbals.

"You do love to read," Patience said as Dougal coaxed a fire to life. "You speak French?"

"I was a schoolteacher. Once you have the Latin, you've a toehold on French, Italian, Spanish, Portuguese, and Greek. I like the look of you here, Patience, among my books and treasures."

No longer Miss Friendly. "Show me the rest."

He dusted his hands, replaced the fireplace screen, and bowed her through the door into the second room.

A sanctum sanctorum. In the corner stood a very large bed—neatly made, a blue and white patchwork quilt over the whole. More books graced another set of shelves, and a large desk occupied the corner nearest the windows. The table beside the bed held three books, one of them open, and on the desk the standish, stack of foolscap, and blotter sat in the same arrangement as on the desk one floor below.

A faded carpet of cabbage roses covered the floor, and a pair of large, worn slippers were positioned by the bed.

Those slippers would be exquisitely comfortable.

Patience peered behind the privacy screen and confirmed that Dougal was a tidy man, even in his private quarters. His wardrobe was similarly arranged, everything in order.

He wouldn't expect her to pick up after him, and he'd set that example for their children.

That mattered, but still, Patience could not find the words to tell Dougal she'd marry him. She'd said yes once before—clearly, unequivocally—and hadn't ended up married.

Perhaps instead of words, deeds might do.

She crossed the room and stood before Dougal. "I care for you a very great deal, Dougal P. MacHugh, publisher. I esteem you greatly, and circumstances have conspired to give me an opportunity to esteem you intimately as well. Take me to bed, Dougal."

His brows rose, suggesting she'd surprised him, and then he raised her hands and kissed them, one after the other.

"Are ye sure, lass?"

"I'm sure," Patience said, stepping into his embrace. Mrs. Horner and the professor would be scandalized, the Windham sisters might not understand, and Patience wasn't entirely sure of her own motives, but she knew exactly where she wanted to spend the night, and with whom.

* * *

The part of Dougal that reveled in words worried that Patience hadn't explicitly said yes to his proposal. Perhaps he should have asked permission to court her, which was how the Quality went about an engagement, except he wasn't a true gentleman, in the strict definition of the term.

And yet, Patience was kissing him as if he were the crown prince of her every dream.

Dougal kissed her back, because she *was* the crown princess of his every dream, also the queen of his mercantile ambitions and the empress of his good fortune.

Patience shivered, and Dougal recalled that his bedroom was damned near freezing. "Come with me," he said, leading her into the front room. "Swing the kettle over the fire, and I'll get a blaze going in the bedroom. There's bread, cheese, and apples in the window box. I'll be but a moment."

He needed that moment to regain his self-possession, then gave up the exercise for hopeless when all he could think of was Patience warming up the bed with him. He turned down the covers, traded boots for slippers, made sure the fire was off to a good start, then prepared to persuade a lady to accept his proposal.

Patience sat on the sofa, staring into the fire. "There's much I don't know about you," she said. "How old are you?"

Dougal took the place beside her. "I'll be thirty-two on St. David's Day. What else do you want to know?"

"You don't care how old I am?"

"You've reached the age of consent. A few years one way or the other aren't relevant. I would like to know what day you were born."

She drew her feet up under her skirts. "The viscount valued my youth."

Him again. "The viscount was a shallow, greedy, arrogant young fool. Cuddle up, Patience."

The dubious glance she shot him confirmed that in addition to many other failings, the viscount hadn't bothered to share simple affection with the woman he'd proposed to. Dougal hefted Patience into his lap and drew his grandmother's quilt around her.

"Like so," he said. "Cozy and friendly. Ask me more questions."

"When will you take me to bed?"

"Your enthusiasm for this venture warms my heart, Patience. May I remind you, you haven't eaten since noon. If we're to put that bed to its best use, you'll need your strength."

She straightened enough to peer at him. "You'll need yours too."

"I live in that hope." Dougal also hoped he'd be able to restrain his passion enough to please his lady, and he further hoped the snow didn't let up for a few days, because recovering from his good fortune might take that long.

"Tell me about your family, Dougal."

Over tea, cheese toast, and sliced apples, he obliged as Patience pulled pins from her hair. MacHugh the saddlemaker was his cousin, as was MacHugh the stationer. MacHugh the fishmonger wasn't related as far as they could tell, but the trail was promising, three generations back on the Irish side.

Cousins Hamish, Rhona, Colin, and Edana might visit London in the spring, though Hamish had no use for city life. Dougal's younger sister Bridget was walking out with the blacksmith's son.

"So many people," Patience said around a yawn. "Do you suppose the bedroom has warmed up?"

"Aye. I do admire your ability to focus on a topic, Miss Friendly."

She was back in Dougal's lap, a warm, lovely weight of female cuddled in his arms. She'd put away a good quantity of food, while the wind had rattled the windows and spindrifts of snow had whirled from the rooftop.

"I like this," she said. "I like that you're affectionate. I suspect I am too."

Please, may it be so. "Let's find out, shall we?"

Dougal rose with Patience in his arms and carried her to the bed. For all that she'd asked after his relations, his education, his favorite books, and whether he knew how to ride a horse, she still hadn't officially, entirely, unequivocally accepted his proposal.

He settled her on the bed and closed the door, the better to keep in the heat. "Do you need help with your hooks and stays and whatnot?"

"Hooks, yes, but I favor jumps," she said, pushing off the bed and giving him her back. "I have experience, you know. The viscount saw to that."

She swept her braid away from her nape and stood before Dougal, her back to him, a tender, private part of her exposed for the most mundane reasons.

"You must not tell me the viscount's name," Dougal said, starting on the three thousand hooks marching down the center of her back. "Not ever."

"You can't call him out. He's a titled gentleman, and he'd decline to meet you, owing to the differences in your stations. That tickles."

"I'm not about to give some useless prat of a title a chance to injure me," Dougal said, "but between the MacHughs, the MacQuistons—my mother was a MacQuiston—the MacDuffs, and the MacPhersons, all of whom I claim as relations, the viscount's every debt, inane blunder, stupid wager, or expensive mistress would soon become common knowledge if you tell me his name. My competitors would pay dearly to publish that sort of tattle."

Patience peered at Dougal over her shoulder. "You don't publish tattlers. Why not?"

"It's not my calling. How do you ever get dressed in the morning?"

"My housekeeper assists me, and not all my dresses are this impractical."

Her chemise was a surprisingly frothy, frilly affair peeking up over her jumps. Dougal was not a connoisseur of lady's underlinen, but he wanted to see Patience some fine day wearing only that chemise and a smile.

Though stockings might be a nice touch too. White silk with red garters.

"All done," he said, wrapping his arms around her waist. "I haven't a sheath, Patience. Do you know what that means?"

He felt the heat of a blush rise over her skin. "It means the apothecary on the corner is a gossip, among other things. Can't you… wait?"

Dougal kissed her nape. "Withdraw, you mean?"

"Is that the term for when you don't spend?"

Her blush would have scorched the entire West End. "*Coitus interruptus* gets the notion across as well. The idea is to prevent conception. I'll withdraw."

He paused between kisses in case she had any other comments, questions, or pithy observations to offer, but the lady had gone quiet. Dougal acquainted his lips with the soft skin below her ear and the pulse beating beneath that.

The simple act of kissing her neck had him aroused. He slid a hand down over her derriere and gave her a gentle shove in the direction of the privacy screen.

"Use my tooth powder, and I'll heat you some wash water."

Patience moved off to the privacy screen on a soft rustle of fabric, her braid swinging gently above her fundament.

Dougal went into the front room, opened a window, and breathed in a half-dozen lungfuls of frigid air. He was considering whether arctic air wafting over his open falls might aid his flagging self-restraint when *God Rest Ye Merry, Gentlemen* floated from the bedroom on a soft hum.

He warmed an ewer of water from the steaming kettle on the pot swing, sent up a prayer for fortitude, then brought Patience her wash water.

"Will you undress, Dougal?" she called from behind the screen.

He passed her his nightshirt over the top of the screen. "In a moment." *Will you become my wife?*

Tonight, he would become her lover. For now, that was Christmas gift enough. By morning, he had every intention of becoming her fiancé.

Though for that to happen, she'd have to say yes to his proposal, wouldn't she?

CHAPTER SIX

Late on a bitter winter evening, Patience delighted in her own personal springtime. The soft breeze of Dougal's breath at her nape had been her only warning that a man could kiss a lady in places every bit as interesting as her mouth. The sensations that followed had been sweet, surprising, lovely, and so...

Words failed. Patience suspected they'd fail frequently when it came to Dougal P. MacHugh's lovemaking. His nightshirt bore the scents of heather and lavender, his blue and white quilt put her in mind of the sky on a fine May morning.

He came around the privacy screen, his manly wares on display from the waist up.

Gracious, everlasting angels. "What was the point of combing your hair, Dougal?" She would delight in mussing it up for him.

"To be presentable for my lady. My nightshirt has never looked so fetching. I haven't a warmer to run over the sheets."

Patience had cuddled in Dougal's lap for the better part of an hour, and nothing—nothing at all—compared to the snug, cozy intimacy of his embrace.

"I suspect a warmer won't be necessary."

"I wish I had one, though," he said, starting on the buttons of his falls. "Seemed like an extravagance for a bachelor. For you, I want only warm sheets, fresh sachets, and a steaming pot of chocolate in the morning."

He might have been reciting the legend of Beowulf for all Patience could heed his words. The tone, though—the intimate, casual tone—did odd things to her insides. The placket of his falls draped open, and he stepped out of his remaining clothing all at once.

He folded his breeches over the privacy screen, giving Patience a good view of his backside.

"I've seen statues," she said. "The Elgin Marbles, for example."

Dougal, as naked as God made him, banked the fire. "Are you a connoisseur of ancient sculpture, then?"

Patience's breath had developed a hitch to go with the peculiar leaping about of her heart. "I have a lively sense of curiosity, which I suspect you are generously obliging."

The viscount certainly hadn't. He'd fussed about under her skirts, told her to close her eyes, and then commenced slobbering, poking, and muttering mangled French allusions to flowers and honeybees.

"I am a great believer in the power of knowledge," Dougal said, hanging the cast-iron poker on the hearth stand and facing Patience. "I also favor deliberation over a heedless rush."

Patience had lost the ability to fix her gaze where a lady should. She'd apparently acquired the eyes of a lover, because every inch of Dougal fascinated her. His arms, his knees, the distribution of hair over his chest, and... elsewhere.

"That ancient sculptor would have needed a deal more clay if you'd been his model."

Dougal scratched his chest and yawned, looking magnificently male and oh so gloriously comfortable with it. "I beg your pardon?"

"If you were one of those Greek fellows, in the museum. The sculptor would need... perhaps the Greeks were a diminutive lot. I'm babbling. Are you giving me time to change my mind?"

Had Patience been cold earlier? The sight of Dougal in his natural glory pooled heat low in her belly.

He stepped closer. "You can change your mind, Patience. If you ask me to share that bed with you and not touch you the whole night through, I'll do it. Don't adhere to an earlier decision out of stubbornness, pride, or some notion that Mrs. Wollstonecraft would approve. Become intimate with me solely because you want to."

Dougal's regard was the least lover-like expression Patience had ever seen on a man. He was serious, almost somber.

"You could share a bed with me, having proposed marriage to me, and simply roll over and drop off to sleep?" She didn't like that idea at all. Her fists were clenched with the effort to not touch him, to not lean in and taste him, not feel him body to body.

"I'd be daft by morning," he said, threading a hand beneath Patience's braid. "You might find me lying in the snow stark naked on the roof of the awning, only George to guard my carcass, but if you tell me to keep my hands to myself, I will."

"I'd rather you made the effort to warm up the bed with me."

He swept Patience up against his chest and deposited her on the bed, then came down over her.

"Do you have any questions, Patience?"

She loved Dougal for that. For making one last gesture as the man who believed in knowledge, the lover who was determined her role would not be passive.

"When can I take off this nightshirt?"

He shifted to the mattress beside her and pulled the covers up over them. "When the sheets aren't as cold as the rooftop, I'll be more than happy to assist you with that nightshirt."

"You are so warm." Warm like sunshine on daffodils, like a soft breeze on green fields.

To see Dougal behind his desk, polishing his spectacles, working at his ledgers, or reading the broadsheets put out by his competitors, Patience would not have suspected him of warmth.

But when he left the last of his crumpet for Harry, petted the lazy old cat, or strutted about his quarters in the altogether for Patience's benefit, she saw a generosity of spirit that kindled both tenderness and desire.

"I'm having my cousins knit you some proper stockings," Dougal said, working an arm beneath Patience's neck. "Your feet are… they wake a man up."

"Sorry."

He cuddled her close. "I wouldn't change a thing about you, Patience. If you've cold feet, I'll warm those up too."

Too? Well, yes too. Dougal rolled to his side and recommenced the kissing at a lazy, daundering pace. At first Patience tried to hurry him, to urge him on. She went so far as to put his hand on her breast—surely that was part of it?—but Dougal made no move to… *move.*

"I think the sheets are quite comfortable now," Patience said as Dougal traced her eyebrows with his nose.

"I think you are in much too big a hurry. We haven't a deadline here, my love. If, for example, you wanted to touch me—my chest, say—you have as much time to do that as you like."

My love. What a delightful pair of words. "Touch… your… chest."

The sheets were toasty by the time Patience realized that Dougal had presented himself as an assortment of sweets. She could select the curious textures of his chest—springy hair, odd little nipples, solid muscle, and a steady heartbeat—or she might prefer the satisfaction of sinking her fingers into the silky abundance of his hair and clutching tightly, the better to delight in his kisses.

Or those kisses might be her choice—soft, tender, passionate, playful. Dougal's kisses were like spices wafting from a busy kitchen. Tantalizing, heady, exotic.

So much he offered her, and so generously.

This is how lovemaking is supposed to be. In the midst of this abundance, Patience felt both anger and sorrow for the young woman who'd been willing to settle for a mere prancing title.

"They lie to us," she whispered. "The parents, governesses, and dancing masters. They lie, Dougal. And thus we lie to ourselves, until the truth is so obscured, a young woman dares not recognize it."

Dougal shifted over her. "My feelings for you are honest, Patience. I love you. All that I am, all that I have will be yours forevermore."

She kissed him, for having listened to her, for the very deliberation that had so frustrated her earlier.

"If you don't get me out of this blasted nightshirt, Dougal, I will—"

He sat back, a rearing lion of a healthy male. "Sit up, then, lass."

Patience wiggled to her elbows, and there was an awkward moment when her breasts were first bared to her lover. The awkward moment didn't last, because she was too busy studying the part of Dougal that would now require *far* more clay than those puny Greeks in the museum had.

"Touch me," Dougal said. "I adore your curious mind."

They touched each other. Patience learned the contours and textures of the aroused male, and Dougal obliged her with all manner of caresses and kisses to her breasts. She also learned that lovemaking could happen in a variety of positions—Dougal claimed most of his knowledge was theoretical, which diplomatic untruth she allowed him.

No man who brought a lady this much pleasure was working entirely from theory.

And Patience was through with testing theories anyway.

"Enough talk," she panted, for Dougal's attentions to her breasts left her breathless. "Enough Latin, cant, and anatomy. Are you laughing at me?"

"I'm delighting," Dougal replied, bracing himself on his arms above her. "It's no' the same thing a'tall."

His burr grew thicker, along with other parts of him. Patience positively reveled in that knowledge.

"Make love with me, Dougal. There's a deadline now. A tight, pressing deadline."

"Never that," he said, hitching closer. "This is the easy part, Patience. We take all the time we please, maybe even have a wee discussion as we go."

"This is not an editorial meeting, Dougal, in the name of all that is—oh, that's lo-ve-ly."

A woman who made her living with words did not speak in syllables, but as Dougal joined with Patience, she lost even that ability. Sighs were all she had left, along with soft moans, kisses, and all manner of caresses.

The sensation as Dougal joined with her was one of fullness, of intimacy so overwhelming and right, Patience gave up trying to label it and surrendered to the glory of being an adult female at her pleasures. Dougal's stubborn unwillingness to hurry became a determination to cherish, and how Patience treasured him for that.

"Patience, stop thinking. Feel the rhythm, *be with me.*"

Dougal punctuated his words with a particular emphasis to his thrusts, and celestial choirs could not have distracted Patience from the resulting sensation. She met him the next time, went seeking that same exclamation point of arousal, and found it.

Again, and again, and again, until she was the one creating the rhythm, and all she knew was that to find where it led, she must be closer to Dougal.

Pleasure coalesced where they joined, a bright, astounding, precious sunburst. Dougal didn't leave her hovering in view of the beautiful vista either. He stayed with her, knowing somehow exactly how to make the joy last, how to be both the breeze that held her aloft and the connection that let her fly free.

A sense of vindication gilded Patience's repletion when the soaring moments settled gently back to reality. She'd guessed that lovemaking should have been much more than she'd been allowed to know. The viscount had betrayed her in many ways, but the self-doubt he'd created was at last allowed to die.

He'd been like those statues in the museum. Not enough clay, no real life, no individual features, so thoroughly had privilege and arrogance worn away his humanity.

This lovemaking with Dougal was real.

This was love.

Dougal slowly withdrew, and as Patience held him close, he spent where it would cause no risk of a child. He was being responsible, and yet, a part of Patience resented his self-possession. She wanted the limitless passion for him too. Wanted to be the tether that kept him safe while he soared, whether his passion was conjugal, commercial, or—she suspected he was a fine writer himself—creative.

And she could be that for him. She absolutely could be.

He lifted away from her some moments later. "I've made a wee mess."

"I like it," Patience said. "It's a lover's mess. It's what consideration and keeping your word feel like and smell like." Not exactly a fragrance, but to Patience, it was the scent of knowledge.

"God, you are ferocious." Dougal kissed her nose and retrieved a handkerchief from the nightstand. The tidying up was the work of a moment, and then he subsided to the mattress and pulled Patience into his arms.

"Are ye warm enough?"

"I'm warm enough." At long last, she was warm enough. "Tomorrow, we'll talk about a wedding date, Dougal, and perhaps a wedding journey north in spring."

He kissed her temple. "I'd like that. I'd love that, in fact."

Patience couldn't keep her eyes open, so she wrapped her arms around her beloved and surrendered to dreams in which neither Mrs. Horner nor Professor

What's His Name figured *at all.*

* * *

"Patience is missing baking day," Megan Windham said, pacing before the hearth, a newspaper rolled up in her hand. "We've had not even a note from her. She has shared baking day with us every year for the past dozen at least. We always finish with her lemon cake, so it's warm for her journey home."

"We have done holiday baking with Patience since before my come out," Elizabeth said from a stool beside the music room's great harp. "Which means the tradition goes back to antiquity. Perhaps yesterday's foul weather dissuaded her."

Elizabeth made more and more references to her age, and Megan had no idea what to do about it. Based on the look Charlotte and Anwen exchanged, they didn't either.

"Patience knows she could have bided with us overnight," Megan countered. "She's stayed here before when the weather turned disagreeable."

"The weather is glorious now," Charlotte observed from the window. "Blindingly so. Perfect weather for a snowball fight."

Sun on heaps of freshly fallen snow made the morning brilliant, and yet, Megan was worried. "Patience lives alone, or the next thing to it. What if she's fallen ill? She could have sent us a note."

"She has a housekeeper," Charlotte said, moving away from the window. "Patience enjoys great good health, most of the time."

She'd had a nasty lung fever the previous spring.

"We should take her some lemon cake," Anwen said, knitting needles clicking away. "That's not hovering, not assuming the worst. We're being neighborly if we bring her some lemon cake."

Megan considered that suggestion, though as far back as she could recall, Patience had visited them—they did not venture into her neighborhood to visit her.

"Do we have her direction?" Somewhere in Bloomsbury, as best Megan could recall. Not far from Mr. MacHugh's offices.

"It's off Holborn, near the museum. I recall visiting her grandmother there, years ago."

A guilty silence greeted Elizabeth's admission, but Patience hadn't been eager to entertain callers. Whether she was self-conscious about a humble dwelling, or too pressed for coin to offer a proper tea tray, the message had come across clearly: *Receive me, don't visit me.*

"Patience has been working very hard at a time of year when most of us have less to do," Megan said, stashing the rolled up broadsheet into the coal bucket. "Mr. MacHugh ought to be ashamed of himself."

"I think Patience likes her work," Elizabeth murmured, fingers drifting across the harp strings. "I daresay she likes Mr. MacHugh too—admires his pragmatism, his grasp of mercantile matters. Those broadsheets are selling like hot rum buns."

Elizabeth was closest to Patience in age, and possibly in perspective. "You think Patience *likes* Mr. MacHugh?" Megan asked.

"Lemon cake," Charlotte said. "This definitely calls for a neighborly delivery of lemon cake."

Anwen's knitting needles slowed. "Bloomsbury is halfway across London, and the snow will make traffic difficult."

Could Patience be smitten with her Scottish publisher?

"It's not like her to miss a baking day," Megan observed. "We should bring her a loaf of stollen too, in case she might want to share with her friends at MacHugh and Sons."

All three of Megan's sisters smiled at once.

"That's very seasonal of you, Megan," Elizabeth said, rising. "We'll wait until after lunch, so the streets have a chance to clear, and then we'll pay a holiday call on our good friend."

"And maybe buy a few broadsheets on the way," Charlotte added. "See what argument Patience and the professor have got into now. Hard to imagine they have anything left to dispute, the way they've gone at each other this past week."

* * *

Patience remained in bed for long, lovely moments after Dougal had risen. He was off to the chophouse to fetch breakfast or possibly lunch, while Patience was trying to find the energy to move.

When, if ever, had she been this relaxed before? This well rested? This happy? The professor's last special edition would come out today, and she wished him nothing but success with his sales.

Dougal had made love with her again before he'd left the bed, and while he'd been careful, he'd also been playful.

"I am ticklish about the ribs," Patience announced to the room at large. "So is Mr. MacHugh."

One of the many revelations of the past two weeks.

Patience shoved the covers aside, pushed her feet into Dougal's slippers, and finished the cup of tea he'd brought her before he'd left. Dressing was an awkward undertaking, but Patience did the best she could with her hooks— she'd managed without help on many previous occasions—and made her way downstairs to the office. From the street below came the regular scraping of merchants clearing their walkways. Sunshine poured through every window.

"Good morning," Patience said to George, who occupied his usual spot on the mantel. "I am in love."

George squinted at her.

"Try to contain your jealousy, cat. You know all manner of details about my beloved that I do not—yet. You know what hour he comes down every morning, when he goes up to bed, how many meals he's eaten at his desk, and what his favorite poem is."

So much she and Dougal had yet to learn about each other, but how lovely to look forward to learning it.

The bell on the front door jingled, and Patience's heart leaped. She patted old George despite his lack of enthusiasm for the day—he was not in love, poor beast—and went into the clerk's room.

"Harry, good day."

"Morning to you, Miss Friendly," Harry said, stomping his boots. "Amazing how quickly the merchants will shovel out when there's custom to be had, isn't it?"

"Did you have far to come?" *And will you tell all the other clerks that you found me here alone?*

"Not far at all. I live down the street, share a room with Wilkens. Dougal offered to let me bide with him, but a man needs a bit of privacy sometimes— and to get away from this place."

That man being young Harry, apparently. "Mr. MacHugh should be back shortly. He went to the chophouse."

"And himself didn't even start the stove," Harry groused, hanging his cap, coat, and scarf on a hook. "My auntie would box Dougal's ears for leaving a lady to freeze, but Dougal is ever one to keep his mind on business. That's a great lot of snow out there, isn't it? Did you have any trouble making your way here?"

"It was slow going at first," Patience said, opening the stove and finding only a few coals still burning. "Will the others be in soon?"

She wanted to have the place to herself and Dougal, but she also wanted the professor to know that MacHugh and Sons wouldn't let a little thing like a snowstorm stop them from publishing their broadsheets.

"Poor old professor," she muttered, pushing the coals to the back of the stove with the poker. Whatever else might be true of Pennypacker, he hadn't had as lovely a night as Patience had. "Where are the spills, Harry? This fire will take a little help to get going."

"I put them in Detwiler's desk," Harry said from Dougal's office. "George gets up to mischief when he's left here by himself for too long."

Harry came to the doorway of the office, George cradled in his arms.

"That cat shredded some of my columns, Harry MacHugh, and I rewrote them so I'd have the last word with the professor. We all have to do things we'd rather not."

"Hear that, cat?" Harry said, scratching George under the chin. "You're on dangerous ground. Any more bad behavior, and old Dougal P. MacHugh, publisher, will banish you to the tavern next door."

The cat was no more impressed with that threat than he was with anything else. Patience left off hunting for the spills.

"Harry, what does the P in Mr. MacHugh's name stand for?"

"P is for Pennypacker," Harry said, moving off toward the front door. "My auntie's people are Pennypackers. Have a farm south of Dunkeld. Shakespeare passed through there once upon a time, so they say. C'mon, George. The Bard got all his ideas for The Scottish Play while he was in the area, so my auntie claims."

Patience subsided into Mr. Detwiler's chair, struck by the coincidence of her nemesis having the same name as her prospective mother-in-law. The publishing community was close-knit—all of the publishers belonged to the same clubs, and they regularly met for meals, for example. One of Dougal's competitors could easily have learned of his mother's antecedents and chosen the name to plague him when devising a *nom de plume* for the professor.

"Such teasing is a bit juvenile," she muttered, opening the last of Detwiler's drawers. A neat stack of paper sat inside the drawer with a layer of spills peeking from beneath it. "Hidden from bored tomcats."

Patience put the papers on the desk and set about encouraging the fire in the parlor stove back to life. It took kindling, fresh coal, and a trip to Dougal's office to light the taper, but she managed.

Ten years ago, she would not have known how to light a decent fire, even with all the tools right at hand.

She tidied up the stack of papers she'd taken from Detwiler's drawer and saw Dougal's handwriting. He had beautiful penmanship, such as she would have expected from a former schoolteacher. No blotting, crossing out, inserting, or revising. She might have been looking at a final copy of one of her own…

The piece was signed: *Professor D. Pennypacker.*

Patience was still sitting at Detwiler's desk several minutes later when Dougal bustled through the door, bringing a gust of cold air with him and the scents of bacon, toast, and coffee.

"You're up and about. I'm almost sorry—no, I am sorry. Good of you to get the stove—Patience?"

She didn't want to look at him. Didn't want to see the truth in his eyes.

"I found these," she said, brandishing the pages. "The signature is Pennypacker's, but the name is your mother's, and the penmanship is yours. *Dougal, how could you?*"

He set his parcels on Detwiler's desk and hung up his coat and scarf, while Patience wrestled with the screaming need to pitch his infernal pages into the parlor stove.

"You're angry," he said when his coat was hung just so on a hook next to Harry's. "I can explain."

He wasn't starting with an apology, or with a denial, the two strategies that might have allowed Patience to hold on to her temper.

"You have lied to me, manipulated me, played me for a fool, and probably laughed at me all the way up those stairs, Dougal MacHugh. You are Professor Pennypacker, am I right?"

The doorbell jingled again, and Harry came in, stomping loudly.

"*Am I right, Dougal?* Did you lie to me?"

"I dissembled," Dougal said, "but if you'll listen, I can provide some perspective, and perhaps then you'll see—"

Patience marched up to him and struck him across the chest with his papers. "I'll *see* that I misheard you, I was mistaken, I misinterpreted, I misconstrued, though I have it from the most self-assured authority that my command of English is superb. You never once told me that you were Pennypacker, and this whole exercise has been a farce at the expense of my dignity."

Harry's gaze slewed from Patience to Dougal.

"Harry, get out," Dougal said. "This is a private discussion."

"Wait for me, Harry," Patience said, tossing Dougal's columns at him and retrieving her cloak and scarf from the next room. "I'm leaving, and I doubt I'll be back. I cannot abide a liar, Mr. MacHugh, much less a man who lies for his own self-interest."

She nearly ran out the door, leaving Dougal standing alone, his lovely penmanship scattered at his feet. Harry—bless the boy—snatched up the parcels of food and came after her. The streets were a mess, with only narrow paths shoveled clear, but few people were abroad to hamper her progress.

"Harry, you needn't accompany me. In my present mood, nobody will accost me and live to tell of his folly."

"If I don't accompany you, what do you think my chances of surviving Dougal's temper are, miss?"

"Dougal cannot blame you for a mess of his own creation. He lied, Harry. I know he's your cousin, but he was not honest with me. This whole exercise, day after day of writing and revising, his lectures about how competition would pique the readers' interest, all that blather about increasing the print runs—I doubt he increased them, he just wanted me to think… I feel like an idiot."

Patience felt like a naïve, gullible, gormless dupe, her future in tatters—again.

"You're not an idiot," Harry said, nearly losing his balance on a slippery spot. "But I'm seeing you home, and I thought we might fortify ourselves with a bite of warm toast along the way."

"Touch that toast, Harry MacHugh, and you'll return to Perthshire in a pine box."

He passed her one of the parcels. "Yes, miss."

Patience tolerated his escort as far as her own street, then took the second parcel from him and sent him on his way. Only when Harry had disappeared around the corner did she let herself begin to cry.

CHAPTER SEVEN

Patience's sitting room bore a faint odor of bacon, despite the day being more than half gone. Other than that, her surroundings were reassuringly genteel. Megan and her sisters had arranged themselves about their hostess—Charlotte and Elizabeth flanking her on the sofa, Megan and Anwen opposite on chairs a trifle underendowed with padding.

"We were concerned," Megan said, though, in fact, she was relieved. She'd pictured Patience living in a garret, cobwebs for curtains, mice her only company. The town house was in good repair, not a speck of dust to be seen. The rugs were worn, not tattered; the furniture comfortable, rather than elegant.

Patience was managing, in other words.

The lemon cake, alas, had met its fate.

"I'm sorry for causing you worry," Patience said. "I became absorbed in the writing, and the cat shredded my columns, and one doesn't…"

"A cat?" Charlotte prompted, peering about.

"King George. Dougal—Mr. MacHugh—brought him all the way from Scotland. Said George was his first employee. Mice like to nibble the glue in book bindings, though what good is a mouser who likes to nibble paper rather than mice? George also has a taste for cheese."

Anwen put the last slice of lemon cake on a plate and passed it to Patience. "You've been taking meals at the publisher's establishment?"

Patience set the plate down without taking a bite—*of her favorite lemon cake?*

"Mr. MacHugh was more than happy to keep me fed while I undertook my little scribblings. He escorted me home at the end of the day. He sent Jake out to the main thoroughfares rather than the nearest corner. He let the lads come up with holiday rhymes."

Even Elizabeth looked concerned at this recitation. "Holiday rhymes, Patience?"

"You know." She took a breath. "Deck the halls with tales of folly, fa-la-la-

la-la, la-la-la-la. Mrs. Horner will make it all jolly, fa-la-la-la-la… How I despise that man."

Elizabeth slipped an arm around Patience's shoulders and sent her sisters a bewildered look.

Megan was afflicted with poor eyesight, but her hearing was quite good, and Patience did not sound like a woman overcome with loathing for her publisher. She sounded hurt and lost.

"Patience," Megan said, "what's wrong? We're your friends, and we want to help. I thought you respected Mr. MacHugh and despised that professor fellow."

"They are the same man!" Patience said, bolting to her feet. "Dougal MacHugh was writing the professor's columns, purposely creating a competition with me, regularly taking the opposite view of matters to stir up interest among the readers."

Charlotte took a surreptitious bite of the lemon cake. "Did it work?"

"Yes, it worked," Patience cried. "If I can believe Dougal, the print runs more than doubled, Mrs. Horner is the talk of the pubs, and Jake nearly sells out before he's reached the end of the street."

"But," Megan said, "your trust in Mr. MacHugh is shaken because he concocted this scheme without letting you in on it. Badly done of him."

"That's the worst part," Patience said, turning a pot of anemic violets in the window. "He didn't bring me into it, but he did bring himself into my affections."

Well, thank the angels and celestial ministers of grace.

"One suspected you esteemed your publisher," Elizabeth said, twiddling the fringe of a pillow that might once have been pink. "If you return his sentiments, where's the problem?"

Truly, spinsterhood had got Elizabeth in its foul clutches. "The *problem*," Megan said, "is that if he lied about the professor's columns, is he also lying about his regard for Patience? Patience has little cause to trust the constancy of the courting male."

Patience flopped to the sofa and shoved the remaining half slice of lemon cake closer to Charlotte's knee. "I don't think Dougal would play me false, but then, I thought I was engaged once before. Do you know what the worst, worst part is?"

"Tell us," Anwen said.

"I love to write. I love being Mrs. Horner. In her shoes, I feel as if all the vicissitudes I've endured, the reversals of fortune, even the dratted engagement to his lordship, have some use. Others can benefit from my experiences, and I want that. I don't have what I was raised to think is indispensable—a fellow to order me about, provide me children, and require my fealty in exchange for a place in his household."

Great heavens. "Is that what marriage is supposed to be?" Megan asked. Neither she nor any of her sisters had attracted the affections of a suitable *parti* in their early Seasons. Uncle Percy was a duke, though, and the Windham family well-fixed. Megan and her sisters could afford to be choosy, though perhaps Patience had a point.

"Marriage can be unsatisfying," Patience said. "My mother was helpless to interfere when Papa went out and bought a phaeton we didn't need. Were it not for my grandmama's thrift and generosity, my fate would have been sorry indeed."

In that light, a woman's fealty might not be to the man she married, so much as to the coin he provided. How un-lovely.

"Aren't you forgetting something?" Megan asked.

"I forgot my common sense," Patience said, sitting very straight. "Mr. MacHugh has ambitions for his establishment, and my columns figure in those ambitions prominently. I shouldn't blame him for making the most of the talent he had at his disposal."

"You'd never heard of Dougal MacHugh three years ago," Megan said. "How did you manage?"

"I wrote pamphlets on deportment, tutored young ladies in their French and pianoforte, walked Mrs. Hutching's pug on rainy days, and practiced economies."

"You didn't need Mr. MacHugh," Megan concluded. "You still don't. Mrs. Horner can write for one of MacHugh's competitors, she can put out her own broadsheets, she can write a book, or do all three. You have managed, Patience—you, not your settlements, your husband, a kindly uncle, or some dashing swain. You. You have a home, a profession, and a bright future thanks to your own hard work."

"She's right," Elizabeth said. "In some regards—I will deny it beyond this room—I envy you."

"You envy *me*?" Patience said. "I reuse my tea leaves. I forego a fire in my bedroom most nights. I tune my own pianoforte rather than pay somebody or allow a man into my home for the purpose."

"*Your* tea leaves," Charlotte said around the last mouthful of lemon cake. "*Your* bedroom, *your* pianoforte, *your* home. And you manage all of this with the coin you earn with your wits and wisdom. No wonder Mr. MacHugh is enthralled with you."

Now there was a lovely word: enthralled.

"He wasn't honest with me," Patience insisted. "And he proposed marriage to me."

"How dare he?" Anwen murmured—with a straight face.

Charlotte hit her with a pillow. "One shouldn't make light of a man offering marriage."

"Was the marriage proposal honest?" Megan asked, because that mattered.

"I'll never know, will I?" Patience replied. "Was he offering marriage to secure Mrs. Horner's ability to earn coin, or offering himself, in good times and bad? Dougal is very shrewd."

Heaven help the man if his suit rested on shrewdness. "We are at your disposal, Patience, if you need assistance in any regard." Megan rose, and her sisters did likewise. Anwen looked preoccupied, Charlotte disgruntled—Charlotte was frequently disgruntled—while Elizabeth's gaze as she peered around the cozy parlor was wistful.

"We'll visit again next week," Megan said. "Perhaps Mrs. Horner will have some advice for you by then that will resolve the situation with Mr. MacHugh."

"Perhaps," Patience allowed, seeing her guests to the front door. No butler, no porter, no footman—no *man*—mediated between Patience and those who called upon her.

What must that be like? The entire street of widows and spinsters likely operated the same way, and Megan guessed they looked out for each other. They gossiped too, but mostly, they looked out for each other.

Patience was handing around scarves and holding cloaks when a knock sounded on the door.

"I have no company for years, and now I'm Piccadilly Circus North," she said, opening the door.

A young woman stood on the stoop, a baby in her arms, a valise by her side. "I've come to call on Mrs. Horner. Is she home?"

"I'm home," Patience said. "Please do come in. My guests were about to depart."

"Patience?" Elizabeth murmured, but what harm could a woman and an infant do?

"Thank you very much for the call, my friends," Patience said, kissing four cheeks in turn. "You've given me much to think about, and I'll look forward to seeing you again next week."

A farewell, rather than a dismissal. Megan got Charlotte by the arm and steered her sister out to the street. The Windham coach waited at the corner, though none of Megan's sisters moved in its direction.

"I think we should pay a call on a certain publisher," Elizabeth said.

"See for ourselves," Charlotte added. "If he's a dunderhead, we'll know it."

"Even if he's not a dunderhead," Anwen said. "He's probably feeling like one."

"We're only three streets away," Megan said. "Come, ladies. I've never paid a call on a publisher before."

* * *

The lads had straggled in as the morning wore on. Even Detwiler had made it in before noon, but nothing about Dougal's day had gone right. He'd had to fetch George down from the top of the awning, Jake had slipped and cut his knee on a patch of ice, and the bakeshop had remained closed.

"For Mrs. Horner to take the day off was brilliant," Harry crowed, swinging into Dougal's office uninvited. "Every other broadsheet I had has already sold out, and folk are clamoring for her final column tomorrow. They're more interested in our advice than in Father Christmas's visit."

Harry had been a font of nervous cheer since assuring Dougal that Patience had arrived safely to her home and that she'd taken breakfast with her.

"I'm not angry with you, Harry," Dougal said. "I was dishonest, and that's ungentlemanly. Sooner or later, Patience would have learned my middle name." At the altar perhaps. What a drama would have ensued then.

Harry took the seat opposite Dougal's desk. "Why did you lie to her, Dougal?"

George hopped up on the desk and spread himself out on the blotter. The cat's expression was more critical than curious. *Yes, why lie to the woman you want to spend the rest of your life with?*

"I have no excuses. I made an expedient decision last summer in the best interests of the business—and its employees—and then didn't rectify the situation. I don't blame Patience—"

"Excuse me, Mr. MacHugh," Detwiler said from the doorway.

"Yes?"

"You've callers, sir. Ladies."

What else could go wrong on this blasted day? "Send them in, Detwiler. Harry, see if the bakeshop is open yet. We could use some crumpets."

Detwiler ushered in the single greatest concentration of female beauty the offices of MacHugh and Sons had ever seen. Four red-headed females assembled in Dougal's office, four fine young ladies. They weren't individually stunning, but each woman was attractive, and everything, from her bonnet ribbons to her gloves, to the trim on the collar of her velvet cloak, murmured of good taste and excellent breeding.

"Dougal P. MacHugh, ladies," he said, bowing and coming around his desk. "Won't you have a seat? I've sent the boy for sweets, and I'm always—"

"Don't bother attempting to charm us, *Professor Pennypacker*," said one of the ladies. She wore blue spectacles and the plainest cloak of the four. When she'd taken a seat, the others did likewise.

Dougal remained on his feet, for these lovely creatures were ladies. They weren't Patience, though, and Dougal wanted to pitch the lot of them into the snow and go find *his* lady. If he'd made Patience cry...

"May I ask who has the pleasure of reproaching me?"

The women exchanged a look, then George leaped into the lap of the one wearing the spectacles.

"What a delightful creature," she said as George's purr reverberated across the office. "We are just come from a call on Miss Patience Friendly, sir, and as her friends, we must express concern regarding your dealings with her. Because no one is on hand to see to the civilities, I will introduce myself. I'm Megan Windham, and these are my sisters, Elizabeth, Charlotte, and Anwen."

Dougal bowed to each in turn, while in the back of his mind an ominous bell tolled. A publisher knew London Society, though he rarely mingled among its titled members. Windham was the family name associated with the Moreland dukedom, and these people were Patience's friends.

Her very unhappy friends.

"Ladies, what may I do for you?"

"Do have a seat," said Miss Charlotte Windham. "We're intent on a thorough scold."

"I deserve a thorough scold."

"You do," Miss Elizabeth Windham said. "If not a birching and pillorying. Have you any idea the extent to which Patience's trust was abused by her former fiancé?"

Dougal could dissemble again, could puff up with male pride and mutter about not discussing Patience behind her back. Fat lot of good such a course had done him before.

"I am aware of that history, and believe that in my way, I may have exceeded even the viscount's perfidy."

The smallest sister, the one with the unusual name, peered at him. "Whatever will you do about it? For matters in their present posture will not serve, Mr. MacHugh."

The lady's family was immensely powerful, and her observation might quietly threaten the ruin of Dougal's business. More to the point, however, these women would be *disappointed* in him, and that, added to Patience's disappointment, was unbearable.

A panting, red-faced Harry appeared in the door, holding up a parcel as if it were a trophy.

"Would you ladies care for some crumpets?" Dougal asked, rising and taking the parcel from Harry.

"No, thank you," said Miss Megan Windham. "We have come here for answers, Mr. MacHugh. You have wronged our friend, and we will hold you accountable."

Dougal stashed the parcel in a drawer. "Ladies, you needn't hold me accountable. I hold myself accountable."

"Pretty words," Elizabeth Windham snapped. "What will you *do*, Mr. MacHugh?"

"I'm a publisher. I publish words."

George left Miss Megan's lap and took up residence two sisters down the row, on Miss Elizabeth's lap.

"They had better be the right words," Miss Megan said.

An idea came to Dougal as he surveyed these gorgeous, fierce women. They were what Patience should have become—secure in the knowledge of wealth and station. Before these women—before all of London—Dougal could assure Patience of his regard, and his remorse, and perhaps that would be enough.

"I'd thought I'd start with, 'I'm sorry,'" he said, "and repeat it thousands of times. Ten thousand times, at least." The printer would have a fit, but he'd find the means to fill the order.

Miss Megan flicked a cat hair from her sleeve. "That's rather a lot of apologizing. Quantity of sentiment alone is merely melodrama. What *qualities* will these words convey?"

* * *

Patience had sent the mother and baby on their way, the loaf of stollen with them. The woman had refused coin, saying she had enough, thanks to Patience.

Christmas Eve arrived after a sleepless night—not quite sleepless, because Patience had dreamed of Dougal returning to Scotland, George silently reproaching Patience all the way up the Great North Road.

Christmas Eve dawned, a bright, drippy, un-merry business, though Patience's housekeeper filled the kitchen with more chatter than a flock of newsboys discussing the next special edition.

"The coal man showed me his copy of the professor's column," Mrs. Dingleterry said. "I read it twice to be sure, then ran right out and bought us our copy. You must be very pleased, Miss Patience."

The professor's last column had come out yesterday.

Patience was not pleased. She wanted bacon, toast, and coffee, hot from the chophouse. She wanted to hear Wilkens and Harry arguing about what the words to a Robert Burns poem implied about young women who sang down by the burnie-o, and she wanted... she wanted badly to see Dougal.

Which was ridiculous. Dougal had wronged her. Period. The end. Stop the press.

Patience left off staring at the teapot. "What did you say about the professor's column?"

"There it is, right there," Mrs. Dingleterry said, setting a broadsheet down by Patience's elbow. "He wishes Mrs. Horner a fine holiday and thanks her for all of her wisdom. Poor man's in love, and all of London will be waiting on the reply from our Mrs. Horner, though her column today is just more of her usual good sense. I'd give anything if his letter were real, Miss Patience. Believe me, I would. I know how hard you work and how much your readers mean to you."

Patience pulled the paper closer, her teapot forgotten.

To my dear readers,

I wish you all a Happy Christmas, but confess that my own holiday cannot aspire to joy, or even to contentment. I have wronged somebody whom I esteem greatly, and thus my yuletide is beclouded by remorse.

Mrs. Horner's words are no stranger to this page, and yet, as you well know, I quote that good lady only to take issue with her advice. Her place in your regard was firmly established, and then, several months past, I decided to insinuate myself into the conversation you and she enjoyed. I advised, I commented, and were that the limit of my presumption, I might wait upon Mrs. Horner's generous forgiveness for my poor manners.

I undertook to criticize, though, and to argue with a lady, and not because I genuinely disagree with her sound wisdom. In many cases, I was guilty of playing devil's advocate, because I knew discord would earn your notice, and I coveted that notice and the coin it would earn me.

I envied Mrs. Horner your loyalty and saw a way to turn her diligent efforts to my advantage. I am ashamed of the course I set and can take only the smallest comfort in the knowledge that ~~*Mrs. Horner's wise words may have seen greater circulation as a result of my ploy.*~~

Renown and its attendant benefits, however, can never replace trust or respect, and I respect Mrs. Horner so very much. I humbly apologize to her for my conduct and hope she will receive my words in the wise and compassionate spirit for which we all esteem her so greatly.

Mrs. Horner, if you look with any favor at all upon the author of these words, please accept my thanks for all of your efforts and my sincere wishes that you should prosper in the New Year in all that you undertake. With humblest apologies, I remain faithfully,

Your most sincere admirer,
Prof. D. Pennypacker

"That wretch!" Patience shot to her feet. "That fiend. He'll sell twenty thousand copies of this. Callow swains will study it as a perfect apology, and the readers will deluge him with letters. Where is my cloak?"

"In the front hall, miss. The same as always. Are you well?"

"I am... I am... I am about to provide the professor a holiday greeting he will never forget."

"But you haven't had anything to eat!"

"I'll get something at the chophouse. Why don't we ever decorate for the holidays, Mrs. Dingleterry?"

"Because you say it's a silly, sentimental expense?"

"And you listen to me?"

"The professor says you're wise and kind and all that other. Shall I buy some greenery, miss?"

Patience fished in a pocket and produced some coins. "Yes, and invite all the other ladies over to help you decorate. You might bake some lemon cake too, because the scent is divine."

And if Patience could not find a way to make peace with Dougal, she'd need at least a consolatory slice or two—or three—of lemon cake. And hearty servings of stollen, crumpets, and tarts too.

CHAPTER EIGHT

"We've sold out?" Dougal asked.

"The professor and Mrs. Horner have both sold out," Detwiler said, settling into the chair across from Dougal's desk. "The printer is doing an extra run as we speak, and the name of Dougal P. MacHugh is on the lips of every publisher in London. They're all saying you're brilliant, and next Christmas, they will conduct an epistolary courtship by broadsheet."

"Let them," Dougal said, taking off his glasses. "This time next year, I might well be teaching school again in Upper Achtermachtaltiebuie."

"Is there an Upper Achtermachtaltiebuie?"

"Go home, Detwiler. I'll see you Monday, no earlier than noon."

Detwiler pushed to his feet. "I'm sorry, lad. You tried your best. Hell hath no fury like a spinster—"

Dougal rose and leaned over the desk. "Patience Friendly is *not* a spinster."

Detwiler braced his hands on the desk. "Spinster, the proper legal definition for a woman as yet unmarried. *Old maid.* A woman past the usual marriageable age, rarely applied to men in the same situation but sometimes used to designate the occupation of one who spins."

Dougal leaned nearer. "Patience Friendly is a *writer*, a *brilliant* literary talent with a *genius* for the publishing business. She is an *excellent* editor and a woman of *unshakable* integrity, whom I am *proud* to have associated with this establishment. She is also *my fiancée* until she tells me otherwise."

"You needn't shout," said a familiar female voice. "Though your sentiments do you credit."

Patience stood in the doorway, but not a version of Patience whom Dougal had seen before. Even holding George in her arms, this woman outshone the Windham sisters for self-possession, and though her ensemble was several years out of date, the quality and style were unmistakable.

"Detwiler," Dougal said. "*Happy Christmas.*"

"Oh, right. Happy Christmas to all." Detwiler took his time shuffling out the door, and when he paused to pet the cat, Dougal nearly howled.

Patience kissed the old buzzard's cheek, sashayed into the office, and deposited George on the mantel.

"Mr. MacHugh, we have business to discuss."

Dougal did not want to discuss business, but if Patience had asked him to recite *Tam O'Shanter* backward, he would have given it a go. He was so damned relieved to see her on her mettle, ready to give as good as she got, while he was damned if he had the first inkling—

Inspiration struck. "I have crumpets."

She wrinkled her nose. "Speaking as a brilliant literary talent, I'm not interested in your *crumpets*, sir. Shall we be seated?"

Dougal came around the desk and gestured to the table, then held Patience's chair for her. He'd missed the scent of her, the rustle of her skirts, the energy she brought to the office—and that was before she'd metamorphosed from Mrs. Horner into this, this force of nature.

"You smell like lemons and spices," he said, taking his own seat.

"This is a business discussion, Mr. MacHugh. Has the professor sold out?"

"Aye. In record time. Mrs. Horner right behind him."

"Mrs. Horner has a reply for him." She passed over a sheet of foolscap. "She'll beat his record."

My dear Professor Pennypacker,

While I appreciate the gracious sentiments contained in your epistle, I must take issue with two of your assumptions, for they will otherwise trouble my holiday exceedingly.

Firstly, you assume that I cannot appreciate a point of view differing from my own, which foolishness I attribute to an excess of delicate gentlemanly sensibilities. A woman who holds the public's trust takes upon herself a great responsibility. Knowing that you will step forth with well-considered criticism from time to time eases the burden of that responsibility for me.

Nobody is right all the time. Nobody goes through life without an occasional error. What a dull world we'd have if we permitted each other no room for foibles, thoughtful discourse, or respectful dissension.

Secondly, you assume that our readers cannot enjoy offerings from more than one writer, as if their appetite for succinct wisdom was limited, rather than expanded, by our mutual efforts. The good citizens who enjoy my column should be encouraged to find others they like as well. When do we ever have too much wisdom, too many insights?

So I must thank you, Professor, for your contribution to an enjoyable and enlightening exchange. My holiday wish is that we shall have many more differences of opinion and that you shall offer the benefit of your thinking whether it agrees with my own or respectfully conflicts with it.

My wish for the readers is that they will take comfort and pleasure in the knowledge that not one, but two, articulate and compassionate authors are available to address their difficulties and concerns.

I look forward to the day when our swords figuratively cross again, Professor. Until that day, I remain, with all best wishes, your good friend,

Mrs. Horner

Dougal read the letter twice, finding not a single comma he could bear to move. "Mrs. Horner and the professor are *good friends* now?"

Patience tugged off her gloves and took the sheet back. "Very is such a weak word, but good friends struck the balance between dignified and warm, don't you think?"

Dougal took the letter back and set it carefully aside. "Patience I want to be much more than your good friend. I am exceedingly sorry I lied to you. It won't happen again."

"You were being my publisher," she said. "You fed me crumpets to inspire my productivity, and you fed me a challenge when my readership was ready for one. Had I known the professor was a creature of your imagination, my responses might not have been so vigorous."

Well, yes, and yet, a lie was a lie. "Are you making excuses for me?"

She rose and went to the window, and even her posture struck Dougal as more regal. "I understand what you did, Dougal. I might wish you'd brought me in on the scheme, but I suspect you initially lacked confidence in it. The professor was an experiment, a lark, a private risk. I tried selling my watercolors once upon a time—I signed them Placido Amadeus. When few people bought them, the failure belonged to a fictitious Italian man, not Patience Friendly."

"Exactly," Dougal said, getting to his feet. "What if the professor's words garnered ridicule? What if you demolished him in a single column? What if he took a position that revealed his ignorance of all matters parental and domestic? Where would his publisher be?"

Patience turned to face him. "I wrote to the professor."

"I beg your—" Her words weren't difficult to decipher, and yet, Dougal's mind stumbled over them. "*You* wrote to Pennypacker?"

"I wrote to you," she said, striding away from the window. "If I wasn't confident of my response to a reader, if I wanted to test my judgment, or offer the reader a choice of approaches, then I'd put a comparable situation before the professor."

"The philandering brother-in-law was you? I thought the readers were pitting us against each other."

"I changed my handwriting, my tone, my everything, lest my letter sound too much like Mrs. Horner to a man who'd read every word she'd written. I meant what I wrote in my letter, you see. To bear sole responsibility for guiding a reader through a difficulty is a heavy burden. The professor was the only person I could turn to, and he never failed to share the load."

"You wrote to the professor..." Dougal caught her hand as she marched past him. "You fanned the flames of controversy *on purpose*. You considered Pennypacker your colleague. You, you—"

"I mispresented myself. I lied. I'm sorry, Dougal. I'm—"

He caught her up in his arms. "You're a genius! You're brilliant. You're the most clever, insightful, delightful—" Dougal kissed Patience on the mouth, and a few other places, and then set her back on her feet, but kept his arms around her. "You beat me at my own game, Patience."

She sighed, then slipped free. "No, Dougal. I've thought about this. Mrs. Harmon Dandy came to see me."

"Who? Oh, her." The gin widow. "She didn't learn your direction from me."

"She followed me home earlier this week. She wanted to leave a note for me here at the office, but then saw Harry walking me home and suspected that I am Mrs. Horner. You did a fine thing for her, Dougal, but you might have told me."

Dougal had the nagging sense that his brilliant, ingenious, though not always entirely honest, author was maneuvering toward a conclusion.

"I sent her to my cousins in Perthshire, Patience. They have a large household and won't mind making accommodations for a new mother who's an accomplished seamstress." Thank goodness for wealthy relations who weren't above the occasional charitable act.

"You probably saved that baby's life, if not the mother's too. I'm endlessly grateful, but we must learn to trust each other, Dougal. We must be partners pulling in the same direction. We each have strengths and abilities, but we're stronger together. You can't write as Mrs. Horner does, and I can't browbeat the printer into doing a special run on Christmas Eve."

"He refused you?"

Patience nodded. "He said the professor had used up the entire crew's store of holiday generosity and for no amount of money would they stay late on Christmas Eve. You would have talked him 'round, wheedled, negotiated. You're a fine publisher, Dougal, and I'm a literary genius, but we cannot succeed without being in each other's confidence."

"I will make a fine husband as well, Patience, if this trust you speak of can go both ways. I think Harry should read law, but he'll never listen to that suggestion from me. He might if you brought it up."

Her brows knit, her expression suggesting Mrs. Horner was on the job, figuring the best way to pass along advice so it might be heeded.

Dougal ran his finger down the center of her forehead. Mrs. Horner hadn't solved the greater problem Dougal had created, but Patience had. He would always love her for that, for giving a promising piece of work one more polishing, for making it the best it could be, despite all the effort involved.

Patience trapped his finger in her own. "Did you mention crumpets earlier, Dougal?"

What did crumpets have to do with—? "Fresh from the bakeshop. Shall we share them, Patience?"

"The lads have all gone home?"

"And Detwiler. I heard him lock up on the way out." Thus earning a Christmas bonus.

"Are we to be partners, sir? MacHugh and MacHugh?"

Oh, that sounded lovely. Dougal stuck out his hand. "Partners, MacHugh and MacHugh. Might I suggest we take the crumpets upstairs to further discuss our plans for the new year?"

Patience took Dougal's hand in both of hers. "We might have to add another MacHugh to the name of the business, Dougal. Would that fit with your plans?"

Dougal snatched the parcel of crumpets from the drawer and tossed them to her. "We can add as many junior MacHughs to the name of the business as you like, Patience, but how about we enjoy our crumpets first?"

"Upstairs," she said. "At a meeting of the senior editorial board. I quite like that idea."

Dougal liked it too, enough to carry his senior editorial director up the stairs and forget all about the crumpets until at least an hour later. The meeting continued, intermittently, well into Boxing Day. They took a break to admire Mrs. Horner's response to the professor when it sold out in minutes early that afternoon. By then, the bakeshop had run out of crumpets.

And stollen.

And tarts.

The senior editorial board never ran out of agenda items, though, and both members thereof had a very, very fine Christmas—every year.

To my dear readers,

I always get a boost of inspiration when a story is set at Christmas. It's the coziest time of year where I live, even if there's no mistletoe nearby. A novella also seemed like the perfect way to introduce the Windham cousins, Elizabeth, Megan, Charlotte and Anwen. These four ladies will get their happily ever afters in The Windham Bride series, and the first of those stories—*The Trouble With Dukes*—comes out December 20. Truly, Christmas will come early for me this year! I've included an excerpt from **Trouble** for you below. Our heroine is Megan Windham, and our hero is Hamish MacHugh, the cousin whom Dougal holds in such affectionate regard.

If you can't wait until December for your next dose of ducal romance, Elizabeth Hoyt's *Duke of Pleasure* will be on sale November 29. Because we've all been very good this year, I've been given permission to include an excerpt from that marvelous tale below.

Finally, I'm exceedingly pleased to be able to offer you a sneak peek from the second Windham Bride story, *Too Scot to Handle*, which doesn't come out until July 2017. How will we manage to wait that long, when Lord Colin MacHugh is not known for his patience?

We will read many, many excellent romances, that's how! If you want the latest on all my releases, sales, signings, and other adventures (yes, I'm planning another **Scotland With Grace** tour in 2017), **sign up for my newsletter by visiting:** GraceBurrowes.com/contact.php, **follow me on Twitter: @ GraceBurrowes**, or **like my Facebook page**: Facebook.com/Grace-Burrowes-115039058572197.

Happy reading!
Grace Burrowes

The Trouble With Dukes by Grace Burrowes (Dec. 20, 2016)

Confirmed spinster Megan Windham has offered to teach the Duke of Murdoch how to waltz…

"A couple usually converses during a waltz," Megan said, as she and the duke started on another circle of the music parlor. "How do you find London, that sort of thing?"

Murdoch's sense of rhythm was faultless, but he'd apparently misplaced the ability to smile—at all.

"Find London? You go down the Great North Road until you can't go any farther, then you follow the noise and stink. Can't miss it. I prefer the drover's routes myself. The inns are humble, but honest."

Megan's mother was Welsh, so a thick leavening of Celtic intonation was easily decipherable to her. She switched to Gaelic, as she occasionally did with family.

"I meant, does London appeal to you?"

Nothing had broken His Grace's concentration thus far. For dozens of turns about the room, despite Westhaven's and St. Just's adventuresome maneuvers with Murdoch's sisters, and Valentine's increasingly daring tempo, the duke had become only more confident of his waltzing.

One simple question had him stumbling.

And when a large fellow stumbled, and tried to right himself by grabbing onto a surprised and not very large woman, and that woman stumbled…

Down they went, though Megan landed on His Grace, an agreeably solid and warm place to find herself. His sporran had twisted itself to his hip, and his arms remained about her.

"Miss Megan," Lady Edana cried. "Are you all right? Hamish turn loose of her, for pity's sake, you'll wrinkle her skirts, and break her bones, and tramp on her hems, and *get up*, you can't simply lie there, a great lummoxing lump of a brother."

"Get up now," Lady Rhona chorused. "Oh, please do get up, and promise you'll never attempt to waltz in public again. Wellington might be at her grace's ball, or the king. Oh, Ham, *get up.*"

His Grace could not get up as long as Megan luxuriated in the novel pleasure of lying atop him.

"I'm fine," she said, kneeling back after enjoying two more instants of Murdoch's abundant warmth and muscle. Westhaven hauled her to her feet by virtue of a hand under each elbow, glowering at her as if she'd purposely yanked fifteen stone of Scottish duke to the floor.

St. Just extended a hand to Murdoch and pulled him upright, but not fast enough to hide a flash of muscular thigh from Megan's view, not fast enough by half.

The duke righted his sporran, bowed, and came up... *smiling.* "Miss Meggie, my apologies for hauling you top over teakettle. You speak the Gaelic."

All the rainbows in Wales, all the Christmas punch brewed at the Windham family seat, couldn't approach His Grace's smile for sheer, charming glee. That smile dazzled, intrigued, promised... oh, that smile was quite the weapon against a woman's dignity.

Megan fired off a shy, answering volley of the same artillery. "My mother is Welsh, and I enjoy languages. Welsh and Gaelic aren't that different to the ear."

"Nobody speaks the Gaelic in an English ballroom," Murdoch said. "Not since the Forty-Five, probably not ever." He made it sound like a great feat of courage, not a simple courtesy to a newcomer.

St. Just and Westhaven watched this exchange like a pair of oversized pantry mousers placing bets on the fate of a fugitive canary.

Bother the glowering pair of them.

Nobody smiled at Megan Windham the way Murdoch was smiling. Even without her glasses, she could see the warmth and approval in his eyes, see all the acceptance and admiration a woman could endure from one man.

"Nobody ends the waltz by falling on his partner," Westhaven snapped. "Lord Valentine, if you would oblige. The duke is in want of practice, assuming Cousin Megan is none the worse for her tumble."

Megan had tumbled hopelessly, right into a pair of bottomless blue eyes, a pair of strong arms, and... those thighs. Ye manly waltzing gods.

"I'm fine," Megan said, putting her hand on Murdoch's shoulder. She was apparently becoming a proficient liar, because having seen his great, beaming benevolence of a smile, she might never be fine again....

Order your copy of *The Trouble With Dukes!*

Read on for a special sneak peek from **Duke of Pleasure**
by Elizabeth Hoyt (November 29, 2016)

Bold. Brave. Brutally handsome. Hugh Fitzroy, the Duke of Kyle, is the king's secret weapon. Sent to defeat the notorious Lords of Chaos, he is ambushed in a London alley-and rescued by an unlikely ally: a masked stranger with the unmistakable curves of a woman….

* * *

Now once there were a White Kingdom and a Black Kingdom that had been at war since time began….
—From *The Black Prince and the Golden Falcon*

January 1742
London, England

Hugh Fitzroy, the Duke of Kyle, did not want to die tonight, for three very good reasons.

It was half past midnight as he eyed the toughs slinking out of the shadows up ahead in the cold alley near Covent Garden. He moved the bottle of fine Viennese wine from his right arm to his left and drew his sword. He'd dined with the Habsburg ambassador earlier this evening, and the wine was a gift.

Firstly, Kit, his elder son—and, formally, the Earl of Staffin—was only seven. Far too young to be orphaned and inherit the dukedom.

Next to Hugh was a linkboy with a lantern. The boy was frozen, his lantern a small pool of light in the narrow alley. The youth's eyes were wide and frightened. He couldn't be more than fourteen. Hugh glanced over his shoulder. Several men were bearing down on them from the entrance to the alley. He and the linkboy were trapped.

Secondly, Peter, his younger son, was still suffering nightmares from the death of his mother only five months before. What would his father's death so soon after his mother's do to the boy?

They might be common footpads. Unlikely, though. Footpads usually worked in smaller numbers, were not this organized, and were after money, not death.

Assassins, then.

And *thirdly*, His Majesty had recently assigned Hugh an important job: destroy the Lords of Chaos. On the whole, Hugh liked to finish his jobs. Brought a nice sense of completion at the end of the day, if nothing else.

Right, then.

"If you can, run," Hugh said to the linkboy. "They're after me, not you."

Then he pivoted and attacked the closest group—the three men behind them.

Their leader, a big fellow, raised a club.

Hugh slashed him across the throat. The leader went down in a spray of scarlet. But his second was already bringing his own club down in a bone-jarring blow to Hugh's left shoulder. Hugh juggled the bottle of wine, seized it again, and kicked the man in the balls. The second doubled over and stumbled against the third. Hugh punched over the man's head and into the face of the third.

There were running footsteps from behind Hugh.

He spun to face the other end of the alley and another attacker.

Caught the descending knife with his blade and slid his sword into the hand holding the knife.

A howling scream, and the knife clattered to the icy cobblestones in a splatter of blood.

The knife man lowered his head and charged like an enraged bull.

Hugh flattened all six foot four inches of himself against the filthy alley wall, stuck out his foot, and tripped Charging Bull into the three men he'd already dealt with.

The linkboy, who had been cowering against the opposite wall, took the opportunity to squirm through the constricted space between the assailants and run away.

Which left them all in darkness, save for the light of the half moon.

Hugh grinned.

He didn't have to worry about hitting his compatriots in the dark.

He rushed the man next in line after the Bull. They'd picked a nice alley, his attackers. No way out—save the ends—but in such close quarters he had a small advantage: no matter how many men were against him, the alley was so cramped that only two could come at him at a time. The rest were simply bottled up behind the others, twiddling their thumbs.

Hugh slashed the man and shouldered past him. Got a blow upside the head for his trouble and saw stars.

Hugh shook his head and elbowed the next—*hard*—in the face, and kicked the third in the belly. Suddenly he could see the light at the end of the alley.

Hugh knew men who felt that gentlemen should never run from a fight. Of course many of these same men had never *been* in a real fight.

Besides, he had those three *very* good reasons.

Actually, now that he thought of it, there was a *fourth* reason he did not want to die tonight.

Hugh ran to the end of the alley, his bottle of fine Viennese wine cradled in the crook of his left arm, his sword in the other fist. The cobblestones were iced over and his momentum was such that he slid into the lit street.

Where he found another half-dozen men bearing down on him from his left.

Bloody *hell*.

Fourthly, he hadn't had a woman in his bed in over nine months, and to die in such a drought would be a particularly unkind blow from fate, god*damn* it.

Hugh nearly dropped the blasted wine as he scrambled to turn to the right. He could hear the men he'd left in the alley rallying even as he sprinted straight into the worst part of London: the stews of St Giles. They were right on his heels, a veritable army of assassins. The streets here were narrow, ill lit, and cobbled badly, if at all. If he fell because of ice or a missing cobblestone, he'd never get up again.

He turned down a smaller alley and then immediately down another.

Behind him he heard a shout. Christ, if they split up, they would corner him again.

He hadn't enough of a lead, even if a man of his size could easily hide in a place like St Giles. Hugh glanced up as he entered a small courtyard, the buildings on all four sides leaning in. Overhead the moon was veiled in clouds, and it almost looked as if a boy were silhouetted, jumping from one rooftop to another…

Which…

Was insane.

Think. If he could circle and come back the way he'd entered St Giles, he could slip their noose.

A narrow passage.

Another cramped courtyard.

Ah, *Christ.*

They were already here, blocking the two other exits.

Hugh spun, but the passage he'd just run from was crowded with more men, almost a dozen in all.

Well.

He put his back to the only wall left to him and straightened.

He rather wished he'd tasted the wine. He was fond of Viennese wine.

A tall man in a ragged brown coat and a filthy red neckcloth stepped forward. Hugh half-expected him to make some sort of a speech, he looked that full of himself. Instead he drew a knife the size of a man's forearm, grinned, and licked the blade.

Oh, for—

Hugh didn't wait for whatever other disgusting preliminaries Knife Licker might feel were appropriate to the occasion. He stepped forward and smashed the bottle of very fine Viennese wine over the man's head.

Then they were on him.

He slashed and felt the jolt to his arm as he hit flesh.

Swung and raked the sword across another's face.

Staggered as two men slammed into him.

Another hit him hard in the jaw.

And then someone clubbed him behind the knees.

He fell to his knees on the icy ground, growling like a bleeding, baited bear. Raised an arm to defend his head…

And…

Someone dropped from the sky right in front of him.

Facing his attackers.

Darting, wheeling, spinning.

Defending him so gracefully.

With two swords.

Hugh staggered upright again, blinking blood out of his eyes—when had he been cut?

And saw—a boy? No, a slight *man* in a grotesque half mask, motley, floppy hat, and boots, battling fiercely with his attackers. Hugh just had time to think: *Insane*, before his defender was thrown back against him.

Hugh caught the man and had another thought, which was: *Tits?*

And then he set the woman—most definitely a *woman* although in a man's clothing—on her feet and put his back to hers and fought as if their lives depended on it.

Which they did.

There were still eight or so of the attackers left, and although they weren't trained, they were determined. Hugh slashed and punched and kicked, while his feminine savior danced an elegant dance of death with her swords. When he smashed the butt of his sword into the skull of one of the last men, the remaining two looked at each other, picked up a third, and took to their heels.

Panting, Hugh glanced around the courtyard. It was strewn with groaning men, most still very much alive, though not dangerous at the moment.

He peered at the masked woman. She was tiny, barely reaching his shoulder. How was it she'd saved him from certain, ignoble death? But she had. She surely had.

"Thank you," he said, his voice gruff. He cleared his throat. "I—"

She grinned, a quicksilver flash, and put her left hand on the back of his neck to pull his head down.

And then she kissed him.

ORDER YOUR COPY of **Duke of Pleasure**!

Lord Colin MacHugh and Miss Anwen Windham share an interest in a certain Home for Wayward Urchins. After a morning gallop in the park, they tarry on a bench, discussing the children, and touching on a few other topics...

Anwen unpinned her hat, or whatever the thing was. A toque, maybe. Her wild gallop had set it slightly askew.

"You think the boys will consider working in the garden a reward?" she asked. "I thought house servants ranked above the outdoor servants?"

Colin took her hat from her, examining the collection of pheasant feathers and silk roses that had probably cost a footman's monthly wages.

"I think we do best that which we enjoy most." He enjoyed kissing and that which often followed kissing *exceedingly*. "If a boy is to spend his entire life at a job, it had better be a job that he has some aptitude for. Let the fellow with a passion for horses work in the mews, and the fussy young man who delights in a perfectly starched cravat become a valet. It's all honorable work."

He was being a Scottish commoner with that sentiment.

"That's sensible," Anwen said. "Sense is what the orphanage needs. Not good intentions, or idle talk. Common sense. What are you doing with my— Lord Colin?"

He'd pitched the thing with feathers into the bushes five yards off, so it hung from an obliging branch of the nearest maple.

"Come," he said, taking her by the hand. "The squirrels have no need of such fetching millinery, and the grooms are busy with the horses."

"Right," Anwen said, rising. "Enough serious talk, for now. I'm full of ideas, and can't wait to put them into action."

"Exactly so," Colin said, leading her into the deep shade beneath the tree. "Time to put a few well chosen ideas into action."

Also a few foolish ones.

He made sure they were safe from view, drew the lady into his arms, and kissed her, as a snippet of her earlier words settled into his imagination. She'd said he'd given her hope.

She'd given him hope too.

* * *

Nothing penetrated Anwen's awareness except *pleasure*.

Pleasure, to be kissed by a man who wasn't in a hurry, half-drunk, and all pleased with himself for being brave enough to appropriate liberties from a woman taken unawares by his boldness.

Pleasure, *to kiss Lord Colin back*. To do more than stand still, enduring the fumblings of a misguided fortune hunter who hoped a display of his practiced charms might result a lifetime of security.

Pleasure, to feel lovely bodily stirrings as the sun rose, the birds sang, and the quiet of the park reverberated with the potential of a new, wonderful day.

And beneath those delightful, if predictable pleasures, yet more joy, unique to Anwen.

Lord Colin had bluntly pronounced her slight stature an advantage in the saddle—how marvelous!—and what a novel perspective.

He'd *listened* to her maundering on about Tom, Joe, John, and Dickie. Listened and discussed the situation rather than pontificating about her pretty head, and he'd offered solutions.

He'd taken care that this kiss be private, and thus unhurried.

Anwen liked the unhurried part exceedingly. Lord Colin held her not as if she were frail and fragile, but as if she were too precious to let go. His arms were secure about her, and he'd tucked in close enough that she could revel in his manly contours—broad chest, flat belly, and hard, hard thighs, such as an accomplished equestrian would have.

Soft lips, though. Gentle, entreating, teasing…

Anwen teased him back, getting a taste of peppermint for her boldness, and then a taste of *him*.

"Great day in the morning," he whispered right at her ear. "I won't be able to sit my horse if you do that again with your tongue."

She did it again, and again, until the kiss involved his leg insinuated among the folds and froths of her riding habit, her fingers toying with the hair at his nape, and her heart, beating faster than it had at the conclusion of their race.

"Ye must cease, wee Anwen," Lord Colin said, resting his cheek against her temple. "*We* must cease, or I'll have to cast myself into yonder water for the sake of my sanity."

"I'm a good swimmer," Anwen said. "I learned very young, and one doesn't forget. I'd fish you out." She contemplated dragging a sopping Lord Colin from the Serpentine, his clothes plastered to his body….

"Such a sigh," he said, kissing her cheek. "If ye'd slap me, I'd take it as a mercy."

"I'd rather kiss you again." And again and again and again. Anwen's enthusiasm for that undertaking roared through her like a wild fire, bringing light, heat, and energy to every corner of her being.

"You are a bonfire in disguise," he said, smoothing a hand over her hair. "An ambush of a woman, and you have all of polite society thinking you're the quiet one." He peered down at her, his hair sticking up on one side. "Am I the only man who knows better, Anwen?"

She smoothed his hair down, delighting in its texture. Red hair had a mind of its own, and by the dawn's light, his hair was very red.

"No, you are not the only one who knows better," she said, which had him looking off across the water, his gaze determined.

"I'm no' the dallyin' kind," he said, taking Anwen's hand and kissing it. "I was a soldier, and I'm fond of the ladies, but this is... you mustn't toy with me."

Everlasting celestial trumpets. "You think I could *toy* with you?"

"When you smile like that, you could break hearts, Miss Anwen Windham. A man wouldn't see it coming, but then you'd swan off in a cloud of grace and dignity, and too late, he'd realize what he'd missed. He wouldn't want to admit how foolish he'd been, but in his heart, he'd know: I should ne'er have let her get away. I should have done anything to stay by her side."

I am a bonfire in disguise. "You are not the only one who knows my secret. *I* know better now too, Colin." She went up on her toes and kissed him. "It's our secret."

A great sigh went out of him, and for a moment they remained in each other's arms.

This embrace was lovely too, but different. Desire simmered through Anwen, along with glee, wonder, and not a little surprise—she was a *bonfire*—but also gratitude. Her disguise had fooled her entire family, and even begun to fool her, but Lord Colin had seen through all the manners and decorum to the flame burning at her center.

"I'll guard your secret," Colin said, "but if we don't return to the horses in five minutes, I'll be doing that as the late lamented Lord Colin. Your cousins have a reputation for protectiveness."

Anwen stepped back and plucked her millinery from the branch above. "We were looking for my hat, blown into the hedge as I galloped past." Along with her wits, her heart, and her worries.

Most of her worries.

"Just so," Lord Colin said, taking her hat, and leading her past the bench and back to the bridle path. "Hat hunting, a venerable tradition among the smitten of an early morning in Hyde Park. That excuse will surely spare my life."

By the time Anwen's cousin, Lord Rosecroft, trotted up on a handsome bay, Anwen was back in the saddle, her skirts decorously arranged over her boots, her fascinator once again pinned to her hair. The grooms trundled along at the acceptable distance, and the first carriage had rolled by, the Duchess of Quimbey at the reins.

"Anwen," Rosecroft said. "My apologies for losing track of the time. Denmark here was going a bit stiff to the right, so a few gymnastics were in order. Lord Colin, good morning."

"My lord," Colin said, bowing slightly from the saddle. "That's a beautiful beast you have, and it's a glorious day for enjoying nature's splendors, isn't it?"

Rosecroft's mother had been Irish, and when he wasn't being an overbearing big brother and meddlesome cousin, the dark-haired Rosecroft claimed a portion of Gaelic charm. His smile was crooked, his pat on the horse's shoulders genuinely affectionate.

"I'd rather be admiring nature's splendor back up in the West Riding," he said, "but I think I can report to my superior officers that today's outing was in every way a success."

He turned his smile on Lord Colin, who smiled right back.

Order your copy of **Too Scot to Handle!**

Made in the USA
San Bernardino, CA
26 October 2016